IN SEARCH OF LOVE

NIVEDITA VEDURLA

Dedication

To the person holding this book, you are a beautiful gift.
Cherish yourself above everything else.

Contents

Contents

Acknowledgements

Every passion has a purpose to fulfil and pursuing it, results in perfection of work. I feel truly blessed by the Almighty who has given me a passion to write stories. Each story is different like the different phases of our life. No matter what we do, no two people's life can be the same. I resorted to writing as a way to express myself, but gradually, it became an integral part of me.

I am thankful to my parents, my parents-in-law, and my husband for encouraging me in pursuing my passion. It is my family members' love and support, that has played a major role in shaping my stories. Their love, emotions, and way of living life are the foundation of my stories.

I would also like to thank the kids in my family, Viraj, Swaranjali, Swayam, Vagmi and Veera; their innocence has always kept me hooked and reflected as warmth in the stories that I pen down.

Coming to the wings that give me the ability to make my stories come to life, I would like to acknowledge my gratitude towards my editors, Amrita Kriti and Janki Thakkar. Their contribution for this book and my life cannot be expressed. I am thankful to them for being in my life and helping me as a true friend.

Last, but not the least, I am thankful to my readers, who are my biggest motivation and encourage me to continue my journey as an author. I hope you enjoy reading the book and find the love that you've always wished for in your life.

CHAPTER I

Natasha

The night seemed short as I twirled and danced with Jai on the yacht. It was the first time when I felt a connection with him. Somewhere deep inside, the feeling of affection took root, making me want to turn this fake relationship into a real one. *Is it because I feel lonely, now that Samira has found a beau, or am I influenced by her love for Chad?* Whatever be the reason, the man brought about indescribable emotions that made me feel warm and fuzzy.

It was almost three in the morning when the yacht party ended. Everyone returned to their hotel rooms to retire, except for Jai and me. He instructed the captain to take the yacht further into the sea for dolphin sightseeing. We relaxed on the deck, our eyes rooted to the water shimmering under the moonlight to catch a glimpse of the elegant aquatic mammals. Suddenly, one jumped across right before our eyes!

I cheered joyously when another one jumped past in the opposite direction.

"It's just like how it happens in fairy tales when the girl gets her Prince Charming!" I remarked, overcome with those tender emotions of love and fantasy. The sound of the sea, the mellow and radiant rays from the moon, and the charismatic guy before me was like a perfect romantic set-up. I had an instinctive urge to wrap my arms around his neck and whisper, *You are my Prince Charming!*

Jai was leaning on the railing. He frowned at me with a sideward glance and chuckled while shaking his head. "I knew you had a soft heart but didn't expect that you would believe in fairy tales!" He leaned in closer and eyed me with interest. "So then, are you waiting for your Prince Charming?"

I returned his gaze; the handsome face held a smile that made my heart race. But the meaning behind his words was like a splash of cold water. It made me realise that he didn't believe in fairy tales. I turned my gaze back to the sea. "I read in a book; what you seek, seeks you. Tonight's ambience is right out of my imagination... I am sure the rest of it will also be true one day, and I'll have a family of my own." As I uttered, I caught a glimpse of another dolphin jumping high up in the air, across the radiant full moon and then diving back into the water.

"You want a prince to come and rescue you? But I don't see you in any kind of distress!" His eyes danced in amusement as he laughed aloud.

I frowned, unable to grasp his meaning.

"Normally in fairy tales, isn't the woman in a dire situation for the prince to come and save her?" His eyes wrinkled at the corners, making him look even more handsome than usual.

"Yes," I chuckled. "You are right. I'm not in distress because I can help myself," I said, eyeing the dolphins at the horizon. "My belief is that there will be someone who will stand by me and be true to me." I was sure my wish would undoubtedly come true.

"You sound as if you are asking for a dog!" Jai shook his head in disbelief. "Only dogs can be so faithful. Do you think in today's times, people stay true to their promises?"

His question and way of thinking didn't bother me. If I would be able to clear out things for him, maybe tomorrow he would believe in it too. "Yes, there are people who are as faithful and loyal as a dog because they are in love, and in love, everything is possible. By the way, dogs aren't bad. On the contrary, I believe they are far better than humans. So please don't demean them!" I couldn't help but laugh at his stupid comparison and also on my confidence that one day this so-called egoist, Jai, would surely change.

"Ah, love... Here comes another magical word!" He sniggered and then faced the sea, taking a sip of his drink.

I could clearly see that the word was not an easy one for him. He seemed disturbed, as if he wished the word didn't exist at all.

"J, love isn't just a word. It's a strong emotion, which can make or break a person," I voiced, intending to make him understand my view.

"Hmm, how does this so-called love start? When do you come to know you are in love?" He returned his gaze to me and asked.

I rested my hand on the yacht railing, my eyes focused on the sea. "When you care for a person, the absence makes you miss that special someone in your life. You want to share all your life with that person, and just one kiss from them is all you need to survive."

My hand unknowingly touched his on the railing, and a spark flowed through my body, making my heart race. Withdrawing my hand immediately, I glanced at him and held my breath. It took me a few moments to control my surging emotions and utter, "I know all this won't make sense to you until you fall in love, so..." I paused as I tried to find the right words, but I felt him regarding me with an intense look. Feeling flustered, I looked away and wondered for a while, *What was running in his head?* Hesitantly, I continued aloud, "So, I think-"

Suddenly, he pulled me in his arms and pressed his warm lips on mine.

As if it was not enough ignition to stop my blood flow in my veins, he snaked his arms around my waist. My brain told me to push him away and remind him that this was not in our contract! But my eyes instinctively closed to relish the touch. The greed I had been suppressing all evening, surfaced and I let the feeling sink in.

This was the first time someone had kissed me so passionately. It was only a few hours since I realised I had fallen for Jai. And magically, all my innermost wishes were getting fulfilled. Nervous yet excited, I clung on to him and let the warm feeling envelop me all around.

The intensity of the kiss made me swoon. Then, just as abruptly, he released me. I felt instantly dejected at the loss of his touch. My lips trembled, longing for it, but his eyes had withdrawn as if his mind was overcome with guilt.

I pursed my lips to calm the trembling when he unexpectedly moved closer and claimed them once again. My heart danced rapidly with happiness.

This time, the kiss we shared burned like a bright flame within, enlightening me slowly. It was like something I had never imagined. Of course, I've seen many people kiss and have even experienced a few. But this one felt surreal as if he had unleashed his passion, which, in turn, was igniting the primal desire locked in my body all this time.

His big and warm palms moved to caress my curves, rubbing through the fabric of my light cotton floral dress. I knew I was inviting trouble, but all rational thoughts vaporised under his teasing fingers. I felt my chest expand and gasp for air when his lips effortlessly caressed my nape as if they knew my desires and were waiting to be free. In that split second, I was all his, electrified to the deepest core of my body and waiting to be one with him.

Before I knew what was happening, he quickly guided us through the narrow passage of the yacht and then to a small cabin below the deck.

Shutting the door with his legs, he swiftly landed us on the bed. His hands made their way under my clothes and shed them one by one, while his mouth titillated my skin, making me float in moans.

I was lost in a tide of passion that was sweeping across me. Though he devoured each inch of my exposed skin, it wasn't long before we felt the urge to satiate ourselves overpowering everything else. The moment our core made a connection, tiny tears of pain and joy escaped my eyes. I concealed them, hiding my face onto the soft pillows. All the pain gradually mellowed out, and my head started to whirl in ecstasy as if I was drugged. Warmth exploded within my core, and I lifted my head up, latching onto him for support as he traversed to the deepest part of me. Though the inhibitions and fear for the future of our relationship still stood firm at the back of my mind, I was lost in a blissful state, sensing him filling me with his warmth.

We danced to the melodious tunes of desires shooting through us as we made out in the small cabin, right in the middle of the sea. Our bodies rocked back and forth, just as tides passed through the silent waters, making them gleam with joy under the brilliant moonlight.

As exhaustion spread all over me and my head dropped onto the pillow, I felt movement next to me. I opened my eyes to find him lying down beside me with his hand outstretched. The subtle smile on his lips and gentle gaze was all I needed to crawl into the crook of his arm.

I felt at home and didn't know when I drifted off to a peaceful slumber.

CHAPTER II

Natasha

Six Months Later

Fairy tales don't last long. Life opens your eyes right when you start believing in them and feel high about them. My fairy tale was also short-lived, crashing me to the bottom of an endless abyss. Unable to find a scaffolding to help me stand up, I withdrew to my cocoon, away from all friends and well-wishers. This was the first time going home seemed like a burden. The pain was quite inevitable. The innumerable things running in my mind made my heart feel more and more anguished.

Did he really not feel anything for me? This question stifled my chest, making me want to return to him and ask, but I could not summon the courage. *Moreover, if he would have felt anything, he would have acted on it. Right?*

But now, can I really forget him? I had thought this fling would end on a happy note. *People with soft hearts should never get involved in a casual affair. While I lost my heart to him, he was just playing the part to get his money.*

I sat in the waiting lounge for my flight, to return to my hometown, to my Ma. Heartbroken, I read my boarding pass for the tenth time in that minute, but nothing registered; in a dazed state. I never believed money could bring pain until now, when I actually wanted to trade love for money. However, love can be sacrificed, but my *Ma* could never be. She needed me more, and it was my responsibility to look after her the way she had always done for me.

It hadn't been easy for my *Ma* to raise me. She worked three jobs, as a school teacher during the morning hours, as a cook in the evening, and as a teacher at night school for adults. She was always on her toes to save more money for my education and well-being. It was her desire that I fly high in life, and because of that, when a company in Perth sent me an offer for a job, she spent all her savings and even took out a loan for my trip.

Alas! My fate tricked me, and the company turned out to be fraudulent. Though I found out before spending more money as a deposit at the company, I didn't have enough to return to India. With some effort, I procured a job and decided to stay on to clear *Ma's* debt.

A few months later, when I applied for higher studies at Curtin University, I met Samira. We clicked right from the start, and soon became inseparable. We became bosom buddies, caring for each other with our hearts while sharing everything from room, books, clothes, and even working at the same jobs.

Thanks to her and *Ma*, I could complete my education, but that happiness didn't last long. Life gave me another grief *Ma* was diagnosed with cancer.

Isn't it foolish to fancy my life as another Cinderella story despite these hardships?

A ground staff member of the airline appeared before me. "Ma'am, are you Miss Natasha Meher?"

When I nodded absentmindedly, she continued, "We've been calling out to you for some time now. The flight has started boarding."

"Huh? Okay..."

My delayed reply made her scrutinise me for a moment and she asked, "Ma'am, are you all right?"

"I-I'm okay," I replied to her in a hoarse voice and stood up, holding the boarding pass tight in my hands.

As we passed through the automatic glass doors, I caught a fleeting sight of my reflection. With no makeup, dark circles under the eyes, drooping shoulders and unkempt hair tied in a messy bun, I appeared far from the Natasha I had known myself to be. Just one person had brought such a drastic change in me! If I would have encountered Jai in some other circumstances, would it be possible to make him realise how much I loved him?

My eyes welled up at the thought, and everything blurred.

A sudden call on my phone made me stop in my tracks. Anticipating it to be Jai, my heart rate quickened. *Did his feelings for me finally dawn onto him?* I wiped away the unshed tears hurriedly at the thought and rummaged for my phone in the purse. With a nervous yet radiant smile, I glanced at the caller. The next moment, all hope turned to dust. It was not him; it was Samira, my bestie. I bit my lower lip as the dwindled hope left a baring pain, stifling my chest.

For one weak second, I wanted to reach out to her and hold her hand for support, but then, shame engulfed me. *How can I confess to her what happened? What will she think of me?* Moreover, it was her wedding. I didn't want to spoil her happiness which she had witnessed after such a long time.

I was sure that if I told her the truth now, she would feel crushed and maybe sad throughout her wedding proceedings. *I'll speak to her once the marriage is over, and tell her the truth. Or perhaps I'll not talk at all... Maybe, I should close this chapter of my life and simply move on...*

I switched off my phone and silently thanked God for arranging the money. It was time to look after my *Ma*; after all,I didn't have anyone apart from her. As the finances were now straightened out, I informed *Ma's* doctor to begin her treatment.

Tears gushed down my cheeks as all the pleasant memories came to mind, knowing well that memories were all that I was ever going to have.

I followed a long to-do list on reaching India. Firstly, I rented a place in Mumbai, got it set up, procured a new sim card, followed by taking care of other basic essentials, and then brought down my *Ma* for treatment.

Dreams and desires could wait, but responsibilities could not. Once *Ma* would become hale and hearty, none of my heartaches would matter. The pain would become a thing of the past. *After all, Ma is my best friend, and with her around, I don't need anyone else to make me happy.*

Such was my *Ma's* love. I smiled, thinking of the happy times I've spent with her, nestled away in the lap of the beautiful mango tree courtyard. Though I still remember the harsh times of my early childhood, they were all erased by the love and care of my *Ma*. She had gone to the extent of giving up her own family just for the sake of me! *It is now my turn to leave everything and live just for her.*

CHAPTER III

Natasha

"So, Miss Natasha," the middle-aged interviewer addressed me and glanced at me while going through my resume. He then asked, "Why did you leave Perth? You must have been earning good money there. Why did you return to India?"

Nervously, I clasped my hands underneath the table and answered, "Sir, my *Ma* has been diagnosed with cancer. I had to return home to look after her."

"Oh!" He remarked while nodding in understanding and asked, "I hope she is doing fine now?"

"Well her treatments and therapies are still on."

"Uh-huh. I'm sure your mother will recover soon," he replied, appearing to be interested in my situation. "So, who else is there to look after her once you join work?"

"I've hired a nurse to take care of *Ma*."

"I see," he replied, glancing at my resume again.

Although he didn't look rude, I could perceive from his body language and my job-hunting experience in India that he wasn't keen on hiring me. He probably felt I would not give my hundred per cent to work because of my mother's condition.

"Sir, don't worry, I will do my best in the job. The lady looking after *Ma* is well versed with her, so I am at ease." I shifted in my chair and tried to convince him about my dedication to work.

Though his mind seemed made up, unlike other interviewers, he did go through my resume and asked a few more questions regarding my prior experiences. Probably, he was looking for more genuine reasons to reject me.

As predicted, he asked, "Why is there a gap after your education in Perth? What were you doing during those nine months?"

"I was looking for a good opportunity but didn't get any," I lied. I couldn't possibly tell him that I was seeking a fairy tale in a fake marriage. Or that I had even given up my job because my fake father-in-law asked me to help in his business instead of working in my fake husband's company. *'It won't look nice working in the same company where he is the boss while you work as an administrator,'* he had said. *'And he won't pay you better than me!'*

I had laughed at it and agreed to his condition, only to realise he never intended for me to work at his firm. In fact, he never invited me to join while I waited for him for four months.

When I had asked Jai about it, he had replied, "It was Dad's way of asking you to stop working and stay at home."

"But he is the owner of such a big company. How can he be so narrow-minded? I don't think it's true," I responded, rolling my eyes. *Why would his father do this to me?*

Jai flashed a sarcastic smile at my naivety. "Then tell me, how else could he proclaim to the world that his daughter-in-law is at home enjoying at the expense of his hard-earned money?"

I gave him a small smile, assuming that he was testing me. "You are just playing around with me!"

"So, why hasn't he asked you to come to his company and start working?" He raised his brows, forcing me to deliberate a valid reason. Then, with a wry smile, he added, "Natasha, I know him well. He is my father, and I know how he plays his tricks."

Spellbound, I gaped at him.

Jai had continued, "Take my advice. It's already been four months since you left your job. So, it's no point speaking to him about it anymore. In a month, or so I will get the money, and you can leave this place for good."

The interviewer cleared his throat and placed my resume on the table, breaking my chain of thoughts. "Natasha, I would like to help you," the interviewer began and then added, "But it's against our company policy to hire someone with a gap of more than three months in their career."

"Thank you for your time, Sir," I replied mechanically and stood up to leave. Just as I was about to step out of the door, I turned and said, "Sir, you know what?"

He looked up at me with a questioning gaze.

"Companies always want the best candidates to work for them, but they are not even ready to give them a chance, ignoring their small flaws!" I complained, feeling utterly reproachful towards the interviewer and other interviewers like him. I was tired of all the rejections after facing multiple rounds of interviews in various companies. It was demoralising and disconcerting. I had to let out the steam which had gradually built within me.

"It's not like that. We-" the interviewer fumbled, taken aback at my outspokenness.

Before he could utter his excuses, I added, "It's okay, Sir. Not your fault. Maybe the day when companies in India will start doing this, people will no longer consider relocating to foreign countries for jobs." After speaking my mind, I walked away from there, feeling a sense of relief and satisfaction.

Since my return to India, I had been on my toes looking after *Ma* and getting her treatment done. Four months went by in a flash, and by the time I decided to look for a job, I realised I had a total nine month gap since completing my MBA. *Only if I had worked in Jai's company instead of trusting his father!*

I wonder whether having skills is more important or having a perfect resume with referrals and without gaps.

With the rising medical bills for *Ma's* treatment, my financial situation gradually plummeted towards that of a beggar. I had to get a job urgently. But the question was, where do I look for one?

The third interview of the week and the twentieth of this month turned out as unsuccessful as the others. Depressed, I took a seat in a coffee shop. Desperation was leading me nowhere, and the companies' rules left me utterly frustrated.

I put my hands down and decided to look for other ways to earn money.

Sipping my coffee, I caught sight of a pamphlet stuck on the notice board, 'Looking for fresh faces for a popular Media agency.'

I wasn't sure whether I was qualified to be a model, but since I had no other options available, I decided to give it a try.

After noting the details of the advertisement, I did some research about the company and about the kind of modelling they usually do.

On the audition day, I changed into a pair of denim jeans with a red tank top instead of fitting into a dress that I wasn't comfortable in. Then, adding a bit of lipstick and mascara, I twirled around, feeling my best.

However, the moment I stepped in at the venue and glanced around, all my confidence vanished into thin air. Research cannot instil the belief that experience gives! I mumbled to myself, feeling dejected.

The girls appeared five to six years younger than me and much taller in height. Though my physical features were no less, I wasn't as skinny as them. All my conviction dwindled, and it felt like a big mistake to come here.

But I was in a dire state. *Beggars can't be choosers*, I thought to myself and found an empty seat in the waiting area. The place was abuzz with all sorts of people. Some of the women there were with their agents, while some were on their own. Some seemed like acquaintances and chatted with animated expressions, while some were quiet. Some appeared nervous, pretty much like me, and some looked confident despite the noise.

The more I observed, the more out of place I felt. Therefore, to calm my anxiety, I took out a book from my bag and started to read.

"What are you doing here?" I heard someone asking while I was immersed in the book.

I didn't look up, assuming that the person must've spoken to someone else. But then the person called out, "Are you trying to hide from me, Natie?"

The voice, coupled with the name, rang a bell in the deep recesses of my memory, making me look up briskly. The familiar face brought about an instant smile. "Akash! What a surprise!"

"I would be delighted if you'll say you've come to meet me!" he remarked, his eyes glistening with mirth.

I smiled as I stood up. "Yeah, kind of. If you are the organiser of this campaign or the judge for selecting a suitable model, I would have to say I've definitely come to meet you."

"Good one!" Before he could say anything more, someone called out to him. He glanced in the direction of the sound and nodded. Then, turning back to me, he added,

"Sorry, I'll be back in five minutes."

"How do you know him?" A girl sitting next to me asked as I took my seat.

"He is my college friend. Why?" I asked her.

"He is a famous Advertising Director, one whom everyone knows in the modelling industry," she replied, admiration evident in her voice.

"Oh! I didn't know," I mumbled, a little taken aback at the mention. Just then, a woman approached me and handed me a form with the instructions to fill in my details. As I scribbled in my replies, the girl sitting beside me asked again, "Have you done any assignments before?"

When I shook my head to say 'no', she looked at me with disbelief and added, "Don't you think you are a bit old to start with this profession?"

My brows knit together in annoyance at her rude comment. But before I could reply, the woman who had handed me the form, instantly answered, "Miss, we are looking for fresh faces, irrespective of age. All we need are people who can give a favourable impression. And if we go by looks, she is well suited and can give a tough competition to many!"

I looked at her with appreciation when she winked at me and added, "Take my advice, don't let others decide what you will become. I've been there and know it well."

"Thanks a lot!" I handed her the form with a smile on my face. Whatever fear and inhibitions I had in my mind about my suitability for the campaign was gone after the lady's remark.

Some strangers do make an impression of a lifetime on you!

I sat down, thinking over her words when my phone began to ring.

"Hey, Akash here," I heard a man say. "Don't talk, just go out, and my assistant will guide you to come from the other side of the gate."

"What, why?" I was perplexed by his suggestion.

"Just listen to me, and go down right now. I will explain later," Akash instructed and hung up. I acted as per his instruction, though not sure why he asked me to do so.

Ten minutes later, a man guided me to a room where Akash was seated behind a huge desk. The same lady who had asked me to fill the form was standing beside him.

"One tea, please," Akash said to the man who escorted me and introduced me to the woman. "This is my friend, Natasha, and Natie, this is Tanisha, my assistant. Tanisha, I want you to groom her up to be a model. Please see to it that the agency approves of her. I want her as the face of our new campaign."

"She looks good, but I think she has no experience." Tanisha looked from him to me.

"Yes, she is a fresher," Akash nodded, appearing optimistic. I stared at him in disbelief. *What was he so confident about? Tanisha's expertise or my skills?*

Tanisha appeared perplexed. "I don't think we have enough time to brief her. Is it possible if we put her in another work instead of this one?" Concern adorned her eyes which were bound by thin spectacles. She stepped towards Akash, her frail figure accentuating her simple white floral mid-length dress. She looked more knowledgeable and mature than the rest of the staff I had met.

The enthusiasm she had poured out for me in the waiting area had left a good impression on me. I felt like helping her out of the impossible predicament. "Akash, it's okay. I just came here to try. You don't have to worry. I'll be fine," I tried explaining.

Completely disregarding my words, Akash said pointedly to her, "Tanisha, she is smart and quick. And much better than the dumb girls we work with. All I want is for you to tell her the basics, and she will be fine." He turned towards me and added, "Natie, you don't need to worry. I know you can pull it off!"

"But the auditions have already started. We don't have time to groom her!" Tanisha put forth her objection in a panicky voice.

"I'm the Advertising Director, right? Leave that problem to me! I know how to set up things. Let the auditions be there; we'll have two contestants for the final selection for the agency panel." With these words, he stood up and rushed out.

Upon hearing Akash's impossible expectations, Tanisha turned pale.

"I'm sorry to land you up in trouble," I apologised, feeling bad for her.

"That's fine," she grimaced with an unhappy look. "I'm used to it by now." She placed her notebook on the table and sighed. She then looked at me, her lips curling up.

A smile cropped up on my face. I could correlate the expression many times with mine. Whatever mess you are in, put up a smile and sigh, 'life is harsh.'

"He is an excellent friend. I hope he isn't a bad boss," I tried to lighten her mood.

"At times, I am fed up with his attitude, but sometimes, I think he uses me to vent out his frustration!" she remarked with a frown. "Forget it! We don't have time to discuss him right now." Then, taking charge of the work assigned to her, she pulled a chair, sat down and added, "Let's start with what you know, and then, I'll brief you with all you need to know."

Tanisha heard me as I told whatever I knew about what was expected of me and was patient enough to answer my queries. Then, she led me to the stylist for a bit of make-up.

An hour later, Akash gave me a call to come over to the audition hall.

"He is asking me to come over," I said, getting cold feet.

Tanisha nodded her head and said assuringly, "Relax. You'll do well."

I kept the phone down and clasped her hand, "I don't want to audition anymore!"

"Take my word, you'll do a splendid job!" Tanisha patted my arm and added, "Remember, not everybody gets this opportunity. If Akash believes in you, then you have it in you!"

Her words were consoling, but the fear of facing the experienced judges adept at finding flaws made my confidence go low.

As soon as the light flashed on my face, I cringed and thought of running away. "You can do it!" Tanisha's voice from the side passage made me take back the thought. I slowly walked towards the centre of the stage with a forced smile to face the judges, only to tumble down and fall flat on my face.

There was silence all around, and my heart raced. Soon after, the sound of laughter resounded in my ears, making me go red with embarrassment. Feeling utterly humiliated, I got up and rushed out. As I entered backstage, people glanced at me and snickered while discussing in whispers; they had probably witnessed my fall. Hiding my face with my hands, I tried to find a place where I could sneak in. Blindly hurrying into an empty room, I closed the door instantly.

"Natasha, come over right now!" Akash's voice boomed in the corridor outside.

"Please let me go. I can't do this," I replied back, nervousness engulfing me, making me wish to dig a hole and hide within.

"Natasha, open up," Akash softly knocked on the door. "There's nothing to fear. I'm right here for you."

I opened the door, but the terror of facing the crowd made me numb.

"Akash, I can't do this!" I pleaded with him, my eyes restlessly eyeing him and the stage. "I had assumed it would be easy, but facing the crowd had made me go blank."

"I know you can do it. Remember who you are!" Akash cajoled, his grip tight on my wrist, not giving me the slightest opportunity to run away. I looked at him, trying to recall what was so heroic I had done in my life that Akash was so confident.

After a brief pause, he continued, "I've never met someone as confident as you! You remember, right after you joined college, you suddenly had seizures one afternoon and then had fainted?"

I nodded, wondering where he was going. The incident was as clear as day in my mind because it was one of those occasions where I had no control over myself. "Yes, everyone was laughing at me when I returned the next day," I said, giving a sigh.

"True, the next day when you came to college, everybody looked at you as if you had committed a crime," he added. He held my arms and continued, "You stood in the middle of the classroom, stared at everyone and said, 'Yes, I suffer from seizures, and it's not something I wanted to be born with. It's hard, but it doesn't stop me from moving. So if you have little courtesy, don't make my problem appear big, just because you don't suffer from it!'"

"You remember?!" I asked, taken aback as he repeated my words verbatim.

"You made an impact straight on my heart with your words. I've spent six years in college doing double graduation, but I never met anyone as bold and strong as you!" His eyes glistened, reflecting his deep-rooted respect for me.

I was hooked to his gaze for a second but then looked away abruptly. "I'm not that strong now. Life has thrown me around, and I can't even meet my own eyes." With my head cast down, dejectedly, I mumbled, "I'm lost, unable to find myself."

"C'mon, you can't give up without even giving it a try. Ok, let's do this. Forget about this campaign. But in the next one, you have to give your best!" His encouraging words made me sigh with relief. At least it was over for now.

"Till then, I'll make sure you are well prepared, ready to face the crowd and the camera!" he said with a smile. "Give me ten minutes. I'll wrap up everything, and then we'll go for some coffee."

I smiled at his back as he rushed away towards the audition hall. It had been around four years since I had last met him, and he was still the same, always willing to help and giving me the strength to shine. A few of my close friends often teased me with his name and tried to convince me that he was not just fond of me but had more profound feelings. But we never brought that topic up in our friendship.

Right now, finding love and living a fairy tale life had taken the backseat. I didn't want to think along those lines. Moreover, Jai still occupied my mind and a sizable portion of my heart.

Whenever I thought of my time with him, I couldn't believe that anything about our relationship had been fake. Even though it all started with a win-win arrangement, everything about us was far from mere pretence. At times, I was taken aback by his honesty and genuineness. He even shared his plans when he was going on a secret date to meet a girl he had met at a party. I had hoped that he wouldn't get intimate with her because I wanted him to be mine, but alas, it was just a wish, and wishes are like tampered feathers of a butterfly that cannot fly.

I swiped my phone screen at the sound of a notification.

No antidepressants and alcohol. Only exercise, yoga, and a healthy diet. It's an order from Jai:)

My face automatically curled up in a smile, and a few drops of tears escaped my eyes. Ever since I fell in love with him, my feelings only grew with each passing day. I wished to be with him forever. I accompanied him to parties and get-togethers, giving him company in drinks till dawn, hoping that he would reciprocate my feelings one day. But there were no signs from him.

As a result of all that drinking, I collapsed on the floor one night. My eyes stared far away while I couldn't feel a thing. Then, a few seconds later, I felt warmth seeping into my body, and I blinked, regaining consciousness.

I stared at the dark brown orbs, eyeing me with concern. "Let's take her to a doctor," I heard someone say and then felt being lifted up in someone's arms. I was in no position to see who it was, but my senses recognised his touch. Jai's fingers kept caressing my face and my hair while holding me in a protective embrace. Feeling safe in his arms, I succumbed to tiredness and passed out.

Quite sometime later, when I opened my eyes, I found myself lying on the car seat. When he noticed I was awake, he said, "You fainted all of a sudden."

"Oh, I didn't realise," I uttered.

"Don't worry. We are going to a doctor now," he added with a smile.

"Have you ever collapsed like this before?" asked the doctor as he examined me.

"I suffer from seizures. It was frequent until college, and then I didn't have any fit for a long time. I thought that I had recovered but don't know how it returned," I replied in a low, raspy voice. I glanced sideways at Jai, trying to read his thoughts. *Did he find me repulsive, much like many of my college mates, or did he pity me for being sick?*

Much against my suspicions, he blinked at me with assurance in his eyes.

"Are you facing any kind of stress?"

When I shook my head, he asked, "Any new habits or changes in your lifestyle?"

A lump formed in my throat as I knew it was due to my increased alcohol intake and irregular sleep.

"Are you taking proper rest?" he asked as he looked at me for answers.

"I think that's the issue, doctor." Jai suddenly spoke up. "She's not resting well these days and has been partying all night! You're right! Her lifestyle has drastically changed over the past month."

I was speechless and clenched my jaws. *Is it because I love partying and drinking, or is it all because of him?* I did it all to be with him so that he would appreciate my presence. But he seemed to be accusing me of changing my lifestyle!

The next second, I let out a sigh. It was not Jai's fault. He clearly wasn't aware of my feelings, and neither was he aware that I did it all for him. *Love makes people do things, which they wouldn't do otherwise.* To add to it, I was hopelessly romantic about him, dreaming of being one with him, emotionally attached to him, painting fancy pictures of our future together. *Sometimes, my heart feels like a fragile piece of red crystal that will be shattered because of my fairytale beliefs! But, for once, I wanted to believe in them, and I wanted nothing but this man in my life!*

If someone asked me the reason, I wouldn't be able to name it. In matters of the heart, we can't tell why it functions out of the way, just for a few people in life.

"What are you thinking about?" Jai asked as we left the doctor's cabin.

When I shook my head, he continued, "Remember, no more late-night parties and too many drinks."

"Hmm," I uttered dejectedly. *My only way of being with him has been restricted. How am I supposed to stay with him now?* He was busy during the daytime with his office and spent his evenings socialising. *When would I spend time with him now?*

"What happened to you? Don't take so much stress. Just take care of your health," he said, ruffling my hair. He then added, "Give me your phone."

When I unlocked and passed him my phone, he typed something and handed it back. "I have added a weekly reminder for you for the next year so that you sleep on time. Also, no alcohol, and it's my order! Understood?"

He never commanded me, so this time when he uttered such a sweet order, I couldn't help but smile and nod my head. "Yes, sir."

"Are you fine, Natasha?" Tanisha's voice interrupted my chain of thoughts.

"Yes," I nodded. "I'm okay now, but I was too scared earlier. I'm sorry I let all your hard work go to waste," I added, looking at her with pitiful eyes.

"No worries, everyone gets nervous the first time they go on stage. Many great models too had to go through this phase in their lives," she said sweetly.

"Thanks, Tanisha," I said.

"Shall we go?" Akash asked, coming inside. "Tanisha, take care of the rest of the event and let me know if anything comes up," he ordered her, pulling me out along with him.

"Sure, I will." Tanisha pursed her lips and pretended to smile. I could make out that she didn't like the tone of Akash's voice. but having no option, she obliged without complaints.

I picked up my purse from the table and dismissed the reminder that Jai had set on my phone, letting go of the memories that left lingering pain within me.

CHAPTER IV

Natasha

I was up early the following morning as I couldn't catch a wink all night, all worked up about the events that had shaken up my life in the past one year. Last evening at the coffee shop, Akash had told me about his next campaign with a luxury car manufacturer. He wanted me to accompany him to his next meeting scheduled today with the executives from the car company. They needed a fresh face to relaunch their brand in the Indian market, and Akash insisted I could do well in this.

I refused him straight away, but he insisted and added that it was not an audition but a meeting. Only if they liked my appearance would I have to face a camera test. The campaign dictated outdoor shooting with limited staff, so I didn't have to be nervous and jittery. "You should relax and be at ease," he added.

"Are you sure I will be able to do it?" I asked, sounding like a trapped rat in a cage, crying for help desperately.

"You will do well. I just have to check if things are ready at their end," said Akash. "I will confirm with you tonight."

Despite his encouragement, I was unsettled and anxious, which reached a new peak when Akash called up late in the night. "Listen, this is your chance. There will be only a handful of people for the camera test, so I'm sure you'll not have stage fright," he said. "I will pick you up at 10 a.m. sharp tomorrow."

He disconnected the call and left me to my devices. I shook my head, wondering why I ever went for the audition in the first place. Then, with plans to wake up early the following day, I closed my eyes to sleep. Just then, Jai's face flashed before my eyes. He had once said exactly the same thing to me while he was convincing me to accept his proposal of our fake marriage.

"Natasha, this is your chance to take care of your *Ma* and also lead a happy life," he had said, ushering me inside his cabin. Though he worked as an HR executive in Chad's company, he also had a retail outlet that sold luxury designer clothing. So after the coffee shop closed down, I started working for him as an intern to manage his inventory. That's when he came to know about my plight and offered me the contract marriage proposal.

"I can't. I will fumble and ruin everything. Please ask someone else," I said, feeling awkward to portray a beautiful relationship as fake.

"You don't have to be so nervous. I'll be there with you at all times. Besides, you just have to focus on the guests at the wedding. I promise I won't let you have stage fright." His dark brown eyes pleaded to me innocently. I found myself caught up in the moment. I could say nothing to avoid agreeing to his terms.

"I don't think I will be able to make it-" I started to say, but he suddenly took my hand in his, leaving me dumbfounded.

"Look, you are my only hope. My father will never lend me money if I don't marry soon, and I can't get anyone as suitable as you," he explained.

"Why me when there are so many other women?" I asked, feeling helpless. I could not possibly agree to his audacious proposal, nor could I summon up my courage with an irrefutable argument to deny it.

"First of all, you are an Indian, and secondly, you fit most of the criteria of a good daughter-in-law. My mom will like you for sure!" Still holding my hand, he tried to persuade me earnestly.

"Give me some time to think," I mumbled, trying to free myself from his grasp.

He withdrew his hand slowly, "Okay, sure, take your time," and got up to go back to his chair.

"By the way, one day should be enough to think, right?" he asked, catching me off guard.

I rolled my eyes in disbelief.

He made a funny face and confessed, "Don't take too long. I may die waiting."

I laughed at his gesture and got up to leave, "I'll let you know by tonight." I don't know why I asked for just a few hours to decide something this important!

However, he didn't even allow me to think it over for the night. He barged in while I was checking on the logistics of the day. "So, it's a yes, right?" he asked in his ever so persistent voice, without any hint of embarrassment or awkwardness.

"I was busy doing my work all day, didn't even get time to think about it!" I remarked, keeping my notebook down on the table. His pressure tactic was getting on my nerves now.

"Then let's discuss the plans over a cup of coffee," he stated, shutting the machine I was working on and picking up my purse as if he was already my boyfriend or fiancé.

Despite his alacrity, I kept seated in my chair, still not eager to accept his proposal.

"Be assured, you won't regret it." He flashed a smile, a small dimple adorning the side of his cheeks. Still holding my purse, he turned around and strolled towards the exit.

"You are too persistent on this," I said while trying to suppress my smile.

"It always takes effort to get what you want!" The charm of his smile had me hooked long ago. With my lips curled up, I followed him, convincing myself that there was nothing wrong in trying.

However, when we sat in the coffee shop, I couldn't help being in awe of his personality. Captivated by his alluring voice, I was lured by his words. "Look, I know you are a sensible girl. Whatever you are doing for your *Ma* is commendable! Life is giving you a chance to make more money and be happy. I think you should accept the offer, which is right before you."

"What if everyone comes to know, and later on, they accuse me of being a bad girl?" I asked what was nudging me in my heart. "And then, there are bound to be certain things I will repent later."

"Firstly, your *Ma* will not come to know about us being in a fake relationship, and secondly, I assure you there will be no intimacy between us until both of us are willing to take that chance," he said in a casual voice. "So there is no raising a finger on you and calling you bad."

I felt goosebumps visualising the scene of us being together on the bed, exploring each other intimately. I mentally shook my head to ward off the weird imagination and uttered a low, "Okay." For consolation, I added in my mind, *this should not happen again.*

"Thank you so much. I always knew you were smart. I will start making the arrangements and see to it that it is a secret," Jai smiled, leaving me spellbound.

Before I could stop him, he had picked up his phone and called someone. "Come to meet me tomorrow. Natasha is ready for the agreement. We need to get the paperwork in place and make it quick," he instructed on the phone.

I rolled my eyes in surprise. I wanted to snatch the phone away from him but stopped myself. What he had said made sense. It was not possible for me to arrange for *Ma's* treatment in such a short time unless I agreed to Jai, even though the proposal sounded to be preposterous.

A notification on my phone made me traverse back to my present. Everything was gone, and now I was on my own, trying to start a new journey. Even though I had tried to be strong, Jai's memories sometimes kept forcing me to become weak. I was finding it extremely hard to get over him.

And that's the reason why I couldn't sleep the whole night. I kept twisting and flipping myself on the bed, trying to persuade myself to get a good rest. But before I knew it, it was morning already.

I wonder how easy it's for someone to enter your mind in the middle of the night and disturb your entire sleep without them being physically present with you.

CHAPTER V

Natasha

As promised, Akash reached my doorstep at 10 a.m. sharp. I bid goodbye to my mother with a kiss on her cheek and left home with Akash. A few minutes later, he stopped the car in front of a styling boutique. He had told me about his plans for my quick makeover, but I didn't expect it to be such a posh place.

Flustered about the charges I'd have to bear at the expensive place, unknowingly, I uttered, "But I haven't got enough money with me."

"Leave that on me," he said, stepping out of the car.

With the lavish interiors, reflecting mirrors, a small water fountain at the centre, and staff ready to put five-star hoteliers to shame, I realised the payment for these services was beyond my means. "I think we should go somewhere else."

"Natie, leave everything to me," Akash held my hand to stop me from running off. "This boutique is owned by my agency. You are my guest here."

"I can't take such a huge favour from you," I shook my head, trying to pull my hand away.

"Don't be a kid! You know such a thing doesn't exist between you and me!" he remarked as he grabbed my arm and forced me to take a seat. Then, to the stylist who had appeared at his arrival, he instructed, "Style her so that she looks simple, elegant, and stunning."

He turned to me and added, "Natie, be at ease. I will come in a short while with a relevant dress." With these words, he left me in the company of the stylist.

I kept staring at my image reflecting in the mirror as the stylist worked on my hair. She styled it in a simple knot with curled ends. The makeup she applied was light and enhanced my features without giving a hint that I was loaded with expensive cosmetics.

I'm not sure whether it was to ease my nervousness or it was in her nature, the stylist chatted non-stop while she worked. She explained the features of each product she used on me. Thanks to her, I did not realise how time went by.

When I looked at my reflection, in the end, I found it hard to accept that it was me. I turned my head left and right in disbelief, only to realise that she had cast magic upon me and turned me absolutely beautiful. I loved it!

Behind me, Akash's familiar voice rejoiced, "Just the way I had imagined. Good job, Cynthia!"

"Thank you so much," I said to the stylist and turned towards Akash. He was smiling widely and had a paper bag in his hand. He extended his hand and added, "Change into this. We need to be at the venue in thirty minutes."

The premium brand label on the paper bag made me feel the burden of the expenses he incurred on my behalf. As I reluctantly eyed the bag, Akash pursed his lips.

"Natie, come on. There's no time to argue right now. Pay me back when you become an international model!" He clapped his hands to make me buck up and get going.

"Okay," I mumbled and walked towards the changing room with heavy steps.

I took the black dress out of the bag, slid it over my head and adjusted the narrow straps running down my shoulders to my back, holding the dress tight onto my frame. The thin band on the waist added to the charm. As I stared at the mirror, the reflection smiled back at me with appreciation.

"Thanks for the dress," I said to Akash as soon as I stepped out. "It looks wonderful!" There was no doubt that his choice was perfect.

"Most welcome," he replied with a satisfied smile. "I just knew it would suit you!"

As I took a seat in his car, my mind started wandering around in circles. I didn't know whether the chance I was taking was good for me or not, but I knew I had to give it a try. It was impossible to work in India as a receptionist and earn a decent living.

Neither did I know how long it would take for *Ma* to recover entirely. I had to make sure I made enough money to provide for her medical bills and everything related to her well-being. She was my top priority.

We arrived at a business park, and Akash stopped the car in the basement parking of the tallest building. As soon as the elevator doors opened on the topmost floor, the name 'Ninja Motors' greeted our sight. Beyond the main doors, the receptionist was seated, probably expecting our arrival. She greeted us with a warm smile and led us towards a conference room.

Soon, a man in his mid-thirties joined us. He acknowledged us and then spoke to Akash at length about the campaign.

"Mr Mehta, this is Natasha," Akash introduced me and added, "She's a fresh face and totally apt for this campaign."

He nodded, "We'll leave all that in your capable hands. We trust you in this. Let's just wait for my partner and sign the contract."

Just then, the door was pushed open from the outside. "Sorry guys, I am late," I heard a familiar voice echo in the room. A shiver ran down my spine as recognition set in.

"Oh God, not him!" I cast my head down, not willing to face the person who had been plaguing my days and nights since we went our separate ways four months ago.

I heard him say, "Mr Akash, finally we get to meet. I've heard a lot about you!"

"Thank you, same here," Akash replied. They discussed the plan to launch the brand for a couple of minutes while I kept mum with my head down.

Although I tried to listen to all their talks, my mind was clearly not in favour of working with them. I wanted to hide my face and run away from there, but I heard someone calling my name; it was Akash. "This is Natasha Meher, fresh face but perfect for your campaign. I think she would do proper justice to this launch."

I looked up with a plastered smile and uttered a soft, "Hi."

The minute our eyes met, I felt like digging the ground and burying myself underneath, but to my utter surprise, Jai asked in a casual voice with a smirk, "Nice! I think I have seen you somewhere, Natasha?"

"Could be, she has also recently returned from Perth," Akash spoke on my behalf. I glared at Jai for his audacity to ask me such a question and felt like clawing the crooked smile off his face.

"So, miss or is it Mrs Natasha?" he asked with a smug smile.

"It's Miss. We don't do contracts with married women in our company unless it's old models who have been working with us or some other circumstance," Akash replied.

Jai's conceited smile stretched from one ear to the other, and my blood started to boil. He was clearly enjoying the fact that he was privy to my weakness. I wanted to run away, but I stopped because of Akash. If anything slipped out in reply, it would affect my relationship with him.

"Sorry, Jai and Akash, I have to move out." Mehta, Jai's business partner, suddenly voiced in, ending the topic. "I have a meeting lined up. Jai, let me know what you decide. Once the meeting gets over, I'll drop by if required."

Just as he exited the conference room, Jai turned to me again. "How many years into modelling, Missss Natasha?" asked Jai, unnecessarily stretching on 'Miss'.

"She just started with us. Since we are looking for new talent, I thought she would be the best," answered Akash.

"Is she mute?" Jai questioned, raising one brow as he cast his eyes from Akash to me. "Or does she have some other problem?"

"I can speak very well, Mr Jai," I replied, my tone lined with anger.

"Oh, okay," replied Jai and turned to Akash with a sceptical look. "So you are suggesting we use a newbie like her to launch our brand. Are you sure she will be a good idea? I'm sorry, but I don't see any special calibre in her for you to recommend her so profusely."

I could tell that Jai was picking on me. *That's it!* I stood up abruptly, losing all my calm. "Akash, since he doesn't trust us, we shouldn't be working with him," I said, crossing my arms over my chest.

Akash gently held my hand and pulled me down to take a seat. "Natasha, calm down." He gestured with his eyes for me to relax.

"I trust you, but before I make an agreement with your agency, I need to be sure I am involving the right person for this launch," Jai stated, eyeing me. "Perhaps, we should make a decision after the camera test. Frankly, I don't think this advertisement and glamour launch of the brand will help bring more profits, but my partner is adamant in trying, so let's do some photoshoots with your model."

"That's great!" Akash chirped in. "So, when are you available for the camera test?"

Jai glanced at his watch and replied, "It's eleven right now... how about twelve o'clock? I don't have any meetings lined up after this, so if you could arrange a photographer and the camera, we could do it right away." Jai touched his chin, and his eyes danced in amusement. *He was clearly mocking me!*

I sighed, trying to calm myself for Akash's sake and contemplated whether to come clean before him about my relationship with Jai. I could either walk away from the campaign or stay put and watch how things went.

"That's perfect! I'll make the arrangements right away," nodded Akash, standing up. "Excuse me for a minute. I'll make the necessary calls and be right back."

"Ak-" I opened my mouth to stop him.

But Jai butt-in, "Thank you! You can talk here. Miss Natasha, if you don't mind, we can move to my room, next door. It will be more comfortable there."

Akash nodded with a smile in reply as he was already on the phone. He placed a hand to mute his microphone and said to me in a low voice, "I'll be there in ten minutes."

"Come, Natasha," said Jai, standing up and leading the way.

Since Akash had already agreed, I had to step out of the room. But I had no inclination to follow Jai to his cabin.

"I think I'll be fine here," I said, stopping outside the conference room and pulling out my phone from my purse.

"Oh, you don't want to come to my cabin? But weren't you perfectly alright with sharing a room with me for six months?" Jai sniggered, opening the door to his room. "I don't mind waiting for Akash here outside. The only thing is it's far more comfortable in my room."

"Why?" I asked, annoyed at his remark. "I did what you asked for. So why are you taking a dig at me now?"

"Come on! Taking a dig?" he retorted, pulling me inside the room and closing the door behind. He slumped in his chair and vented out, "You hid your face and pretended as if I was a stranger! Then you said 'Hi' as if you didn't know me at all!"

"I did it because there is nothing between us anymore," I countered, feeling miserable inside. I took a deep breath and placed my arms on Jai's table. "And yes, I acted like a stranger because I didn't want to dwell in the past. What I do with my life is none of your business, Mr Jai Sharma."

"You are absolutely correct," Jai replied, not the least bit rattled by my reply. "But how can you act like a stranger when we were such good friends?"

"I don't know about friendship or whatever it was between us. I just know I don't want our relationship to be disclosed to my *Ma* or anyone else here in India," I snapped back at him.

"In that case, let me clear it to you. The case has not yet been approved by the-" Jai stopped mid-way as the door was pushed open.

"The arrangements are done. My team should be here in twenty minutes," said Akash. He glanced from me to Jai, perhaps perceiving the tension between us.

"I'll wait in the conference room," I immediately replied and walked out.

"Sure, then I'll be here. Call me when the things are ready," said Jai to Akash.

"This man is quite weird," said Akash as he joined me a minute later. "Natie, are you ready?" he asked me, and I nodded. "Don't be mad. In this line, you will find many clients who will get on your nerves, but we must be calm until we show them what we truly are," he added and patted my shoulder. "This can be your biggest break."

"A few more projects like this, and you'll become a star," he kept blabbering while I kept thinking about Jai and what he had said. I couldn't understand why he expected me to behave as his die-hard friend when what we had between us was nothing of the sort that friends do with one another. Besides, it wasn't friendship between us that transpired at the end. It was more than that...

Whatever it is, I don't give a damn about his so-called friendship!

CHAPTER VI

Jai

Just when you feel everything is falling in place, you come across problems that you had not imagined even in your dreams. The sole reason for marrying Natasha was to make my Dad fund my dream project. He promised that he would remit the money only after I got married.

Marry, then money. These words reverberated in my ears.

I felt suffocated at home and went to work. Not 'Tech-Empower Agency', where I worked under the scrutiny of big brother, Chad, but my own retail shopping outlet, not very far from there.

Despite my efforts, this retail outlet could not be made into a huge success. The city of Perth was overwhelmed with similar outlets at every corner. After making average sales for four consecutive years, I realised that I could not expand the outlet with the net annual profit I had envisioned earlier. There was absolutely no future in this business. To avoid my parents' constant nagging and the stress building up from my failure, I sought to work with Chad in his company.

I learned many things from him, but the sense of ownership never existed in his company. I had to follow his rules, which, at times, left a sour taste in my mouth.

When I intended to launch a luxury car company in India and asked my Dad to invest, he refused straightaway, stating that it was not profitable. Moreover, he added with a regretful face, "I invested a good amount for your retail business. Look what you've done to it! You should have worked harder to make a profit and used that money in your car business!"

I stood quiet, with my head hung low, feeling utterly helpless!

"If you had partied less and not hung around with your friends day in and day out, you would have saved millions and used that in your company!" Dad berated me with a scowl.

I felt like saying, *'Forget it! I don't need any of your money!'* And I almost walked away, but then stopped. The car company was my dream, and I couldn't do anything except listen to his accusations to fulfil it anyhow.

"Still, I will lend you money on one condition," Dad added, flexing the newspaper he was reading. He eyed me as if instructing an employee and not his son.

I stood rooted to the spot to hear his condition, even though I was hundred percent sure it would never be a conducive one.

He folded the newspaper, kept it aside and looked at me as he said, "If you get married within the next six months, you can have the money."

"Six months?" I shrieked. It was beyond my comprehension how he had come up with such a ridiculous clause to lend me the money! *Is he crazy? He is speaking of marriage as if he is picking up groceries from the supermarket!*

"Yes. You do have a lot of female friends, and I'm sure they are all worth dating. So just pick one amongst them," he explained.

He sounded as if those girls were dying to marry me while I was the one who was refusing them. *Yes, girls are dying to marry me, but I know I can only spend a week with them. How can I bear their ill attitudes and lack of brain for a lifetime?*

This condition seemed impossible to fulfil and the resulting outcome unacceptable! I really needed his funding, but how could I marry just anyone and be tied up with her for the rest of my life?! Moreover, I was not quite ready to share personal or business life with just about anyone!

I didn't want to argue with him as I knew it was meaningless to do so. The condition did not seem worthwhile. He was someone who forced his ideas upon others but never bothered to listen to their views.

Frustrated, I stormed out of the dining room. Just as I was about to step out of the house, my mother's voice made me stop. "I hope you understand why he has put forth such a condition. You are our only son, and we wish to see you do well."

"Mom! You're in this together with him! This stupid condition of his is absolutely ridiculous!" I grumbled at my mother.

"Once you'll get married, you will get a sense of responsibility. Everything you do will be streamlined, and you will be able to make better decisions," Mom advised, holding my hand, knowing very well that I wasn't interested in marriage.

"Seriously, Mom? Marrying is now like getting into a session with the psychiatrist, or perhaps it brings about a complete change in DNA?" I scowled, releasing her grip over my hand and walking away. "Mom, we are in the twentieth century, but both of you sound like you are stuck in the eighteenth century!"

"Jai, you need to give it a chance," she said aloud, making me stop.

"And if it doesn't work out, then I'll get divorced, is it? So, who will be responsible for the hell I go through in the process?" I asked, making eye contact with her.

She cringed at my words, not expecting me to counter her logic this way.

"No, you didn't think about this!" Unable to hold my fury, I yelled, "And that's because you thought I would adjust with anyone just as you adjusted with that arrogant man all your life."

She helplessly glanced at me, too stumped to reply.

With a look of contempt, I turned around and left. It was a waste of time to talk to her on this topic.

To cool off my mind, I drove directly to my retail outlet. As soon as I reached, I wanted to rush inside my cabin and scream my heart out, but my attention stopped at a familiar face near the reception. I had met the woman quite a few times at The Grind, the coffee shop on the bottom floor of Chad's office tower. She was continuously fidgeting with a file in one hand, her free hand sometimes touching her eyes and sometimes her chin.

"What is that lady doing there at the reception?" I asked Jina, my store manager, as soon as I took a seat.

"Oh, that lady in yellow is looking for a job." She glanced towards the reception and continued, "It seems she is in urgent need of one and is ready to fit in anywhere in the store."

Through the clear glass, I stared at the coffee girl for a few seconds and then instructed Jina, "Get her resume."

With a frown, she asked, "Sir?"

"Get her resume," I repeated and got back to review the papers before me.

Jina returned and handed me the coffee girl's resume. I flipped through her profile. Her name was Natasha, and she is pursuing an MBA at Curtin University. Her name sounded pleasant to my ears. With a smile, I said, "Hire her to do the logistics and pay her decently."

Taken aback, Jina stared at me wide-eyed. Her surprise was understandable as there were no open positions in the store. She currently looked after the logistics, and hiring Natasha to do the same job was clearly not favourable for her. Moreover, I asked her to hire Natasha directly without even an interview.

"Jina?" I raised my brows at her blank look.

Coming back to reality, Jina nodded and left. I'm sure she assumed that the woman was an acquaintance and hence I offered her the job. It wasn't entirely false either. I did know her, but I hired her because I had something in mind for her.

A few minutes later, Jina walked in and placed the contract agreement before me for my signatures. As I looked up, Natasha stood behind her with eyes open wide and mouth agape in surprise at our fortuitous meeting.

"Natasha, please, take a seat." I gestured towards the chair with a smile.

"Ah, yeah... Hi. I didn't know this was your place," Natasha said, regaining her composure.

"Yes, I own this store as well as work with Tech-Empower Agency as an HR head," I replied with a smile as I signed the agreement and slid the papers towards her for her signatures. "By the way, congratulations, Natasha, and welcome aboard."

"Thank you," she said, and then signed the papers, disbelief evident on her face.

"I am Jai Sharma. I hope Jina explained to you about your work here?" Before she could answer, I added, "And let me know if you are happy with the pay package here."

"Oh, no issues with the pay. It is much more than what I used to get working at two places!" Natasha remarked with a pleasant smile.

"Two places?" My brows raised questioningly. I had to know everything about her before approaching her with what I had in mind.

"Well, initially, I worked at only one, but it wasn't sufficient to support my stay and the study loan. So I started doing two jobs," she replied.

"You are also doing an MBA along with two jobs," I remarked, looking at her resume.

"Yes, I enrolled in it as soon as I found the company I had come here to work for was a fraudster. I realised, only further studies could get me a good job," she said and added, "It will be completed in three months from now."

"Hmm," I nodded. Then, to better understand her financial situation, I tried to probe, "Once your college is over, I'm sure you'll do well! You'll be able to earn better and even save!"

"Well, I hope so, for I really need a good salary." Her eyes turned distant, and her voice gradually diminished as she answered.

My gaze was fixed on her face. There was a hint of melancholy in her voice. "Is there a particular reason why you need to earn well?" I asked inquisitively.

She took a deep breath and shook her head. "Just a personal situation." With a small smile, she added, "Nothing for you to worry about. Thank you so much for the job!"

Damn! She sure is in need! I wanted to know the reason and the amount. *But I have to have some patience and not rush her, or she might run away!* "Sure, I know you can manage, but let me know if you need anything. You are now my employee and also an old acquaintance." I tried not to be too nosy.

"Thank you, Jai. I am privileged to be here," she replied.

Just then, Jina, who had left to get Natasha's identity card, re-entered and handed it to her.

"Looking forward to working with you," I said, standing up and extending my hand to her. Then, after a small shake, I turned to Jina and added, "Explain everything to her and make sure she is at ease."

As they left, I sighed, feeling much better. There was still hope. I could keep my dreams alive!

The next few days, I watched her and found her to be indeed the right choice. She was beautiful, slim, homely, and friendly. I just knew she was the one who could fit in with my family right away and also would not create a problem for me. And she was in dire need of money as her mother was suffering from cancer and needed surgery for complete recovery.

Everything went according to my plan, and I even got the money. But as life would have it, the luxury car launch was unsuccessful. The idea didn't sell well with the Indian crowd.

My partner, Mehta, advised me to rebrand the car, targeting the upper-middle-class segment of the population. Hence, the marketing plans had to be revised, and a new advertisement with a fresh homely face was required.

If everything went off well, we would relaunch again, but I had no clue I would come face to face with Natasha. I didn't see her until Akash pointed out a girl sitting next to him, and there she was, as radiant as I had ever known her to be. She looked stunning in the body fitting outfit and the new hair-do.

But why did she pretend as if she didn't know me? We had such a good friendship and had shared everything under the sun with each other. Naturally, I was annoyed, and that's why I teased her. However, the response she gave told me something was off with her. She was not happy to see me there. I never thought she didn't want to see me again.

"Sir, the arrangements for the photoshoot are done," said my secretary, knocking on my door.

"Sure, I'll join in sometime," I said and returned to my emails. After completing the monotonous job of reading and replying, my annoyance dissipated to an extent, and I decided to set out and check the camera test.

When I arrived at the site, the photographer was instructing Natasha to try some poses before the camera. She looked embarrassed and even fumbled a couple of times as she posed.

I caught sight of my partner. There was a deep frown on his face as if he was having second thoughts. It seemed like he was considering whether Natasha was worth the pain or not.

On the other hand, Akash was trying hard to motivate Natasha to bring out the desired look.

"I don't think she can do it. She's lacking confidence. And the fresh look is missing." I tapped my hand on the camera lens of the photographer.

"By the way, is she your girlfriend?" My partner asked Akash, unable to hold his disappointment. "Can't we have someone else?"

By the look on Akash's face, I could read he did have some feelings for Natasha because he laughed it off very casually and said, "Give me some time. She is a fresher, but she will do well."

"Natasha, come here," I called out.

She took slow steps towards me. Her face had a glint of awkwardness as she walked.

"Look, take a day off and come back tomorrow, but tomorrow is the final day of the trial. I don't want any random girl to be the face of my brand. Show us what you've got tomorrow, else we'll be happy to replace," I retorted, feeling irked at the attention Akash gave her. He appeared as if he desperately wanted to do something for her but was helpless.

The more I looked at him watching her with those caring eyes, the more it pissed me off.

Natasha remained quiet, with an uncomfortable look on her face.

"All right, we'll see you tomorrow. Thank you for your time," said Akash as he asked the photographer to pack up, and they left from there.

As Mehta watched them leave, he turned to me and asked, "Will she be able to do it? Why give her another day?"

"I think she'll do fine. She just needs some time to adjust," I said, feeling unsure why I said so. *Is it my confidence in her, or is it my confidence to make her do whatever is required?* I couldn't figure it out. She seemed to be feeling awkward. Was it because of my presence?

That night, I reviewed my current financial situation. It was terrible! The car sales were depressing, and the retail store in Perth was running at a loss. A lot was at stake; we had to make the rebranding work, otherwise...

With a drink in my hand, I imagined things from bad to worse. I had a sudden impulse to run away from everything and go somewhere far away. At that very moment, my Mom called up from Perth as if she knew I was in a lot of stress. "How are you doing? I heard the company isn't doing that great."

"I haven't given up, Mom. I am trying my best not to let you down and make Dad proud," I said, taking a sip of my drink to soak the feeling of sadness and change it to motivation. But it wasn't convincing.

When you are low, your loss of enthusiasm is clearly reflected in your voice, and that's what happened to me. I tried my best to motivate myself, but each word sounded fake.

"I know, Jai, but I don't know why you chose to build this in India when you have all your family living in Perth..." She sounded low.

"I am here for my grandpa, who has always been my guardian angel whenever I was sad and left out," I said, thinking of my childhood. Mom and Dad often fought with each other and left me with grandpa. Those were the best days of my life when I used to see the world from his eyes. Grandpa loved my company, and I, his. With Mom and Dad away, he made sure I was taken care of well. He had appointed a young couple with a son to look after me. When Grandpa was busy with work, I sneaked into their house in the backside of our compound to play with their son, Atul.

Grandpa disapproved of me playing with him as he was not good company. He often roamed around on the streets with other notorious children like him and acted roguish in the neighbourhood. But I still liked playing with him. Because in his company, I had enjoyed learning to climb trees, gate crash other people's houses and even steal fruits from their backyard. I also learnt self-defence, the secret of hitting someone when attacked. Memories are much more fun when you have done something adventurous; it can be bad or good, it doesn't matter.

"You are mad, Jai. I don't understand the logic! He is no more, and you say that you are doing all this because of him," Mom shrieked, irritated by my words. My feelings were always secondary to mom and dad. They just never tried to understand me!

They expected me to always act rationally, but I could never be practical like them where Grandpa was concerned. I owe my emotions to only one man, my grandpa. It didn't matter whether he was living or dead.

Sometimes, even staying where the person you love once lived gives you peace. However, it is futile to explain all this to those who don't even understand those kinds of sentiments.

"Jai, are you there?" asked my Mom, breaking my spell of thoughts.

"Yes, I am. Just a bit tired. Can we talk tomorrow?" I asked.

She whispered in reply, "I hope you get back to your senses soon."

As soon as I kept the phone down, it started ringing again. The number was unknown, but the caller tracing app displayed Akash Malhotra. I had no clue why he called, but I picked up, assuming it might be related to business.

"Jai, I am sorry, but tomorrow we will not be able to come. I've got an urgent personal problem, and won't be able to join you. I hope you understand," he said.

"Okay," I replied and heard his thank you as he disconnected the call.

Was he really having a problem or citing it so that Natasha could get some additional time? His caring look, which he cast on Natasha all day, flashed in my mind. *He sure favours her a lot!* I was sure it was an excuse to give her some time.

But couldn't she just call me if she needed more time? Why did she have to go through him? I will have to confront her once she comes back!

Once Mehta would come to know that they were avoiding us tomorrow to give time to Natasha, he would suggest we change the media agency. I would have to convince him to wait.

Oh God, I don't know why I'm doing this! Maybe just for the simple reason that I knew her personally. She wasn't a bad person, and she once helped me when I needed her. After the morning interaction, two things about her irked me. First, her deliberate act, pretending not to know me, and second, her unapproachable demeanour. *I had to find out whatever was the reason for all this, for I know I will not be at peace otherwise!*

Having said that, I wanted to know if she had contacted Samira, her best friend. At her wedding, Samira had looked at me as if I was the culprit for Natasha's absence.

The last words Natasha told me before leaving Perth was, "Don't let Samira know that I'm in India." She looked hurt as if she was suffering, so I couldn't muster up my courage to ask her for a reason. But as soon as Samira found out about our fake marriage, the former's eyes were full of hatred every time she glanced at me.

It was clear that Samira loved Natasha as much as Natasha loved her. But there was something about Natasha... her eyes always spoke volumes about her feelings. Big brown angelic eyes dropped tears like pearls when she was sad and fluttered down every time she is embarrassed...

I never knew how her eyes looked when she was angry. In fact, I'd never seen her get furious. But today, I got a glimpse of it when I teased her. But then, she looked away, and I didn't get the opportunity to see what they turned into.

I think I've had too much of Natasha today! Before this, I don't think I've ever thought of her so much in a day!

I was sure of one thing, if Grandpa was alive, he would have been happy to meet her.

I dozed off, imagining Natasha and Grandpa together here with me in this house.

"You know he is still here. J, please behave," she said as I pushed her, cornering her up a wall.

"You are my wife. I have all the rights to kiss you and make love to you whenever I want," I said, caressing her cheeks with my thumb.

Her eyes blinked as she tried to hide the excitement which rose in them as she blushed. "Not true. You can't do all this to me whenever you want." She teased my senses with her coquettish gaze. Then, suppressing her smile, she tried to push me away.

I smirked at her futile attempts. "Don't underestimate me. It will take me just a few minutes to turn you on. I love watching you-"

She clamped my mouth from saying the rest. "I don't understand what has happened to you! When did you become a pervert? Let me check on Dadu first." She removed her hand from my mouth and tried to move away.

"Not before I get what I want," I held her hands in mine and gently kissed along her earlobes to her collarbone. She had stopped pushing, and I could hear her breathing getting harder.

My hands dropped down as she laced hers on my back and gave a peck on my lips.

"Later on, J... please, and you can't do this to me, whenever you want. I am not your wife anymore," she said, moving away, her eyes glistening with tears.

"Hey, you are mistaken. There is still something between us," I urged, holding her to me.

She withdrew the grip ever so easily. "Now, there is nothing. We are separated. I am not yours, and you are not mine."

"Goddammit! I will rip those papers and anything that makes us apart!" I screamed, but she had moved a couple of steps away before I could hold onto her.

"It was you who separated us, not any papers. Only you!" She turned around softly with those harsh words and disappeared into thin air.

"Nats," I screamed aloud and tried to run behind her but fell down on the floor. My eyes opened suddenly, and I realised I was dreaming. I had dozed off on the sofa and had fallen down on the floor.

It was a dream. *I guess it's the after-effect of thinking so much about Natasha*, I mumbled to myself and then moved to my bed.

CHAPTER VII

Natasha

"I don't want any random girl to be the face of my brand. Show us what you've got tomorrow, else we will be happy to replace you." The words resonated in my ears, again and again. It was like the nail on the coffin!

I never ever want to see him again! I don't know how I could ever fall in love with that disgusting man! After what I've done for him, he's behaving as if I'm nothing for him!

Yes, I wanted to hide that I knew him, but what was wrong with that? I can't tell everyone I knew him well because we were in a contract marriage. We were faking then!

I felt like replying, 'Haven't you already seen enough of what I've got?' But I bit my lips; I couldn't humiliate myself just for the sake of putting some sense into him. With everything that I had done for him, at least, he could have addressed me with some respect!

But no, it's my fault to find goodness in Mr Jai Sharma. It's like asking the devil to become God!

I tried hard, but my tears didn't stop. Worried about me, Akash, who was driving, restlessly glanced at me multiple times.

"Natie, we can let this one go. We can try the next one," he said as we almost reached his office.

I shook my head and wiped away the tears. "No, I will do my best. I can't run away like a distressed girl. I will show him what I can do."

It wouldn't have hurt like this if someone else had said those words. I was not upset because Jai mocked and demeaned me; rather, it was because I didn't expect him to act so low.

Akash was a little rattled at my reaction. "I know you are a strong girl, but it's not necessary to hurt yourself, seriously. I won't mind dropping the project."

I sighed and looked at him, "Can you stop pretending as if everything is fine? I can see how important this project is to you. If you do well, this project can earn you crores. Plus, you'll make a name. If we back out, people will question your choices."

"Neither the money nor the opinions of others matter to me," he said, stopping the car on the side. "You are important. You are a very good friend of mine, and I can't let you down."

"It's a commercial for a car, and they have big budgets. So how can this project not be important to you?" I asked with a smile at his kind words.

A call on his phone interrupted our conversation. His expression immediately changed seeing the caller's name, and he said sweetly, "Soha! Baby, I'll be home soon, darling. Look, I will get there in an hour." He listened for a while and replied, "Baby, now I have an aunty with me whom I have to drop at the office. She has some work." He turned to me with his hand placed on the mic. "It's my daughter. She wants me to come home and play with her."

For a second, I was taken aback to know that he had a daughter. But then, I remembered that he was four years older than me. We met in college when he enrolled in a Mass Communication course for his second graduation.

I heard his daughter's childish whining from the other end. Though I couldn't make out what she said, my mood immediately lightened.

"Oh no, not Tanisha Aunty. I am with my college friend, Natasha Aunty," he explained to her with a smile on his lips.

She sounded adorable. How could I hold back her father just to drop me back at the office? I gestured at him to let me off and drive home to his daughter. I could very well take a taxi.

I opened the car door and was about to step out when Akash held my hand to stop me from walking out. He signalled with his finger for me to hold on for a second and said on the phone, "But *beta*, she is busy. She can't come home today. I'll bring her some other day."

When he disconnected the call, I raised a brow. "What was the little one asking?"

"She wants you to come home with me. She is baking a cake and wants us to taste it," Akash replied, laughing.

"Cake? How old is she?" I asked inquisitively.

"Six," he replied, then added, "Quite a champion at cakes, considering her age."

His kid sounded super fun. So, to get my mind off all the distressing things, I replied, "I'll be glad to come."

"Are you sure?" he asked with a frown, quite taken aback.

I nodded, shutting the car door.

Fifteen minutes later, we entered a posh apartment in Malad. As he opened the door with his keys, out came a sweet voice from inside, "Darling, I'm in the kitchen."

I stopped and stared at him in complete surprise.

"She calls me darling, and I call her dumpling," he said, suppressing an embarrassing smile twitching at the corner of his lips.

I stood a few steps away from him as we walked into the big spacious kitchen. There was a large counter in the centre. A little girl was seated with her legs dangling and was mixing something with the spatula.

"This Renee doesn't know anything. We will have to change her soon, Darling," the little girl said as soon as she saw him.

Next to her was an old lady pouring the chocolate mix into the bowl slowly. "Oh, as if someone else will be willing to take up your tantrums as nicely as me. Remember, only a fool will be able to withstand all your silly acrobats," she retorted.

"Renee, you are getting old and stupid! You can't understand even my jokes!" the girl remarked playfully, making the old lady frown. "Why do you want me to always help you in the kitchen? You should make all this and give them to me!" The little girl jumped down from the counter to run away.

"You little brat!" The old lady kept the chocolate mix aside and ran after the girl. "Wait, let me first give you a spank, then I will tell you."

The little girl raced around the counter with the old lady on her heels.

Akash glanced at me and then turned to the two people running around like Tom and Jerry. He clasped his forehead with his fingers and said helplessly, "Soha, stop running."

Both of them abruptly ended the chase.

"Catch me, Renee," Soha said, flashing a mischievous grin at her.

But the old lady threw her wooden spatula on the countertop. "Okay, I give up! Don't run, please, Soha."

The little girl's lips turned down. Then, in a sulking voice, she said, "You all are making me so bored! I can run a little bit, can't I? Why am I treated like a doll? Just sit in one place and not do things like a normal girl." She slumped down on a stool with her hands crossed and head hanging.

"You are a drama queen." Akash smiled at her adorable performance of the pitiful act. "Come, meet my friend, Natasha," he said, picking her up in his arms.

She was quite a charmer as she giggled and then settled down on the couch with him.

"Hi, Natasha," she said, snuggling to him and looking at me. "Are you his college friend who used to eat his tiffin at lunchtime?"

"Did he say that?" I asked them, hurdling across the couch to where they sat.

"Yes, he did and also that you were plump. With gaps in your teeth and had no friends," she added.

"Hey, quiet," hushed Akash, while she kept talking. "He also said you never attended any classes and used to take his notes."

I pursed my lips and glared at Akash as if I wished to kill him right there.

He clamped up Soha's mouth. "What rubbish are you spouting! You wanna make us fight?"

She bit his hand.

Akash yelped and removed it from her mouth.

"I am telling her whatever you have told me!" Soha quipped, her eyes glistening merrily.

"So, this is what you tell everyone behind my back!" I countered with a furious look. "I'm going back, and don't ever talk to me!" I stood up, holding my purse. Intending to leave, I turned towards the door.

"He also said you were a gem of a person and one of his closest friends in college," I heard her say.

I paused in my tracks as she added, "It's because you enjoyed his tiffin that he requested *Dadi* to make delicious food for you."

I turned around, my cheeks creased with a radiant smile.

Soha continued, "He also told me that you both did a lot of gimmicks together to earn money to pay your fees."

I slouched back on the sofa and added, "Yes, that we did, and I also used to bring tiffin for him."

She frowned at my correction and clutched his arms, "I know you both are good friends, but you can't ever take my place. He is my darling! Not even Tanisha Aunty can take him away from me!"

Dumbfounded, I glanced from Soha to Akash.

"My dear dumpling, I'm only yours. Natasha Aunty is my friend, and Tanisha is my assistant. Why do you think they will take me?" he teased her, pressing her chin between his fingers.

"I think they will, one day," she reasoned, making a face.

I pressed my lips together, thinking about what to reply when Akash hit her hand softly. She hit him back hard on his chest and shouted, "I am not lying! See how Natasha Aunty has turned so beautiful. What if you fall for her and leave me all alone?"

"I won't fall for anyone, don't worry. Your Dad is safe with you," I replied, feeling bewildered at the thoughts of the little girl.

She immediately jumped out of her father's grasp and came up to me. She held my hand, blinked her big eyes and asked, "Break up?"

"Yes, kind of," I replied, holding my laughter at her sweet gestures.

"Don't worry, you'll get someone else soon. It's better to leave the ones who don't care for you!" She said the greatest of the advices in the sweetest of voices.

"You are correct, my intelligent Soha," I said, cheering her up.

"Oops! What's the burning smell..." she said, peering towards the kitchen with her nose scrunched up. "*Dadi*, I thought you were keeping a watch in the kitchen. Who told you to come and listen to elders when they talk?" Soha jumped up again and rushed towards the kitchen, followed by the old lady.

Akash couldn't hold back anymore and laughed at her receding back. Then, thinking of the old times and the revelations made by Soha, I spanked his hands and questioned, "This is what you thought about me!"

"What rubbish! She was teasing you. Didn't she mention later on? I was the one who toldMomto cook delicious food for you," he defended himself, rubbing his hand.

"But I'm a little confused. Sometimes, she calls your Mom *Dadi* and then sometimes Renee," I asked, watching both of them fight in the kitchen over the burnt muffins.

"She calls her different names so that she feels surrounded by many and forgets her mother." Akash looked over his shoulder towards the kitchen and sighed. "She was three when my wife died in an accident. Then, in the same year, we came to know she has a hole in her heart."

"What?" I almost choked, realising the horror the little one was facing. "It can be treated, right?"

"Yes, but she needs to be at least six for surgery," Akash replied with a distant look. "She turned six a few days ago, and we're planning to fly soon to the US for her treatment. We've been waiting for such a long time, and the doctor had advised not to make her sad, panicky, or tired. Mom and I are always on toes, and because of that, she's our spoilt little brat!" He shrugged his shoulders and added with a smile, "But I don't mind her tantrums. For me, she is my world!"

"Hats off to your Mom's patience," I said.

"Yes, I can be relaxed because Mom is there, but I don't know what will happen when she gets too old. She keeps on pestering me to marry someone, but I'm afraid if I marry, the other person might not look after Soha the way we do," he said, then stood up. "Anyway, that's enough of me. I don't want to bore you with such mundane talks."

"So, what is it with Tanisha?" I asked since Soha had hinted at her name too many times.

"Soha doesn't like her at all. Not that Tanisha is bad, but Soha feels Tanisha gives unnecessary reasons to make me work late, and then I don't get to be with her for more time," he explained.

"Oh, and here I thought that you two were seeing each other," I lamented, trying to tease him.

"No way!" Akash refused forcefully. "First of all, she is my employee. Secondly, she is not my type. She is blunt and outgoing, a complete opposite of me!" he added, shaking his head. "Leave the discussion about her. Tell me, how's Aunty?"

"*Ma* was suffering from cancer, but we got to know about it at the right time. She underwent surgery and is recovering now. At times, we have to visit the hospital for her post-surgery care and therapy to get her back to her previous form. Glad she could come out of it," I said with a sigh, thinking of those dark days when I had come to know of her illness.

"She is quite a brave lady!" he remarked with a knowing smile. Since we were pretty close during our college times, he was well acquainted with *Ma*.

"That she is. I wish I could be as strong as her." The tribulations I was facing were probably nothing compared to hers, but I found it immensely difficult to face them each day.

The sound of giggles behind us made us turn around. Akash's mother and Soha were hiding behind the curtain and listening to our talks.

"Soha, come here. What mischief are you up to now?" Akash asked, waving his hand at her.

"What mischief? We just wanted to give you both some alone time. After all, you both are long-time friends," his Mom replied.

"But why did you two not stay in touch?" Soha suddenly asked, blinking her eyes at us.

"In touch..." Akash thought for a second and answered, "I think work kept us occupied, and whenever I emailed, she didn't reply, so we lost touch," he shrugged.

I bit my tongue in embarrassment. I did change my email address multiple times when I went to Perth.

"My fault!" I raised my hand in apology. "I lost track of time in my effort to make ends meet and earn enough money for *Ma*."

"Now that you both have met, I think you should come here often. I need some company too," complained Soha, taking a seat between us.

Her questions, her tantrums were quite charming, and I fell for her cuteness. It was around nine in the evening when I checked the time and gasped. While eating, talking and playing with her, I didn't realise how time flew by! When I left, I had a bright smile on my face. How long had it been since I had laughed this way and been myself?

When I reached home, I went straight to meet *Ma*. She was lying on the bed, watching TV. The moment she saw me, she shifted her attention to me and adorned a beautiful smile on her face.

"I think you met someone special today!" she remarked as soon as I sat down beside her bed.

"It's a little girl, my friend's daughter. She is so much fun and is quite a charmer." Soha's face flashed before my eyes and brought a smile to my lips. But the thought that she was suffering from such a condition dampened my spirit's the very next second. "She lost her mother at three and then was diagnosed with a hole in her heart."

"Oh, that's bad," *Ma* said instantly. "Have they consulted some doctors? There must be a cure for this."

"Yes, they'll be flying soon to the US for her treatment. But, *Ma*, she reminds me a lot about myself. When I was young, I was also a mischief-maker, often bringing troubles home!" I gently squeezed her hand and added, "But then when life made me go through tough phases, I learnt my lessons. Finally, however, God became kind to me, sending you into my life!"

"You were mischievous, but you were a sweetheart. So obedient, sweet, and understanding!" *Ma* said, a faint smile adorning her cheeks. "You were the cutest one I had ever met. Actually, sometimes I forget that you were not born as a part of me. But I'm thankful to God. I don't know what I would do without you."

"*Ma*, you are just being modest. I know what you had to go through for me," I said, shaking my head. How could I forget that she had to leave her parent's home because of me?

It was a day I would never forget. My parents and older brother left me for some urgent work with my relatives. That was the last time I met them; they never returned. Later that night, I heard my aunt telling my uncle, "They died in the bus accident. Now, what do we do with this girl? You know the money you get is not enough. How do we look after her?"

My uncle sighed and replied, "We have no option. Use her as a help. What else can we do?"

My head buzzed and blanked out. The days just went by. I was wallowing in unending grief at the loss of my parents and sibling.

"Natasha," *Ma* called me lovingly, and I nodded my head, clearing my thoughts.

"Had it not been your relatives who dropped you at my house, I would have never met you," *Ma* said, cupping my cheeks.

To wash their hands off me, my uncle and aunt left me with *Ma* on the pretext of visiting the neighbouring village, and like my parents, they never returned to pick me up.

"But I always regret spoiling your life. You didn't marry and even lost your family because you had to take care of me," I said, bowing my head down.

"Who said I don't have a family? A daughter like you is much more precious than having an entire clan of family." She pulled my hand and engulfed me in her warm embrace.

I don't know where she found all the courage to stand up and fight for me against her family. She gave up her dreams and everything just to live for me! No matter what I did for her, it wouldn't be enough to repay her.

"You are the toughest woman I know," I said, pecking her cheek.

"In life, we do have to make tough decisions. It may transform your life completely, but you have to stand by it, no matter what. People and society will question your beliefs, but you must stay strong," she advised. Then, patting my cheeks, she added, "And when there is a question of someone's life, do what your heart says. Sacrifices are a must when you want to do things your heart suggests as correct."

"Hmm," I nodded, placing my head softly on her chest.

She wrapped her hands around me and ruffled my hair. "People may tell you that you are wrong, but always be true to yourself. Love what you have selected as it's your choice. Our choices define the person who we really are! Love with all your might, and you will never need to cry."

"But what if the person doesn't respond?" I asked, holding her palms in mine and raising my brows playfully. I was asking the question for the sake of my heart, but I didn't want *Ma* to know that I was sad thinking about how this thought had ruined my life.

"Natasha, this universe is round, so whatever you give out will come back to you, one way or the other. But never lie to your heart and never do things you don't feel from your heart." She rubbed my cheek softly and continued, "You were my love, and I don't regret fighting my family because of you. I am happy I stayed true to my love. You are the purpose of my life."

I smiled nevertheless. Even though I had failed in my love, I decided never to let *Ma* know about it. Staying true to your heart doesn't always work out.

The word 'purpose' shook something under me. *Ma* knew the purpose of her life, and that's why it was easy for her to choose and make the right decisions. And right now, she was I purpose of my life...

The housekeeper brought *Ma's* dinner in the room, and I fed her just like how she used to when I was a kid. The moment she took a bite, I said, "My good girl!" That's how she praised me after every bite she fed me in my childhood.

She gave a hearty laugh at my attempt to copy her.

I wanted to feed her well as she appeared dull and frail. The illness and then the vital medicines had taken a toll on her body. After a few more bites, she refused as she felt full. I didn't push her because eating more always made her feel bloated. The housekeeper cleared the dinnerware, and I helped *Ma* clean up. After some chit-chat, she was drowsy, so I tucked her up and returned to my room.

Although meeting Jai had soured my mood, spending time with Soha and *Ma* brought me back to my usual temper.

I had drifted to a peaceful slumber when I got a call from Akash almost at midnight.

"All okay?" I asked, hearing a lot of background noise from the other end.

"Soha collapsed half an hour after you left. We got her to hospital, but the doctor says she's got drained out and is not reviving," he said, sounding utterly helpless. "I am flying her to the US tomorrow morning. I've informed Jai that I cannot come tomorrow, but if you can visit him and explain why we can't work, it will be helpful. Tanisha's held up handling the other clients. She'll contact him later to discuss the matter."

"Sure, I will." I nodded my head mechanically.

Akash rambled on, "Look, don't explain too much. Just tell him to cancel the contract. Money is not important."

Money is not important? The words resounded in my ears. How could that be when he was flying to the US for medical treatment? Instead of promising to convey his intention, I added, "I'll see what I can do. You don't worry about me and take care of Soha. I'll reach the hospital in twenty minutes."

"No," Akash immediately refused. "No need to come. She is in the ICU, and visitors aren't allowed here. Special arrangements are being made to fly her tomorrow, so don't worry. I'll call you later. See you..."

After Akash disconnected the call, I felt stifled in my chest. I wanted to meet the little girl who stole my heart this evening. But since meeting her wasn't possible, all I could do was pray for her recovery.

"Tomorrow is going to be a tough day," I said, sighing and shutting my eyes tight. My insides cringed at the thought of meeting Jai the next day. How would I handle him all by myself?

I had to be strong and tell him we couldn't do it, but I was unsure how much loss Akash would bear for that.

When I woke up in the morning, I received a picture message from Akash of Soha and me playing. It was a picture clicked yesterday with the caption:

The best times I had!

Regards,

Soha

A second later, another notification popped up from him.

This one's from Soha. She asked me to send you the photo with the caption.

Boarded the flight.

Take care.

A few drops of tears rolled down my eyes. I was already missing the little Soha who seemed cheerful and happy last night. Sleep disappeared from my eyes, worrying about her.

CHAPTER VIII

Jai

I woke up in a sour mood after last night's dream. I knew I had a lot of work at the office but didn't wish to go to work. I delayed it, letting my secretary know that I would be late.

I put on loud music and began sketching cars. This was a hobby I had taken up while staying with grandpa. As the garage owner, he often received high-end vehicles for repair. That's when I fell in love with them. I watched them in awe and sketched them onto paper while grandpa busied himself in repairing them.

Whenever I get some time, I sketch cars. It gives me peace and helps clear my mind. By the time I finished the drawing, it was almost noon. The moment I entered the washroom to take a bath, the sound of my ringing cell phone made me trace my steps to the nightstand. Since it was my secretary's call, I answered immediately. "Hello?"

"Sir, Miss Natasha is here to speak to you."

"Miss Natasha," I felt a strange urge to repeat the name as if the truth of the abbreviation used along with the name ticked my wicked mind.

"Tell her to wait," I replied and was about to disconnect when she immediately added, "Sir, she has been here since nine and says there's something urgent she wants to speak to you about."

"Okay, I'll be there in thirty minutes," I said and disconnected the call.

I had thought that she was the reason Akash called up to say he would not be able to come today to finalise the campaign. However, it was pretty strange that he didn't turn up while she was in my office to have a talk.

I quickly showered and went to the office. All the way, I kept wondering why Natasha was here. Did she wish to talk to me in person to clear the air of rudeness that we shared yesterday? I would be glad to be my old self with her if she did. But, ideally, she doesn't deserve to be ill-treated either.

She was sitting quietly in the waiting room near the reception when I entered the office. I could make out that something was bothering her. I asked my secretary to let her in and bring us some coffee.

"Yes, Natasha, tell me, you wanted to meet?" I asked as she walked in.

I gestured towards the chair for her to take a seat. My secretary served a tray of two mugs of coffee with some nuts.

"Here, have some coffee." I offered her a cup, placing it before her.

She fumbled for a few seconds, staring at the coffee mug. I could sense that she had something important she wanted to discuss but was a little hesitant. Then, a few seconds later, she started, "Actually, I'm here to cancel the ad campaign contract signed with Akash's company."

"Why?" I asked bluntly.

She sat quietly with a frown. I guess she didn't expect me to ask this in such a straightforward way. "Akash's daughter is not well. He flew to the US for her treatment. Unfortunately, he doesn't know when he will be able to return, and with him absent, the management of the shooting will be affected, so that's why we would like to cancel the campaign. His assistant will get in touch with you soon to discuss the details."

"Okay..." I said, feeling sorry to hear about his daughter, but all these feelings were overshadowed by her mention of 'we'. *Is she so close to him to be speaking on his behalf? When did she become a team with him and why? Isn't she supposed to talk about 'us'?* That's what I had been expecting since I came to know she came to visit me. I was completely caught off guard as she referred to herself and Akash as 'we'. Was she about to marry him or be partners with him?

"Thank you," she replied, getting up from her seat a minute later.

"But you'll have to bear the charges for breaking the contract." I focused my gaze on my laptop, not willing to give a damn about her reaction.

"How much?" she asked.

"Two crores, the cancellation amount is already mentioned in the clause," I said bluntly.

She sat down for a minute in absolute silence, then said, "But he won't be available, his daughter is sick, and the poor child has no one except him. Without him, we can't proceed. So how do you expect him to pay in this case?"

"A clause is a clause, either he pays or his company. We'll have to look for some other company now. It costs time and money. If he has asked for cancellation, he must be aware that he has to pay compensation for breaking the contract," I explained.

Her face dropped, clearly indicating that she cared for this money as if it was her own. I hated it. Somehow, I didn't expect her to be so loyal to a man she had just met.

"Can you not do something about it?" she asked after a minute. "Tanisha's having a tough time managing his ongoing campaigns and responsibilities."

"You can ask him to suggest someone else from the company to manage the shoot. Or we can work with you acting as the coordinator between the agency and my company," I suggested.

She was silent for a while, contemplating her options. Finally, I knew she had little choice but to agree to my words from her thoughtful expression.

"Let me consult with the company and revert back on this," she answered with a sombre face after some thought.

"Yes, that makes sense. You can ask the company to help you contact the relevant people and-" An incoming call from my partner, Mehta, interrupted my words, and I excused myself before answering, "Just a sec... Hello?"

"What rubbish?" I screamed at the phone, standing up abruptly from my chair, "How can that be possible?" I had lost all my control at the news he shared. "Where did this happen?" I noted the details on a paper as he answered from the other end. "Press? This could ruin our image," I was worried to death now and clasped the phone tightly. "Okay, I'll check the news," I said and then logged into the local news website.

"Breaking news! The Ninja Super Avenue slid down the steep hill uncontrollably. The car brakes failed due to poor traction control. The car stopped only when it hit a pile of sand placed on the roadside. The airbags did not function, resulting in a near-death experience for the driver. He has been hospitalised for minor injuries to his knees and elbows and a concussion."

Frustrated, I called up Mehta for a quick meeting, but he asked me to come down to the company reception as the media personnel had crowded there and were demanding explanations.

What was the cause of this blunder? I kept thinking as I rushed out of the cabin. At the reception, the mob of media personnel had completely surrounded my partner.

When I arrived, the crowd let me into the inner circle and started bombarding me with their questions. But then, my peripheral vision caught sight of Natasha, trying to make her way towards me. She had stepped out of my cabin right after me, and I had expected her to leave, but strangely, she followed me down to the lobby. She tried to squeeze in, but the heavy crowd pushed her around, not letting her pass. I felt a strange urge to protect her and clasped her hand in mine.

"Fuckers," I muttered, reaching out and pulling her into my arms. I tried to keep her away from the suckers who wanted to squeeze her.

The security team barged in and cleared the way to the hall where the press conference was being held.

Natasha sat down next to me on the stage, followed by Mehta and faced the media panel.

"Mr Jai, tell us why your team did not conduct the security check before launching the vehicle. How can you launch something that can take people's lives?" asked a reporter sitting in the front row.

"Ninja Super Avenue has gone through the crash test, front steering impact and has also undergone testing by Global NCAP. It has also gone through Bharat New Vehicle Safety Assessment Programme. It complies with the new automotive safety standards. We have done all the tests to make sure our customers get enhanced safety," I explained.

"Then how did this happen? Is it not the lack of improper testing of a car unit when it is passed to be on the road?" asked a lady from the group.

"All our cars are tested before they are cleared for the roads," I said, trying to sound calm, clasping my hand on the table.

"How can we be sure?" another stood up and argued. "Companies pay money to the compliance teams and get their cars cleared. It's we, the buyers, who'll suffer if we drive such a high-risk car."

"See," I tried to keep my cool and answered, "I am not sure how the mishap happened, but my team will investigate, and we will get it sorted soon."

"'Sorted'? How can we trust you?" another reporter from the far end shot back at me. "Can you drive the car on a steep hill and show us that it is safe?"

"Sure," Mehta, my partner, stood up and countered. "In the presence of the media, our team will test drive down the steep hill. We will show you that the car is safe."

"No, sir. We want the company owner to drive the car with the lady he was holding and cursed us as fuckers!" prompted another reporter.

One thing led to another, and though I wanted to object, all the reporters appeared to agree with the suggestion. They started demanding that the test be conducted by me with Natasha on my side.

Mehta tried to sway their demand, "Listen, we are telling our team will drive the car in the presence of the media and will give you a clean chit."

If I had been asked alone, I would have agreed, but how could I agree to Natasha sitting next to me while I was driving down a steep hill. I didn't doubt my car, but what if something happened and she got injured because of me?

I remained quiet until I heard Natasha's voice. "Yes, we will drive and prove it to you. The car is safe," she said, taking the mike in her hands.

I placed a hand on the mic with a frown on my face. Then, muting the thing, I said to her in a low voice, "Natasha, it's not required."

She gave an assuring smile and said, "I know the car is safe."

"Can we do the test now?" interrupted a reporter. "I'm asking now so that you don't play any tricks with the car, get it fixed in the meanwhile and tell us it's safe."

"We are ready," she replied, switching on the microphone.

With a blank look, I stared at her.

"All right, sir, we will wait for you at the same place where the accident happened, in Malshej Ghat," answered the reporter in the front row, getting up from his seat.

I didn't get time to decide further as they crowded us and asked us to leave with them.

"Why did you agree with them?" I asked Natasha the moment we sat down in the car and were all alone. Super Ninja was tested by the proper means, and for sure, it would pass the test. But that did not mean I could allow her to be at risk.

"I know, there won't be any fault in your cars," she said, looking at the road.

The cars were lined up one after another trying to reach the spot. Mehta was following us behind while we were sitting in the Ninja Avenue Plus, the one my company had launched.

"How could you be sure when the car had just crashed some time back?" I yelled at her.

She remained quiet. My anger grew as I drove past the vans of the media channels.

Frustrated and annoyed, I banged my hand on the steering wheel. "You know you could lose your life for this stupidity?"

"I know how much this car means to you, so I trust that you would have made sure it will be the best," she mumbled.

"Ah, this is too much!" I grumbled, more at my helplessness than at her. "Why do you always have to be so soft-hearted? You didn't have to agree to anything! I would have been so much at ease if it was just me!"

"But if they asked for us, then we should take it up and show them that it's safe," she countered, facing me with a confident smile. "And don't panic. Even if something happens, I won't blame you. It'll be all on me."

"Listen, by doing this, you are just proving how stupid you are and nothing else!" I retorted, exasperated and infuriated. "You already know that it might not be safe, yet like a fool, you agreed to everyone's demands!" It was utter stupidity on her part! I didn't want to be rude, but I could not hold back my agitation. The fact that she was here while I was driving towards what can be said as a straight death sentence, made my heart panic. It was beating too fast for me to contain it.

"For your kind information, I was always a fool, so you just drive and don't worry about me," Natasha replied nonchalantly and turned to face the window.

"I'll stop around the corner. You get down," I muttered as we approached a turning. This was the last way I could save her from acting stupid.

"Okay, but what if something happens to you?" she asked, still looking out of the window. "We should just do it together, or you too get down!"

"You are a psycho!" I hollered, lamenting every second she was with me in the car. "I don't know why you are doing this! Who told you to follow me to the conference room? And who told you to agree to their demands to sit in the car with me?"

"Can you drive without talking nonsense?" she faced me and commanded in a sharp voice. I had never heard her talk like this. Dumbfounded, I stared at her as her eyes turned a shade darker as if I had lit a fuse, furious as never before.

Consequently, I drove quietly while she turned to look outside with her brows furrowed in wrath.

"If anything happens to you, Samira will kill me!" I tried to persuade her, taking a different route in a milder tone.

"If something happens to you-" before she could complete, she received a call. "No, I haven't cancelled. I will do it but would need your help in doing it." Then, after a pause, I heard her say, "No, I don't want you to face such a big loss now when Soha needs you."

I could make out she was talking to Akash from the conversation. But then, why was she taking so much risk for everyone? She didn't have to do it for Akash because she didn't have to pay a penny. Even for me, she didn't have to sit next to me in this car and take such a risk.

I wanted to know why she was doing it for him. Was there something brewing between them? And what did she mean when she said, 'if something happens to you'?

"It's all right. I can manage," Natasha said. "Take care of Soha. Don't worry about me, and just keep me informed." She disconnected the call and kept it inside her purse.

"Why are you doing this for him?" I asked, unable to control myself any longer. "Are you in a relations-"

"He is a very good friend of mine, and he is in trouble. He needs to pay attention to his daughter's surgery right now, and I don't want him to be troubled about money or his reputation," she said, facing me. Her crystal clear gaze was full of honesty and concern.

"What about me? Why are you doing this for me?" I asked out inquisitively.

"Because I know you. You helped me when I needed it," she said without a second thought. It was right from her heart, just the way she answered about Akash.

I clutched the steering wheel with all the force. Her answers seemed genuine, but there was an edge to it like I was an average person for her while he weighed more than me.

Till this time, I thought she agreed to accompany me in the test because she was concerned about me and had something in her heart for the relationship we once shared. But now that she said it was nothing more than returning the favour I did for her, it disheartened me.

She plugged in her earphones to listen to something, shutting me out. I couldn't talk to her anymore and ask what was troubling my heart. Left with little option, I drove in silence until we reached the destination.

CHAPTER IX

Natasha

I knew I didn't have to agree with the reporters, but something snapped in me and urged me to support him. He needed me. I was angry at myself for being such a sucker and getting carried away, but deep within me, I was happy that I could help him somehow.

His behaviour surprised me. Why was he concerned about me? He asked me numerous things and told me that I was a fool, but I didn't react because I knew I was following my heart. Whether I live or die in the accident, I will be happy that I took up the courage to stand up for him, even though I was sure he would never stand up for me.

For me, my love was always one-sided, where the lady had given away her heart to someone, and he was unaware of her feelings.

"Why was I doing this for him?" Of course, I was taken aback when he asked me that, but thankfully I replied with the apt answer for his question.

He looked dull and fearful as we neared the Ghat. I wished I could place my hand on his palm to calm him down, but I feared, 'what if he feels otherwise?'

"Listen, thank you," he said as we were about to climb up the hill. "If I am alive, I will never forget this ever! I will always be indebted to you!"

"Don't worry, everything will be fine," I said, giving him a reassuring smile.

He pulled the car over, turned to me and gazed right into my eyes. "I feel like we will die. I don't have the courage to move forward," he uttered in a low voice. His eyes were filled with horror as if even if we didn't die in the accident, he would surely have a heart attack thinking about the situation.

My heart raced, watching him so scared.

I took a deep breath and faced the valley ahead. Then, in a low voice, I said to Jai, "Close your eyes. Think of your dreams, what you wished to live for always and believe that it will come true. You will live and do well. This is your dream car, and it will succeed." I turned to him. With his eyes closed, he seemed to be visualising while I was instructing. "People will trust your dream," I continued and added, "and God will make your dream a big success. You will get what you really want. Just believe in yourself."

His eyes were still closed for some time. I shut my eyes and said a silent prayer to the Almighty to fulfil his dream and keep us safe.

"Ready?" he asked as soon as I opened my eyes.

I nodded.

"I'm having a panic attack. Can we sing a song?" he asked, trying to smile through his tense expression.

"I can't. Let's focus on the road," I replied, smiling.

"Your favourite is Arjit Singh, right?" he asked.

I nodded.

"You like 'agar tum saath ho' song if I am correct?" he asked next. Then, he instructed the car audio system to play the song.

I watched him singing the song aloud as we descended the steep hill in the car. The ghat showcased beautiful scenery as we passed through it. I lowered the window panes as mist clouded the area.

It was drizzling outside, and I put my palms out to feel the droplets fall on my hand. It was a beautiful experience. A few seconds later, I sang with Jai. We were singing aloud while the song was being played in the car.

About two or three songs later, when the Ghat came to almost an end, Jai finally relaxed. After a turn, he slowed down the car and parked it to the side. His worried expression was gone with the wind, and a smile adorned his lips. Then, stepping out of the car, he screamed aloud, "Hurray!!"

I watched the scenery with peace. In his excitement, he walked over to my side and gave me a bear hug, "Thank you so much!"

Making my system go haywire with the sudden and brief touch, he moved away and added, "We made it without dying!!!"

He pressed my arms tightly, talking to me as if we were friends forever, and there was absolutely nothing wrong between us.

"I knew we would," I said with a genuine smile. "I knew the car would pass the test."

Letting go of me, he added, "Still, thank you so much for trusting me and my car!"

"Any day," I replied, waving my hand at him to not bother. The fanfare of the media had yet to arrive at the spot. Then, with a smile, I turned around to take in the breath-taking view of the Ghat. The lush green mountains, engulfed in floating clouds and the fine drizzle, had filled the air with magic. I spread out my hands and twirled. The feeling was surreal!

I found a waterfall stream flowing down the opposite end and making its way through the greenery. My eyes sprinted with delight. It's not every day you get to take in the majestic view of nature so close. I wish I could soak myself in its beauty forever!

My eyes caught sight of an inconspicuous tea stall at the corner of the road. "Splendid!" I murmured as a tea at the moment seemed just perfect!

When I ordered tea, the shopkeeper asked, "Would you like some noodles? Cheesy noodles with tea taste best in this rain."

I smiled and nodded. I felt Jai's presence very close to me, and small tremors shot through my body.

"Make one for me too!" Jai said to the shopkeeper, catching me off guard.

"How did the accident happen today morning?" he asked the tea-seller as I sat down on the narrow bench placed outside his stall. The cool mist touched my skin as I watched the waterfall cascade down rocks and vanish in the greenery.

"Every day, some or the other accident happens here. It's mostly those people who are at full speed, driving like maniacs or in a drunken state," said the tea seller. Then with a smile, he added, "I noticed a pile of sand this morning while opening the shop, and I was still wondering why it was here when bam! A car came and struck straight into it! Afraid that the people in the car might have been injured, I rushed towards it, but what did I see? The two men jumped out and were even happy!"

My eyes met with Jai's. He gestured at me to stay quiet and let the tea seller continue.

The seller shook his head in disbelief as he added, "After the accident, they came and ordered some tea. They spoke in English and thought I wouldn't understand. But I've been to school, and I know some English! So not only did I hear everything, I even recorded their conversation." He gave a smug smile and continued, "They were bad people! Really rotten! They actually rigged the car to extort money from the manufacturer! Can you believe that! I'm telling you, such dishonest people do not end well."

The man blabbered on as he prepared our tea and noodles. As soon as he was done with the story, Jai said to him, "I'm the car manufacturer. Thank you for sharing this information with us. But can we ask for you to give us the recording?"

The tea-seller frowned at Jai before asking for his proof of identity. Jai immediately showed him his visiting card. Finally, when he was convinced that Jai indeed was the owner of Ninja Super Avenue, he agreed to send him a copy of the video recording at a price. Jai was so happy that he paid him double the amount in cash!

"So, all this drama was for someone looking to make easy money!" he remarked, shaking his head and taking a spoonful of the noodles in his mouth.

"It was scary, though," I confessed, taking a spoonful myself.

"Yum!" he exclaimed, relishing the street food with a contented look. "But on the brighter side, I got to know how much you trust me, and I got to enjoy these hot tangy noodles in this delightful weather with such enchanting scenery!"

"That's true," I said with a serene smile as I twirled the noodles around the fork and ate small bites. I was glad that I stood up for Jai, and he recognised at least some of my effort.

A few minutes later, his partner, Mehta, the company employees, and the media, arrived at the spot. Jai took Mehta towards the tea-stall and told him what the shopkeeper had said. After a brief discussion, they requested the tea-seller to let the media know what he had witnessed and even shared the video clip.

Within minutes of his approval, the tea-seller was surrounded by news personnel, asking him various questions about today's accident. His statement and his video cleared all the accusations against Ninja Super Avenue.

Jai had a relaxed smile on his face when the media finally released the news that the accident was a ploy of the driver to extort money.

"Sir, thank you so much for giving us a test and once again confirming for us that the car is safe to drive," said one of the reporters standing beside us and recording everything on video.

"Ma'am, you were too bold!" a reporter remarked, turning towards me. "Especially at such a time, when your own kin leaves by your side, how come you were so confident, and you stood up to this enormous risk?" he asked, holding his mic to my face.

I was zapped at suddenly being placed in the limelight. I took a second to compose myself and replied, "Sometimes, you just have the gut feeling that you are standing for something right, and this was one such time."

"But Ma'am, in such a time when no one stands for anyone, you stood up. Why?" he asked.

"My *Ma* always says one should stand by the pe- I mean, things that matter to you. I know how much effort Jai has put forth in making this dream his reality, and so I was sure he would have given his best, and stood by his dream," I answered with confidence. I bit my tongue for almost having said 'people' and changed it to 'things' as I didn't want to give away my feelings for Jai, which I had concealed in my heart.

"Do you guys plan to marry anytime soon?" asked the reporter.

I was surprised but knowing well that reporters can ask anything to anyone, I replied, "No, Jai is just an acquaintance and I've met only a few days back."

"Acquaintance and so much trust?" asked another reporter with a mocking smile.

"If I know you and you are correct, I will stand by you as well," I answered with a wink. Just then, my mobile buzzed. "Now, if you are done, I have a call to answer."

Luckily the call brought an end to the interview; otherwise, for sure, the reporter wouldn't have stopped grilling me!

"What? How?" I shrieked in panic at the news from the other end of the phone. It was the housekeeper. She said that *Ma* was having trouble breathing and wanted me to hurry. My first reaction was to call an ambulance, but the signal was weak.

I looked around for Jai, but he was busy answering the reporters. *I wouldn't even get a taxi from here with the low network.* I mumbled while scanning the place for anyone who could take me to *Ma*. Thankfully, I found a cab standing at the farther end of the road. Without waiting for Jai, I boarded it and asked him to take me home. On the way, I called for an ambulance and passed them my address.

CHAPTER X

Jai

Surrounded by reporters, I couldn't get time to thank her, but I thanked her a million times in my heart. For the first time, someone had stood by me through my challenges, giving me strength even though she didn't need to.

I told her multiple times to get down. Someone else in her place would have definitely complied, but she didn't.

I felt a twitch in my heart when she said that I was an acquaintance, but I was more than happy for what she had done for me, so I ignored whatever she mentioned to the reporters. All that didn't matter.

After talking to the media, I looked around for her, but she wasn't there. Mehta said he'd seen her running towards a taxi, looking edgy.

"Was it an emergency?" I asked him.

He shrugged, "No idea."

What could have happened? I discerned for a second and then dialled Akash's number. But he didn't pick up, so I left a message for him to send Natasha's phone number as soon as possible.

Mehta and I returned to the office. We still had to catch hold of the guy who tried to bring us a bad name for the sake of money. Another press conference was held to clear the company's name. After that, an emergency meeting with the investors was held to explain the situation. It took me until midnight to settle all the matters concerning this incident. I slumped down on the bed when I reached Grandpa's place, completely exhausted. Within a few hours, all my hard work had crumbled down; however, I was lucky that I could get hold of the truth at the end, and all was well.

I sighed and closed my eyes. Natasha's voice resounded in my ears, *'Think of your dreams, what you wished to live for always and believe that it will come true. You will live and do well. This is your dream car, and it will succeed!'*

When I had closed my eyes then, what flashed in my mind wasn't my dream car and its success. Instead, it was Natasha sitting next to me in the car, holding her scarf out in the air and screaming, 'I love you, J!' Watching her so ecstatic, there was a bright smile on my face.

I don't know why I was having all these weird dreams or why I was visualising things like a teenager in love when life was far, far away from it all!

I always laughed when my friends during school and college days shared such fanciful dreams. But now I've grown up to know that these don't exist. Instead, they are just hallucinations that intend to weaken us and bind us to things that make us forget our dreams.

The bullshit terms my father poses every time I want something in life, and the loveless parenting that I have undergone prove that all these dreams are nothing but myths of the mind.

However, I was glad that my company's reputation was saved today in the nick of time before the damage could spread like wildfire and spoil my dream of eight years.

The following day when I woke up, Mehta called me up and asked, "Did you know this girl?"

"Which girl? Natasha?" I asked, rubbing my eyes, wondering why he asked.

"Because I don't think anyone will take such a huge risk for someone who had been an asshole to her a day before," he replied.

"I don't know why she helped me, but I'm glad she did," I answered, unable to think of anything else to reply.

"By the way, we've got positive responses from people because of what she said to the reporter. She has been in the limelight and people have been praising her on social media for being such a hearty person!" he said.

"Is it? I will watch it." I switched the call to speaker mode and immediately went online to search social media websites.

"And by the way, the team thinks she's the best choice for rebranding. So you should thank her from all of us," he added.

"Yes, I'll do that!" I replied and disconnected the call.

I checked my messages and found that Akash had replied with her number. I called the number, but it was not reachable. I sent her a text:

Thank you for all the support! Call me as soon as you read this message.

-Jai

I walked inside the office in high spirits when my secretary informed me that someone from Akash's team was there to meet me.

"Hello, Sir! I am Tanisha from Akash Sir's Media Agency," said the lady, taking a seat in front of me.

"Yes, tell me, what do you wish to talk about?" I asked.

"Sir, Natasha called us last night and informed us that she would not be able to take up this assignment due to a family emergency. However, she's asked us to arrange for another model for this campaign," said Tanisha very courteously.

"I will speak to Akash about the replacement," I immediately replied. *But what sort of family emergency did she have?* "Well... you must have her home address, right?" I asked.

"I will ask the team to check and get back to you. Is it fine?" Tanisha replied.

"Sure," I nodded and added, "But we want only her for the campaign. No one else will do."

Tanisha blinked her eyes and replied, "But she will not be available for some time, Sir."

My brows creased up in worry as I asked, "Do you know what sort of emergency it is?"

She thought for a while before answering with a sigh, "She lost her mother last evening, Sir."

"No!" I jolted upright at the news. "Get me her address, quickly." I hurried towards the restroom attached to my cabin. I felt restless. I knew how close she was to her mother. *What should I do? What should I do?* I paced nervously and decided I had to be with her to ensure she was all right! With trembling hands, I dialled the number Akash had sent. "I have to be with her! God, Natasha, pick up your damn phone!" I grumbled at the steady mechanical voice that said, 'The number you are dialling is either switched off or out of network coverage. Please try again later.'

When I came out, Tanisha passed me the address written down on a piece of paper. "Thanks. Give me your number. In case I need anything, I'll call you."

I informed my secretary I was out for some urgent work and hurried towards Natasha's home.

I kept calling her, but her number was still not reachable. Finally, reaching her door, I calmed myself and rang the bell. But after having buzzed multiple times when no one answered, I realised she wasn't there inside.

I knocked on the house next door. "Hi, do you know where your neighbour is?" I asked the lady who answered the door.

"Ah, her mother passed away last evening," said the lady. "She's gone to her native to complete the last rites."

"Do you know which village and the address?" I asked.

"No, I don't. I didn't ask her..." the neighbour replied and added after some thought, "but wait, a person from our building went to her village and came back this morning. You should ask him." She gave me the details of the person and pointed me towards his home.

The man was reluctant to pass on the address as he thought something was fishy. I had to convince him about my intentions and pay him some money to get Natasha's details. The trip was quite hectic and lengthy, but I rarely stopped to take a break because the man had advised that the roads were not safe to travel at night. In my effort to get there quickly, I speeded my car as much as possible. I was never so desperate as I was now, but alas, God's will doesn't work like yours.

I missed a hump in the middle of the road. To my horror, because of the speed, the car flew into the air and turned multiple times before hitting a tree. Though the airbags opened right away, the impact rendered me unconscious.

CHAPTER XI

Natasha

Sitting by the beach, I watched my *Ma's* ashes mix with the waves and become one with the sea. It was already a day since her death. The last twenty-four hours were the loneliest of my life. I wasn't crying, but I knew I was broken beyond repair. I don't know how and when God decided to take away everything from me in a fraction of a minute.

I had rushed home in the taxi, but the ambulance arrived half an hour after my arrival as it was stuck in heavy traffic; the road was blocked because of an accident. By then, *Ma* was very critical. All my hopes were now on the ambulance, but it took another hour to reach the hospital.

As soon as the doctor headed out of the Emergency Room, I rushed over to him. "Sorry, Natasha, we couldn't save her. She had a massive stroke and needed immediate attention. Unfortunately, by the time she came here, it was too late," he said with an apologetic look.

"But how can that be?" I asked him in disbelief. "Didn't you say last week that she was recovering? Then, how did she have a stroke?"

"She was, but cancer is unpredictable," he answered sympathetically. "It eats the body from inside. The strong medication causes many side effects, and sometimes, damages other organs. We can do treatment only based on the symptoms, but it is difficult to detect and treat them in time when there are none."

My legs gave away, and I slumped down on the floor. In a matter of an hour, my entire world had vanished away. A few minutes later, I regained my composure as the nurse helped me sit on a chair nearby.

I peeped inside the Emergency Room. *Ma* was wired up with monitors, but there was no heartbeat, just a flat lI saying that she was no more...

"You can go inside," said the nurse helping me walk as my legs felt as if they weighed several tons.

"I am so sorry, *Ma*, I could not be there with you," I held her frail figure lying on the hospital bed and cried my heart out. "What do I do without you now, *Ma*?"

I vented out all that was there in my heart, but no answer came from her this time. How I wished God would give me just one chance and instruct me, "Don't go out today. Your *Ma* needs you."

Where does all this so-called intuition go when you really need one? I guess I'm not one of those lucky kinds or in the good books of God because he never gave me an intuition. Things always just happened, and I was instructed to accommodate the tragedies.

First, it was my parents and brother, and then, when this angel took me up in her folds after fighting with her family, she was asked to move out of her own home and was thrown away on the streets.

Images of our struggle days and the love with which my *Ma* brought me up filled my heart and eyes, clouding everything else that happened over time.

"*Ma*, open your eyes once and talk to me, please," I begged her a million times, but there was no answer. Her body felt warm as I held it. It was nearly impossible for me to believe she had gone away, just like that.

"Why, *Ma?* I have no one except you! Why did you leave me all alone?!" I wailed, covering my face with my palm.

The nurse standing by the door came over to my side and placed a hand on my shoulder. "Be strong. Perform her last rites where she always wanted to be. It will give peace to her soul," said the nurse.

I recalled my *Ma's* words. She was never happy in this busy city and always wished to return to our village, Diveagar. She wanted to sit by the beach and watch the fishermen catch fish in the open sea.

It was one of my favourite pastimes too. Every time we visited, we sat there for hours together, watching the beach lazily, soaking ourselves with the salt mist of air crashing onto us while the waves submerged onto the beach coast.

After much pleading, a good Samaritan from my apartment agreed to drive me with my *Ma* in his van to Diveagar.

When I set off my foot in the village, people poured into our home and asked about how it all happened. I kept quiet, busy performing the final rites while the housekeeper managed them and answered their queries. It was ridiculous! When she was alive and sick, no one bothered to help, but now that she was gone, everyone wanted to know how she died!

People sometimes act so weird that it's hard to distinguish their real selves. I had seen *Ma* always rush to people in need with whatever she had. She was a teacher and made sure that no kid in the village was left uneducated.

Moreover, when I was travelling to Perth for work, leaving her alone here, everyone assured me that she was in safe hands! But was she? She often worked till late and spoiled her health to wash away her loneliness. She acted jovial over the video calls and lied through her teeth that she was eating well.

A few months later, when I noticed marked changes in her appearance, I called the neighbours and asked them to look after her. But did they? Either they did not, or *Ma* convinced them to lie to me. Whatever the reason, I was left unaware of her problems for a long time.

Right now, I didn't see a reason for complaining to them because it didn't really matter to them. Now that *Ma* was gone, I had nothing for them either. All I cared about now was completing the ritual for the peace of her soul.

Many people came forward to help, and then, I did her last rites in the cremation ground in the evening.

It was twenty-four hours since her body and bones had turned to ashes, and I was here at her favourite beach to let her be one with the sea. No one was there except the peaceful beach, stretched out wide, calling the waves to the shore.

I was watching the fishermen return back with their catch. The sun had submerged in the sea, leaving behind a reddish-orange trail of its rays. It was calm and soothing, just like when *Ma* and I used to sit and watch.

When you sit at places where you have spent time with your loved one or have something they cherished with you, they don't feel so far away. It's like you are holding a piece of them in your heart, binding it to your soul, even if their body has left forever.

There was nothing left in my life, no purpose at all, and without purpose, one shouldn't be leading a life. I sat by the beach and gazed at the sea waves unfolding. Holding her necklace in my palms, I felt her presence engulf me. First, I was immersed in sorrow, and then my mood lifted up, making me feel blissful. The transformation was so quick that I was lost in a fake reality.

I felt as if the waves were calling out to me. I got up slowly and walked towards the sea, soaked in my *Ma's* thoughts. The waves welcomed me. They touched and pulled me inside into the calm. I closed my eyes as peace engulfed my soul, but something drew me out of the bliss, and I was dragged to the shore.

I jerked my hands and legs to go back to my *Ma*, but I couldn't. I opened my eyes to look at what was holding me back. I stared at his concern filled eyes as if he was about to lose something. My eyes closed, and my body loosened the grip. I remembered nothing after that.

CHAPTER XII

Natasha

I woke up with a splitting headache, the one that hurt so much I wish I could just throw away that part so that the pain would stop, once and for all. Feeling parched and hoping that the pain would subside after a glass of water, I sat up. In my groggy state, I got off the bed, only to feel a sudden chill over my thighs.

I looked down and noticed I was dressed in a loose fit top without any lowers. Where were my pants! Why on earth was I not wearing my pants? I gasped and looked around. I was in my room in Diveagar, but how and when did I come here? The last thing I remembered was being on the beach, gazing at the sunset.

I got up and changed into my regular clothes.

"*Ma*, my coffee?" I asked, walking towards the kitchen while tying my hair into a bun. The moment the words left my mouth, realisation hit me. *Ma* was gone, and it had been two days since. I sighed, feeling empty without her presence.

When *Ma* was sick, I'd acted the same way once, calling out to her for coffee out of habit. Her illness hadn't even sunk in yet, and she passed away suddenly.

"Here, your coffee." I heard a female's voice and turned around, surprised. The housekeeper had returned to Mumbai after *Ma's* cremation, so who was in the house?

It was the neighbouring Aunty. She walked over, holding a cup.

"Thank you, Aunty. I didn't realise you were here," I replied with a smile, taking the cup from her hands.

"Actually, *Ma* used to make me coffee every morning. I didn't realise she's..." I didn't finish my sentence as my throat clogged up.

Aunty just flashed an understanding smile and returned to the kitchen.

I took a sip of the coffee and became aware it had the same aroma and flavour as *Ma's*.Puzzled, I glanced towards the kitchen and took another sip. *Yep!* It tasted the same - the perfect blend where milk is gradually added to the cup while stirring the coffee with a dash of ground cardamom on the top.

It was surprising and refreshing! Did she learn from *Ma,* or did *Ma* learn from her? Walking towards the kitchen, I said to Aunty with an appreciating smile, "The coffee is really nice. It's just like how *Ma* brewed!"

"Your husband told me to serve it to you once you woke up. I just reheated it now," she replied with a smile.

"Who?" I asked, almost sputtering the drink out of my mouth.

"Your husband. He left an hour back to get his bandage changed. Seems like his injury is serious," she answered, shaking her head in sympathy. "Since you aren't well, he asked me to look after you while he was away."

Aunty stepped out of the kitchen and took a seat on the sofa. My eyes darted wide, wondering who could be the man claiming to be my husband?

A vague memory of someone holding me and pulling me out of water flashed before my eyes. Just then, a gentle knock diverted my attention to the door.

I was about to walk over and check who it was when Aunty hurried over and answered. The sight of him with a bandage around his head made all the blood in my body flow to my legs as he stepped inside.

"You?! What are you doing here?" I asked as I saw Jai standing in the middle of my living room.

"Thank you, Aunty," he said to the old lady, completely ignoring my questions. Then, he handed her a small paper bag with a tender smile. "I just couldn't hold myself from buying these hot *vadas* on the way back. These are for you."

"Thank you, *beta!* God bless you two!" Aunty took the bag from Jai and left my home.

"How are you feeling?" he asked, walking over to me. He touched my forehead with the back of his palm and murmured. "Good. Looks like your fever is gone."

I was in too much of a shock to reply to anything.

"How was the coffee?" he asked, gesturing towards the cup in my hands. Then, without waiting for an answer, he vanished into the kitchen, returned with two plates from the cupboard and laid them on the dining table. He moved around in my house as if he was perfectly at ease. He seemed to know about everything here!

My brows knit over, not very happy. While I was asleep, he had made himself really comfortable in my home!

Bam! I placed the coffee cup on the dining table and crossed my arms over my chest. "I asked, what are you doing here?"

"Why haven't you finished your coffee? It must have gone cold by now," he said, picking up the cup and taking a sip.

Watching his lips touch my cup flipped something inside me, invoking my vessels to pump the blood harder.

"It's not bad." He licked his lips and placed it back in my hand. "I tried to make it just like how Maria made it for you."

His words made me recall. The coffee did taste like how I used to instruct Maria to prepare. She was the housekeeper at his home in Perth. I took a deep breath and asked again, "Seriously, Jai, what are you doing here?" I pointed at the bandage around his head and added, "And how did this happen?"

"Oh, glad the question changed." He displayed a playful smile and replied, "This happened last night while I was coming here. I banged against a tree, but luckily nothing serious happened. Just hit my head a little," he said, pointing at his head.

My eyes opened wider with his every word. "Are you insane! Who told you to drive all the way here and that too all by yourself! The roads to this village aren't like the ones in Perth!" I retorted, completely taken aback.

"Can we eat first?" Jai scratched the back of his head, glancing at the paper bag on the dining table. "I am hungry to death, and this smell is making my stomach grumble for food." He opened the bag and served the piping hot vada-sambhar on the plates when I didn't reply.

I watched him for an answer, but he ignored me. I walked away from there to the other room when he asked out aloud, "C'mon Nats, eat it while it's still hot. It's delicious. Believe me, they are the best I've ever had till now."

"In some time," I replied, locking myself in the washroom. I had no clue why Jai had come to meet me and why he was behaving like my friend all of a sudden.

I took time to freshen up, having no energy to socialise with anyone.

"How much time will you take?" he asked, knocking on the bathroom door.

I didn't reply and continued at my slowest pace when he banged again, "There is no point in hiding there, so come out soon."

"I also need to use the washroom," he knocked a minute later with urgency in his voice. Although I knew it was all an act for me to come out, I let out a sigh and opened the door. This was the third time he had banged, and I knew he wouldn't let me be alone to think things through.

"Thank you!" he exclaimed as I came out, looking relaxed.

"Did you get me here last night?" I asked, but he didn't answer.

I stood in front of him and asked the same question. This time he looked up and said, "I will answer only after you finish your breakfast."

His unexpected attention and care made me feel uncomfortable. I had been trying to keep myself sane, but his insistence let off a fuse. "Don't you understand? I don't want to eat! My *Ma* passed away, and you are asking me to eat, be happy, but how can I do that!" I yelled, a lone tear escaping my eye.

"I understand, but didn't you say that she was always concerned about you?" He wiped the tear off my cheek and made me sit down next to him at the dining table. "Do you think she would be happy if she knew you were not eating and trying to attempt suicide because of her?" he asked, holding my hand.

I pulled my hand away from his grip. "I don't have anyone else in my life except her. And now that she is gone, I feel lost as if there is nothing for me to do." As more tears welled up in my eyes, threatening to spill over, I turned my head away and clasped my face with my palms.

A second later, I was pulled into a hug. Jai's hands gently caressed my back as he said, "You tried everything you could. Unfortunately, death is never in our hands. But you are a strong woman, Nats. You have to stay strong, even now!"

"I don't know what to do with my life now," I said in between my sobs.

"To live a life, we always need a purpose. If you think your purpose of living was your mother, and since she is gone, you have nothing to do, then..." he squeezed my hand, and I looked up to him as he added, "...find a new purpose to live. Do something of your own, or do something that will give you peace, but don't just say 'I give up', because there are a lot of things you can add a difference to!"

Teary-eyed, I gazed up at him. There was nothing there except concern inked in his eyes. At that moment, he sounded much like my *Ma*, encouraging me to keep fighting and living. The impact of the words made me look down and reflect on what I could do with my life now.

Ma's words resounded in my ears, "Everyone lives for themselves. Try living for someone else. *Make* a difference to someone else's life!"

When I calmed down, Jai said to me as if coaxing a child, "Now, please eat something. I know you must not have eaten anything for two days," he said, breaking a portion of the vada and placing it near my mouth.

"How did you know I am here?" I asked, taking a small bite of the food he held out for me.

"Well, Tanisha gave me your Mumbai apartment address. But when I went there, I was told you had left for your village, so I came as fast as possible. And, I'm thankful that I reached here on time, else I wouldn't have been able to forgive myself," he said, tearing a portion of another *vada.*

I hung my head down. With Jai's timely interference, I missed an opportunity to be with *Ma.* With whatever purpose I'll try to live my life, I could never overcome the love I had for *Ma*...

"When your parents died, *Ma* took you under her care and brought you up. Now that she is gone, I am sure there will be something or someone who will be your reason to live." He placed another piece of *vada* dipped in *sambar* near my mouth.

"Sounds impossible..." I frowned and tried to move away, but Jai held me back and forced the morsel in my mouth.

"When you can believe in fairy tales, Prince Charming and all, then why can't you believe there will be a purpose in your life too?" he asked, spoon-feeding me some *sambhar*.

I looked away. "I stopped believing in fairy tales a long time ago."

He paused for – minute, then added, "Still, I believe -"

"Listen, the word 'believe' from your mouth doesn't sound true." I held his hand to stop him from feeding me and added, "Moreover, I know you very well. Even you don't have faith in these words, so stop trying to paint a fancy picture when you know there is nothing left for me."

"Okay," he replied, and yet again, he tried to feed me. "I was just trying to speak the way you always encouraged me. Now, come on, finish your food!"

"I am done. I'm not hungry anymore," I said with a sigh. "By the way, why did you tell Aunty that you were my husband?"

"I didn't say anything. She assumed so when I came holding you last night," he re–lied.

"Did you by any chance change my -" I paused, thinking about the clothes I was wearing when I woke up.

Jai turned away, refusing to look me in the eye.

"How could you do that!?" I screamed, feeling utterly embarrassed and annoyed.

"I just had to. You were wet and cold. I was afraid you'd catch a fever, which by the way, you did catch! Oh, and I closed my eyes when I did. No other intention than to protect you," he replied with a shrug.

"I just don't get it! Why did you come all this way?" I stood up and glared at him, unable to understand his intentions.

With a tender smile, he met my fiery gaze and replied, "Maybe God sent me to protect you."

Though he looked genuine, he sounded smug! I was so infuriated that I really wished I could eat him alive!

He fumbled around in his pockets and murmured, "Why don't you take a look at your phone and check how many people are worried about you?" He fetched out a phone and switched it on. "This thing was switched off. I charged it for you. I was calling you like a maniac all this while!" He opened the 'Missed Call' list and handed the phone to me. The screen displayed a series of names in red with the number of times they had tried to call me. The first number was from an unsaved number, followed by Akash and Tanisha.

He pointed at the unsaved number and added, "And that is my number. So you better save it and place it in your favourites!" Before I could refute, he continued with a serious look, "Anyway, I know you were all alone and not in the right frame of mind, but you could have told me about the emergency when we were at Malshej Ghat. Right?"

"You were being interviewed by the reporters," I mumbled. "And this was not your problem, so I rushed right-"

"Seriously!" Jai interrupted, looking shocked. "Not my problem? In that case, riding in the car with me and taking such a huge risk was also not your problem. So why did you accompany me?" he demanded, keeping the phone aside.

I didn't reply as I was lost for words.

"And that day, too, you pretended as if you didn't know me. 'Hi', was the only word you said," he grumbled.

It took me a minute to understand he was referring to the meeting at his office with Akash.

"I didn't know how to react. Would you be happy to see me, someone, who was in a contractual relationship with you? I was afraid you'd be petrified that I may reveal your plans," I tried to justify myself.

"Oh really!" Jai ran his fingers through his hair in frustration. Agitatedly, he turned away and then faced me again. "God, Nats! We stayed together for nearly six months! We had a lovely time together! We were such good friends, and this is what you thought?" he asked.

At his straightforward question, I was momentarily at a loss. Finally, I shrugged my shoulders and replied, "I was surprised and didn't know how to react. Honestly, you were the last person I was expecting to meet."

With squinted eyes, he studied me for a few seconds. "Okay, forget about me. Why didn't you call Samira and tell her everything? You know how worried she was about you and how she looked at me after coming to know the truth about us?" he asked, walking closer to me.

"I thought of calling her after her marriage, but then I wanted to move on, so I thought it was best to erase the memories of everything that happened in Perth," I mumbled.

He watched me as if he was disappointed, then, with a heavy sigh, he covered the distance between us. "You were just assuming things and punishing yourself for nothing. We were concerned about you when you vanished into thin air."

"I had told you I would be going back to India," I answered.

"When and where you didn't specify," he countered.

I was silent for a while, as I knew any reply from my end would just add more fuel to this topic.

"From now on, you will keep me informed about your whereabouts and always make sure I know when you are in trouble," he said, pointing his finger at me.

His words brought a smile to my face as I nodded. "Yes, sir."

He calmed down his stature and smiled. "Good. We are going back to Mumbai tomorrow."

"Why?" I asked, surprised, as I had no intention of going anywhere from here.

"What will you do here?" he asked.

"Maybe do some part-time business or try my hands at a small company. Now, I don't need to earn too much as I am alone. So, I guess I'll just settle down here in my *Ma's* home," I explained.

"You are going with me to do the ad shoot for my company. You promised me," Jai said, crossing his arms over his chest.

"Jai, I'm-"

"Do you want Akash to pay my company two crore?" he asked with a questioning look. He knew this would definitely catch my nerve.

With a scowl, I replied, "I don't know all this. I am a terrible model. I tried explaining this to Akash as well, but he just wouldn't listen." I slumped down in the nearest chair, feeling peeved at everyone around me who was trying to make me do things I was not very good at.

"You have earned yourself huge respect the way you spoke to the reporter, so everyone is in awe of you. And be rest assured, I will make sure you give your best for my brand launch," he said, walking towards the sofa. After a few seconds of silence, he asked, "Can you show me around? I may not get a chance to come back here again. Also, I want to try that chilly fried fish that you had said is best here."

I arched up my eyebrows. I never thought that Jai was paying attention to the anecdotes I told him at times. Although I felt nice inside, I couldn't let him know that!

"What happened?" he asked.

I just shook my head and replied, "Give me ten minutes."

When I came out to the living room, wearing a simple long flared pink *salwar kurta* with stripes on its *dupatta*, I saw him standing near the photo frames hung on the wall and paying close attention to one particular picture.

"Hey, is that your parents' picture?" he asked the moment he realised I had returned.

I walked over to his side and gazed at the picture he was pointing at. "Yes, that's my mom, dad, and elder brother. It's the only picture I have of them. This one was taken at a village fair about two months before they died. *Ma* said wherever they are, they must be watching me. So, she has treasured this photograph along with her parents' frame."

I didn't get any response from him, but I continued talking.

"My brother didn't want to go that day," I said, thinking of how he shouted at my parents for taking him along to a relative's wedding.

With a deep frown, he asked after a few seconds, "How did they die?"

"In a bus accident. They were on their way to a wedding in the neighbouring village when the bus met with an accident. That's what my relatives told me. I'm not sure about the details of the accident. I was quite young to understand then."

"So, was your *Ma* a relative of yours?" he asked, turning to look at other photos on the wall.

"No, my parents had left me with the relatives who lived close to our house. But with my parents' demise, I became a burden, so they left me at my *Ma's* place with an excuse that they were going to a wedding at a far off place," I answered. I still remembered that evening when they had made up the lie to get rid of me. I had heard all of their plans of moving out with their essential belongings just to wash their hands off me.

"And your *Ma's* family accepted you, is it?" he asked, looking inquisitive.

"They didn't because *Ma* wasn't married, and they warned her that if she raised me, no one would be willing to marry her," I replied. Of course, *Ma's* family strongly opposed her decision, but she stood by me. "When her family cast her out for not obeying the rules, she didn't turn back and walked out with me along with her..."

Jai listened intently and took the photo frame of my real family off the wall. He observed it closely for a few seconds later and asked, "How old were you when they left you?"

"I was eight," I replied.

I didn't want him to take pity on me, but thankfully when I looked at him, there was only plain concern inked on his face. Then, masking away the flurry he felt within, he said, "That's a lot to take up at that age. Thankfully, God sent you to your *Ma* to look after you."

"Yes, indeed. I don't know what would have happened if I had stayed with my relatives instead of her." Thinking of those early days made me miss *Ma* even more. The stifling feeling in my chest threatened to drown me once again. "Let's go. These things make me sad. I don't want to think about them..."

"Yes, true. Let's go then," Jai said, picking up his wallet and car keys. He glanced at me from head to toe. Then, his eyes widened as he commented, "You look way different in this traditional attire and these..." He pointed at my hairdo.

"It's called plaits. *Ma* used to make them for me, so today I wanted to do it in her memory," I said, holding the two braids in my hand. Her words echoed in my ears, and I said it aloud. "The way you arrange your hair speaks about your personality. Messed up hair speaks about a messed up mind, and perfectly arranged hair talks about your perfectness!" *Well, in short, it was my effort to boost my confidence and buck up!*

"Wow, that's an awesome one. So, I guess your hair today speaks of your strength. You gathered yourself up to be strong," Jai remarked, admiring the neat braids.

Instantly, my eyes caught his. I hoped he was joking, but they had genuineness like he meant what he said.

I don't know how he could always predict what was running inside my head; or, was it the other way round? Whatever he said to me, felt apt to my situation and sentiment.

***

"Yes, I will be coming over by tomorrow, and by the way, contact a good photographer for the photoshoot to start," I heard him say to his partner as we sat in the car.

I was uncertain if I would do well, especially in this present situation when I had lost everything. This photo shoot was something I wanted to avoid.

But before I could tell him that, we heard a few kids running after his car, chasing us. He reduced the car speed so that the kids could catch up with us. As they ran, the expressions on their faces were overwhelming.

"Want a drive?" he stopped the car and asked. The kids were sceptical until he opened the door for them and asked them to hop in.

Jai had a huge smile plastered on his face as he asked the kids about their breakfast, family, and studies.

"I hope your parents won't be looking for you," he said.

They laughed in unison, and one of them replied, "They won't. Our school is over, and now we are free until lunchtime."

"So, shall we have ice cream?" His eyes twinkled with excitement, looking at their faces.

"That will be amazing, *bhaiya*," said the eldest one in the group.

"Let's go, then!" Jai exclaimed and asked me to guide him to the nearest ice cream shop.

We were near the beach, and there was always an ice cream trolley along with a few vendors selling balloons, toys, and other knick-knacks. "One for each," Jai said to the shopkeeper when we arrived. He handed a cone to each one of the kids.

While he was busy, I sat down on a pile of sand nearby and played with the grains slipping between my fingers. Finally, Jai came to me and offered me a cone. "No, thanks," I replied and added, "I am fine, sitting here. You go ahead, have fun with the boys."

"Your loss!" He shrugged and took a seat beside me.

I expected him to talk, but he sat quietly, licking his cone as if he was deep in his thoughts.

"What is it?" I asked.

"I was thinking of my grandfather. We often used to go on such trips like this. We would pick up children from the streets in his car and set out to have fun. He was a famous car mechanic and owned a car repair shop. I used to admire all the fancy cars that would come to his shop and draw pictures of them," he said. His eyes grew distant as if lost in the memory of those long-gone days.

"Staying with him, I learned a lot about cars, but whenever I had to return home to Mom and Dad, I felt like... something precious was being left behind. I had very little time to cherish his company in my life." He fell quiet and silently licked the ice cream.

With a smile, he gazed at the horizon and added, "After years, taking the kids on a ride and sitting here feels nice. It seems like this is what I'd been missing. I have been on trips, conferences, and parties, but none of them was quite like this, sitting by the beach and having ice cream!" He turned to me and then shook his head. "Maybe I'm just thinking all too much."

"What happened?" I probed. It seemed as if he wanted to say something but stopped.

Hesitantly, Jai started to say, "It's just that... I have never said sorry to you. I think I owe you a big apology. I'm sorry for hurting you, Nats. Because of me, you didn't attend your best friend's wedding."

I never expected him to say that. I smiled in return, unable to comprehend a reply for a few minutes.

"I don't think it was your mistake. I had lied to Samira about our relationship. It was me who didn't have the strength to speak the truth to my friend." Although I was pleased that he had apologised, I had already missed the most beautiful moment of my best friend's life. I knew in my heart that it was all because I was too much into him! The grief of losing my fairy tale ending had numbed my mind.

"Can we be friends again?" he asked, extending his hand towards me.

I smiled and shook hands with him. Then, I noticed a crumb of the cone stuck to the corner of his mouth.

I leaned forward to wipe that with a content smile when all of a sudden, he closed the distance between us and kissed me on my lips.

I was taken aback, but the unexpected touch of his lips made me motionless for a second. My circuits zapped at the softness of the feathered experience. A second later, I moved away, realising he had mistaken the gesture and explained, "There was something stuck to your mouth. I was trying to wipe it."

"Oh, I thought…" He looked away, feeling awkward and added, "My mistake, sorry!"

It was all too embarrassing, so I asked, "Shall we leave? The kids must be getting late…"

"Hmm, yes. Let's go," Jai said, standing up in a flash.

"That crumb is still stuck," I said, pointing to his corner of the mouth.

He paused for a second and brought his face forward towards me. "Can you remove it?"

I moved involuntarily and swiped it away. My throat felt choked up with the touch, and I mumbled, feeling sore, "Gone."

There was a smug smile on his face. I felt awkward and sceptical about why he did that.

"So, where do we eat lunch? I want to try the fish chops," he asked, getting back behind the driving wheel.

"Once we drop the kids, we can have it," I replied, a little fearful of what more antics he might try to pull before the kids.

CHAPTER XIII

Jai

As we drove to where Natasha mentioned we would have our lunch, I felt my stomach grumble for food. I think my appetite has gone up since coming to this village. Probably because I was feeling relaxed and was enjoying the simple environment all around.

"Bring in all the dishes of fish you have," I said to the waiter, dismissing Natasha's order of only a select few.

She rolled her eyes and remarked, "Have you gone crazy? How can you order everything?"

"I'm hungry, besides you never know which ones will be delicious," I answered.

"Haven't you heard, too much of everything spoils the broth?"

"Not on days when you feel hungry like a whale!" I grinned, flashing my teeth.

"Your wish!" She let out a sigh and smiled.

An hour later, with my ravenous appetite, I gobbled up most of the dishes laid out on the table. Every now and then, Natasha glanced at me, suppressed her smile and then returned to nibbling her food. What was so funny? Well, I guess it was okay. At least she was in a better mood!

"Do you serve drinks here? I mean alcohol," I asked the waiter when he arrived at our table to clear the plates.

Natasha shook her head as she didn't want any drinks while the waiter smiled brightly and handed me the menu.

After the drinks, I settled the bill, and we returned to my car, ready to head back home. "I feel so full now!" I said, rubbing my hand over my stomach. "I think I've overeaten today!"

Her face blossomed with a naughty smile. What was so appealing about overeating? I wanted to tease her, but I let her be. I liked it when her face brightened up and wished to see her smile more often.

As we drove back, I felt discomfort in my stomach. At first, it was tolerable, but it escalated and even started to rumble with every passing minute. I pressed on the accelerator and hurried towards home. I was in urgent need of the washroom! Damn those fishes!

"Are you okay? You look pale," Natasha suddenly commented, glancing at me.

"Yeah, all good," I said, plastering a smile. If I told her the truth, I was sure she would laugh out loud and make fun of me!

By the time we reached her house, the pain in my stomach had increased tenfold! I parked the car hurriedly and dashed inside the house towards the bathroom at rocket speed.

Five minutes later, when I came out flushing the toilet, she had a concerned look on her face. "All okay?"

"Yes, just nature's call," I smiled, trying to act normal, but the next second, my stomach grumbled aloud, and I had to rush back into the bathroom. But this time, the motion was followed by vomiting, and I knew I had had too much of everything. More than the vomiting and motions, I was mortified at the thought of facing her! This was downright embarrassing! Ignoring her advice, I had ordered too many dishes, gobbled them up and now was suffering due to my gluttony!

"Here, have this. It is an antacid. It might help," Natasha said, offering a syrup as soon as I came out and rested my exhausted self on the sofa.

The medicine worked for only ten minutes, and then I was back in the washroom. Finally, after my fifth visit, she forced me to visit a hospital.

Luckily, she was acquainted with the staff and got me an appointment with the doctor immediately, else with the long queue, I was sure it was better to return to Mumbai to see a doctor than to wait here!

"He is your husband, right? So why did you let him eat so much?" the lady doctor scolded Natasha after I told her about our lunch menu.

Her face flushed in embarrassment, but she kept quiet as the doctor examined me.

"Though the local cuisine is tempting to the tongue, it isn't easy to digest for people not accustomed to it. And since you're not from around here, you shouldn't have eaten so much," said the lady doctor, looking at me. Then, she turned to Natasha and added sternly, "You should take care of your man and always maintain a tight control over him!" She scribbled a prescription and passed it to Natasha. "Bring him to me if he doesn't listen to you. It's become a trend these days for husbands not to follow their wife's orders!"

"Ma'am, I always follow her orders. She told me those dishes were quite rare, and you can't get them in any other state of India," I said, putting my tongue in my cheek.

Natasha clenched her teeth hard and glared at me as if she would eat me raw.

I smiled inwardly. Incensed as Natasha was, she appeared extremely cute and I tried to pull her leg a bit more, "Ma'am, she enjoys troubling me just because I love her too much."

The lady doctor looked at me startled and then at Natasha with glaring eyes, "I didn't think it would be you who needs a punishment."

"Ma'am, please don't listen to him. He is lying. I can take you to-"

I immediately interrupted, "Look at her! She wants to take me there again!"

"Look, mister, I wasn't born yesterday. I can clearly see who the culprit is here, so stop it, else I can give a dosage that you will remember for your lifetime," the doctor scolded me with a scowl.

It was time to withdraw, or the trick would backfire, so I straightened up right away and took the prescription from her. "Okay, doctor."

"And you take care of him well. I don't want to hear any complaints. After all, he is your husband," the doctor added with a warm smile.

Such a nice doctor! I praised her in my mind. "Thank you, doctor. You are too sweet," I grinned. Then, turning to Natasha, I added, "See, take care of me, else I will complain to her."

Natasha's face turned dark, but she didn't reply. As soon as we left the hospital, she couldn't hold back her aggravation. "I don't understand why you are doing this! What fun are you getting by doing all this nonsense?!" Without a second's pause, she continued, "And why did you tell my neighbour you are my husband? She must have gone ahead and told the entire village by now!" she continued grumbling.

"But you are still my wife. It's a fact," I said, taking my seat in the car.

"What?!" she looked at me, startled.

"You still are my wife, and I am your husband, darling. Did you have a memory loss or something? How can you forget we are married?" I teased her as she sat down beside me with a stony expression.

"Please don't joke with me. I left Perth only after we filed for the divorce," she said, sighing and looking out of the window.

"It didn't reach the court, though," I said, starting the car. "So legally, you are still mine, and I am yours."

"How can that be possible?" she asked, her eyebrows perked up. "We both had signed and handed over the papers to the lawyer before leaving."

"Yes, but after you left, my lawyer called to inform that his office had caught fire and the papers were destroyed due to that. He was gravely injured and recommended another lawyer to me," I told her. Observing her serious expression, I added, "This is why the papers have not reached the court, and nothing has been done about it. So legally, we are still husband and wife. You are not happy, is it?" I asked, looking at her tense face.

"Jai, can you stop it? I know how badly you needed the divorce and now are joking around," she said, facing me.

"I needed money, right," I explained, turning towards her. "But I was not so keen on divorce. I liked the friendship that we shared. The only thing I wanted from divorce was to free you so that you could think about your life. And not take us seriously."

"Watch it!!" she shrieked, taking control of the steering wheel as we were about to crash with a truck.

I parked the car to the side, breathing a sigh of relief. Her hands were still on the steering wheel and touching mine firmly. I couldn't help looking at them together and feeling the warmth. All my focus went to the hands that held mine and I wondered, *aren't these the ones that held me firmly whenever I fumbled in the past year?*

I can clearly recollect I had no such friend who was so close to me and cared for me so much.

It was true, and my mind was now stuck at the way her hands held mine.

What was so appealing about her hand mingling with mine? Why was it so overwhelming to be touched by her? I mused and then recalled the kiss at the beach. I had misunderstood her intention and had kissed her. It was a small peck that I had just placed on her lips, but her surprised expression made me move away. Frankly speaking, I wanted to do so much more. I wanted to take her in my arms, mould her into my frame, and kiss her senseless. Heat rose in my body, feeling the intensity of the kiss I wanted.

"Sorry, I got scared," she said, removing her hand from mine and taking away all the heat that emanated from the touch. "Be careful. Don't lose your focus while driving, whatever may be the issue."

After a moment's pause, she asked, "So, we need to do it again?"

I leaned towards her to fulfil her command.

"But how do we do it from here? And why wasn't it sent to court?" she asked, shaking her head.

I immediately pulled myself back. Natasha was talking about the divorce papers, and here I was thinking about the kiss! I felt utterly stupid...

"You will have to come with me to Perth again for that," I lied.

"Can't we scan it and send or maybe courier it?" she asked with a concern inked on her face.

I started the engine and looked ahead. "No, I guess, Perth court doesn't accept that. Physical presence is required in the court before divorce is granted."

"Try once and see if they agree," she urged.

I nodded. I clearly remember how vulnerable she appeared while signing the divorce papers. But now, it seemed she was way too tense because it wasn't finalised. Did something change in her in these six months? Does she love someone else? Or did I read her feelings wrong? The answers to those questions were difficult to even think of. As we reached her home, I was about to run to the washroom when she handed me a few medicines and a glass of water.

After a few minutes, I felt a little better physically, but mentally, my head was in turmoil. I sighed and sat down on her sofa. Unknowingly, my eyes followed her everywhere she went, from the room to the kitchen, even to the bathroom.

Though she was trying to avoid being in the same room as me, sharing the space with her brought a different kind of satisfaction.

I was watching TV, and Natasha was in the kitchen when my phone flashed with an incoming video call. It was from Chad, and I tapped on it to answer.

"Hey, where are you?" asked Chad as soon as the call connected.

"At Natasha's place," I replied honestly. Right then, Natasha magically appeared before me, her hands on her hips and brows knit up in angry glare.

"What!" echoed Samira's voice, and her face appeared on the screen. "Where's Natasha? Is she with you?"

I looked at Natasha with a questioning look, whether she wanted to talk to Samira or not. Instead of answering, she stood there, her lips pursed in a straight line and eyes giving me a death stare for putting her through this.

Gathering all my courage, I placed the phone right before her face. "Here she is."

"Oh hi, Samira," Natasha greeted with an awkward face.

I heard Samira shouting from the other end, "Where the hell have you been these days? Why didn't you call me or come to my wedding? If you had problems with him, I understand, but you could have called me at least! I was worried about you," Samira poured her heart out.

"I..." Natasha fumbled, and her eyes met with mine. She took a breath and added, "I'll call you soon. *Ma* passed away. Give me some time. I'm not in the right frame of mind..."

"What? How?" Samira asked in a shocked voice. The next second, she calmed down and mumbled, "Aunty passed away, and yet you didn't feel the need to call me."

Natasha's eyes welled up. She cast her head down and replied, "I didn't want to disturb you in your new life."

As her tears trickled down her cheek, I felt guilt rising within me. I shouldn't have put her on the call when she had just witnessed her mother's death. I wish I could hug her right away and console, saying, 'I'm right here.' But I didn't have that kind of guts. I was afraid she would push me out anytime.

"Natasha, did you forget everything we have shared till now? How could you think I would be at peace when you are in trouble?" Samira's voice sounded choked up.

"It's decided," Chad's voice could be heard in the background. He came to the screen and added, "We are flying to India to meet you next month."

"Great! Thanks, Chad," Samira replied.

"I'm okay. You don't need to rush, o-" Natasha tried to say.

But Chad interrupted, "I'm booking the tickets. Glad that Jai finally found you after such a long time. That fellow needs a slap, but right now, we need to talk to you first once we reach India."

I remained quiet, aware that everyone would pound me at the end for breaking the damsel's heart.

Natasha and Samira continued to speak, and some thirty minutes later, my presence became completely non-existent. But I was thankful as Natasha had finally calmed down and even teased Samira about her married life.

I pretended to watch the TV, but my ears were all glued to their silly girl talk. At times, Natasha squealed aloud at something Samira had murmured, while at other times, she bit her lips and whispered her reply with a shy look on her face.

A song playing on the TV diverted my attention. As I changed my posture, my foot landed on something fleshy.

"Oh rat," I had just said when Natasha stood up on the chair.

"I will call you later. There's a rat here!" she exclaimed and hung up the call. "What are you doing, standing there motionless! Shoo it away!" she shrieked, skipping to the corner of the wall.

"What should I do? Youshould scare it away," I said, trying to be brave and walk around, when I found another one, and this time, I jumped up on the sofa next to her chair. "How come there are so many here? Have you made them your pets?"

"Why will I do something like that?! Some neighbours must have put 'rat kill', and that's why they have come here," she mumbled, trying to get hold of a stick.

"What will you do with that small stick?" I asked, but she patted on the floor here and there, trying to shoo them off instead of replying.

"Look behind you," I teased her, and she almost fell from the chair. I grabbed her by her shoulders and pulled her up, closer to me.

"Where is it?" she asked, hiding her face in the crook of my neck and urged. "Please do something."

I took the stick from her hand and pretended to *shoo* them away while holding her close in my arms.

"Are they gone?" I could feel her warm breath on my neck. Her eyes were still closed and her face hidden.

"Not yet," I said, my eyes smirking in bliss. "They are coming up, I think."

"What!" She sounded petrified as she clung closer to me. Holding her like this, I was losing my sanity. Unknowingly, my hands started to rub her back.

"Did they go?" she asked.

But my voice was caught up in my throat. Feeling her softness and warmth, the excitement was spreading all the way to my groin. However, I couldn't keep her to myself for long because she moved away. Finally, I opened my eyes and found her glaring at me.

"What?" I defended myself at her glare. "They were just here! Must have run away now."

"I know what you were doing," she said, giving me a scornful look.

I tried to stand for myself and speak up in my defence but under her pensive eyes, I looked away and confessed, "Sorry, got carried away."

It would have been much better if the rats had stuck to their place, but they were long gone.

Getting off the chair, Natasha went to the kitchen and returned with a glass of water and my medicines, "Here, you should take them on time."

"Thanks," I uttered, feeling wrong about the college-goer attitude that I was displaying to her.

For the rest of the night, complete silence followed between us. The only sound was that of the TV. She had moved back to her shell, pretending that I was a guest she needed to take care of.

CHAPTER XIV

Natasha

It was a mistake to let Jai hold me because I feared the rats. But, as he stroked my back, I felt sensations of desire shooting through my body. I wanted to be in his arms, caressed by him just like that and live in the moment.

However, my mind alerted me that it would become a huge problem if I didn't stop him and moved away, pretending it was his mistake. I had to defend my heart and not let him turn me into his puppet again. But the emotional outburst in my body was going out of control. The more I found him relaxed and being himself as he lay on my sofa and watched the TV, the more I was drawn towards him.

I knew it was not intentional, but his casual attitude in my home was like a magnetic pull, alluring and enticing me to drop all pretences and embrace him. Was he telling the truth when he said that our divorce had not been finalised yet, or was he just teasing me? Maybe he just wanted to see my reaction, or maybe not, but what was his intention?

There was just one bed in the house. So, he suggested that he would sleep on the couch. Though it served the purpose for lying down, it wasn't comfortable at all for sleeping. Still, he insisted that he will manage.

I retired to my bedroom but was feeling restless. After an hour, I moved out on the pretext of having water and saw how uncomfortable he was, still trying to settle down. I felt guilty and opined, "The bed is big enough to occupy the two of us. Please come inside." He began saying, "No, it's..."

But I raised my hand and uttered, "It's okay, Jai. You have come this far for me. This is the least I can do."

I moved towards my room, and soon, he followed me. As we lay on the two sides, I became restless and shifted all night, thinking about all the unnecessary problems I'd have to face if I'd have to go back to Perth just to get the divorce.

Once while turning sides, our eyes met. Jai was awake and looked uncomfortable.

"It's a new place. Maybe that's why you are not able to sleep," I uttered.

"Maybe, but why are you not asleep?" he asked, scrutinising me.

"Thinking about *Ma* and my life," I lied. At present, except him, there was nothing else running in my head. He looked like he was about to ask something more, but the moment was interrupted by a call from Akash, and I sat upright.

It was Soha, video calling from the hospital bed.

"Hi, Soha. How are you, baby?" I asked, feeling extremely concerned at her pale disposition.

"I am good, Natie. How are you?" she asked in a frail voice.

"I am good, sweetie." I wanted to reach out to her and cradle her in my arms.

Akash appeared on the screen. "She wanted to talk to you when I told her you lost your *Ma*."

"I too wanted to talk to her, glad you called. How was the operation? When are you both coming back?" I asked, tying my hair into a bun.

"Soon!! The operation was successful. Soha will be able to run and play very soon," Akash said, playfully ruffling Soha's hair.

"Soha, come soon, baby. I'm eagerly waiting for you to return so that I can play all day with you," I said, tears glistening in my eyes.

"When are you going back to Mumbai?" asked Akash, and I looked up at Jai. His eyes were on me, watching me talk to Akash.

I instantly felt goosebumps erupting all over my body.

"I'm returning tomorrow but will come back to Diveagar once the shooting is done," I replied. "Don't worry, I'll be fine."

"Hmm," said Akash and added, "Keep me informed and if you find any problems, reach out to me as soon as possible. I will ask Tanisha to give you a call."

There was magic, that sense of belongingness in our friendship. He always made sure I was doing fine.

"You take care of Soha and yourself. I will let you know if I need anything." The father-daughter duo flashed a smile at me and disconnected the call. I didn't know why I could instantly connect with them, as if they were one of my own clan.

"It was Akash. His daughter is out of danger now," I said.

Jai was still observing me closely. Finally, after some time, he said, "Good, seems like you know them personally."

"Akash is my best buddy. We studied together in college. We used to have a lot of fun doing events and trying out new ventures to source our college fees. I met Soha a week ago. She is a darling," I said with a dreamy smile on my lips. "Just like I always wanted..."

"Just like I always wanted?" Jai repeated my words with a questioning look.

"A daughter like her is all I ever wanted," I confessed. Talking to Akash and Soha took my mind off Jai. In fact,

Akash's words of consolation gave me the strength I had been missing all these days.

"She must be something then," he said with a smile.

"Yes. Soha is a chirpy little girl, and she will make you dance on your toes! In short, she is just awesome!" I beamed. "After speaking to her, I confess, I am feeling a little better." Taking a deep breath, I put my phone aside, closed my eyes and turned to the other side, pretending to be peacefully asleep. But for many minutes, the hair on my neck was nervously standing up as I could feel Jai's gaze on me. The memory of him kissing me and holding me in his arms played havoc on my body as I tried to sleep. When I finally succumbed to exhaustion, unknowingly, I dreamt of something I hadn't experienced for the past six months.

His hands were all over my body, roaming passionately as he explored every fibre of my skin and traversed into the depths of my secret carving. His mouth was devouring the nape of my neck as he inched inside my core. I was sweating as the heat rose from the deepest part of my core, floating in my own world as he plunged deep into me in rhythm. I clutched his back hard for support and moaned his name as I felt numbness sweep across me.

"Hey, you all right?" I felt someone tapping my shoulder, but I didn't want to break the spell and ignored the call.

"Nats, are you fine? Why were you calling my name?" I heard him ask.

I was startled as it dawned on me it was a dream. Feeling embarrassed, I stilled. *Did I moan his name aloud? What a blunder!*

There were only two options before me. Either I could still pretend to be sleeping or lie to his face. But I knew I was terrible at lying, so I pretended to be asleep.

But the man had caught my weakness, and he patted my shoulder again. I held my breath and lay there like a dead woman.

An unexpected coldness touched my cheeks, and I blinked my eyes open. I wanted to push him away, but I felt him lean on my body and kiss my cheek again. This time, I wanted to grab him by his collar and slap him, but I was afraid of answering his questions, so I continued to pretend as if I was deep asleep.

"Perhaps, I could do something more while you pretend to be sleeping," I heard him whisper into my ears. "Maybe kiss you where you like the most," he said, tracing the nape of my neck, then tracing his fingers just above the hem of my shirt. "Or kiss here, where it makes you moan my name."

It was a dangerous threat because then I knew I would lose control. I faced Jai and screamed, "Can you let me sleep?"

"Yes, if you let me know what you were dreaming about," he voiced, a mysterious smile crawling on his face.

This man was making me go nuts now, and I had to stay sane to play my game well. "I was dreaming about Akash, any problem? Or don't I get to dream until I get divorced?"

He stiffened at my reply and glared at me for a full minute. He then remarked through clenched teeth, "You are free to do whatever you want to." The next minute, he got off the bed. It was clear from his posture that he didn't take my words too well. I felt terrible for a while, but I knew I had to toughen my stance. Otherwise, he would have made me succumb to him once again.

The next morning when I woke up, he was awake and ready to leave. It seemed like he had, after all, slept on the sofa last night. "I think we should leave early," he said, looking at his watch. "You can take the day off and rest at your place. Then, once the details of the ad campaign are finalised, I'll let you know, and we can start the shooting."

I nodded in reply and left to get ready.

The drive back to Mumbai was a quiet one. He didn't speak, except asking if I needed to stop for anything.

I felt hungry, but last night's dream and the aftermath had made the air between us awkward. I thought it was better to reach Mumbai in silence.

He dropped me at my place without a word and then left. I stood there looking at him as he passed by, wondering what hurt him so much. Was it the divorce thing that I mentioned, or was it that I dreamed of Akash instead of him.

Either of them worked for me as it would help me to stay away from Jai, and that's what I needed.

His father's final words to me just before my departure from Perth resounded in my ears, and a sob escaped me. I took a deep breath. It was better this way for both of us. Besides, he was the one who had said that what we shared between us was friendship, nothing more than that, so there was no point in keeping my hopes.

CHAPTER XV

Jai

How could she lie to my face? I clearly heard her moan out my name, but she snapped and bluffed that she dreamed about Akash! It was so freaking easy for her to say she was dreaming of him, while like a fool, I couldn't even catch a wink until two in the morning. The whole night I felt tortured, wanting to take her right there on the bed, but I didn't because she had constructed a wall between us.

Natasha dropped all her guards and was so natural while talking to Akash and his daughter as if they were her family! Damn it! She spent six months with me living as my wife, yet she developed no feelings for me! I turned into a stranger the moment she left, and Akash became her newfound happiness.

I drove in silence, anger eating my insides. I don't know why I was feeling so jealous. I felt it was only right for her to leave Perth after filing the divorce. But I clearly had no clue why I was relieved and happy when my lawyer called to inform me that his office had caught fire and the papers were destroyed.

The new lawyer suggested that I could just scan and forward the papers to him once I got them signed; he would take care of the rest. But once I landed in India, Natasha was unreachable, and I didn't know how to contact her anymore. Samira couldn't connect to her either! As the matter wasn't that urgent, I didn't pursue it and let things be.

When we coincidentally met again, for a moment, I felt lucky that I didn't have to go through the trouble of locating her. But today, when she suggested the same things as my new lawyer, to send him the scanned divorce papers, I was astounded at my response. Why did I lie?

A part of me was thrilled to see her in my office. It was as if my deepest wish had been granted and that too without any effort! But contrary to my expectations, she pretended to be a stranger! Damn it! How could she act like that? I was annoyed to the core and wanted to peel off her pretence!

However, my anger dissipated into the air and became extinct when she stood by me for the car test. So when I heard about her misfortune, I wanted to be there for her, as she had been for me.

But now, when I tried to bring us closer, she clearly wasn't interested and even retorted that she was dreaming of someone else!

To keep my sanity, I kept quiet while my mind was running an extra mile. I had to figure out a plan and get Natasha back in my life. I wanted to rest at home for a day, but things were not so smooth at the office yet. After dropping Natasha, I returned home, freshened up and hurried to work.

"Jai, I think we should hire Charles, the famous Italian photographer. He is currently in India, and I believe he can do wonders to re-establish our brand in line with our new target market." Mehta suggested at the meeting held with the marketing team to discuss the action plan of the campaign.

Recognising the name, I nodded. "Sure, let's get in touch with him."

"Ah, great!" he remarked. "I came to know from an acquaintance that he's free these days and wouldn't mind taking up a project if the compensation is satisfactory."

While Mehta spouted praises of him, I searched for the photographer on the internet. Though I wasn't really impressed with his work, his clientele were renowned companies from all over the world. My judgement of the art was probably that of a novice, I thought and glanced at my secretary. It wouldn't hurt to meet him up.

Understanding my gesture, she nodded, "I'll arrange a meeting."

That very evening, we met Charles. I still wasn't convinced but seeing Mehta's enthusiasm, I gave in and hired him to direct our advertisement.

"I think this model will do fine," Charles commented, checking out Natasha's photographs from the camera test session. Though the images were not up to expectation, they were sufficient for the purpose of the meeting. "I suggest we select a backdrop of a beach or a waterfall." He eyed the car catalogue in his hand and added, "As natural as we can."

I liked his idea and nodded, "Interesting. Let's start on this ASAP."

"I'm busy this month but all yours after that," he replied with a complacent look and added, "as long as you fill my pockets well!"

Mehta took it up from here and discussed the compensations while I listened to their sophisticated haggling. I couldn't help but smile inside. There was no one better than Mehta in negotiating when it came to money!

A month later, the details of the campaign were finalised. Morjim Beach in Goa was chosen as the location. Once Charles was hired, the dates for the photoshoot were set. My secretary forwarded Natasha's tickets and accommodation details to her and copied me to the email. Looking at the name, unspeakable emotions surged within me. I was still annoyed with her but was also at a loss. What could I do to make her look at me again?

The ring on the intercom broke my thoughts. "Yes?"

"Sir," the receptionist said, "there's a Mr Atul Shukla here to see you. He doesn't have an appointment but is insisting on meeting you, claiming that you are his childhood friend."

"Let him in..." I responded.

***

"Boss, how are you?" Atul strolled inside my cabin with a big smile and took a seat before my desk. "I don't think you remember me, but when I saw you on TV, I recognised you right away. So, I came here to jog your memory!"

Jog my memory! What a joke! Though I could guess his reason for appearing before me, I refrained from rolling my eyes and asked, "I remember you. What do you want, Atul?"

"Ah! I'm so fortunate!" Dramatically, he slammed his palm on his chest. "Well, then I'll cut to the chase. *Ma's* not keeping well, and I don't have money to take her to the hospital. If you could lend me-"

Before he could finish, I interrupted, "How much?"

He uttered a number and I wrote him a cheque. He thanked me profusely and promised to pay it all back. Inwardly, I scoffed. *He would pay me back? That's another joke!* As long as I lived with grandpa, he often borrowed money from me with similar promises to return them all, and to date, he had never returned a dime! The only reason why I even complied with his demands was because I was indebted to his parents. In the absence of my mom and dad, they looked after me as if I were their own.

"By the way, do you recall any bus accident when you were young?" I asked, looking at him.

"No, why?" he asked with a confused look. Then, after a second's pause, his eyes flickered as if he remembered something but masking it with his usual indifferent face, he added, "if I recall something, I'll tell you, but why did you ask?"

"I just happened to come across someone from your village. Nothing serious," I shook my head and changed the topic. We spoke for a while and added, "Take care of aunty."

"Of course! Don't worry," he said with a snorty laugh and left my office as swiftly as he had come.

For a long time, I stared at the door of my cabin in deep thought. I had recognised the people in the picture of her mom, dad and brother. They weren't dead. In fact, they were very much alive, and it turned out Atul was no one but her older brother. How was I going to break this news to Natasha?

I felt guilty for having learnt this information! Knowing it would break her heart, I could never tell her and neither could I keep it to myself. Now that her *Ma* was gone, she was vulnerable and sharing this would no doubt shatter her!

But I couldn't keep it to myself either. Maybe I could try to tell her in Goa after the shoot...

My attention returned to my laptop screen. I wanted to call and check on her, but I didn't have the courage to face her. What if she said she was busy with her work or was talking to Akash? This was the first time I felt inferior to someone, as if he possessed something that I didn't have.

***

On the day of the trip to Goa, I found Natasha sitting next to Mehta, discussing something in detail.

"Hello," I said and sat opposite them in the waiting area. I had many things to ask her, but I didn't know where to begin. Finally, after much deliberation, I asked, "Where's Akash's assistant?"

Natasha looked at me and asked, "Tanisha?"

"Yep!"

"She'll be joining us later; held up with another project."

"Hmm..." I nodded, again at a loss of topic to converse. "Uh... have you met with Charles yet?"

"Not yet. I don't think he has arrived yet. I guess he is-"

"Found you!" Charles remarked, interrupting us in between. He was dressed in blue chino shorts and an untucked white shirt, with the top two buttons unfastened, revealing his hairy chest. I frowned. Does he think he looks dashing, showing off his hairy chest? I felt immediately repulsive. *I would instead do business with someone who acts professional and dresses appropriately for work than someone who looks like him.* I sighed. It was too late to utter my objections. He was here for my work, and we would be over with him when it would be done. I wondered what people saw in him and how he had made his name. *As long as he gives me results, I am okay with whatever he wears.*

"Hi, Miss Natasha," he said, extending his hand towards her.

She shook his hands with a smile.

Charles held onto her hand and said, "Why don't we sit together in the flight and discuss the photoshoot? It will help us save time and-" He paused and flashed a cheesy grin, "I require an interesting company too."

"Sure, why not?" Natasha replied, shrugging her shoulders.

My secretary had booked her seat next to mine, and I was glad about it. Charles' interference irked me, and I wanted to refute, but I held back my objection. It was essential that she understood the concept of the advertisement.

As we boarded, she sat beside Charles and Mehta next to me. All my focus was on her, and I guess Mehta noticed because he asked, "Do you know her from before?"

"Yes, I-" I paused, noticing something odd in the way Charles was behaving with Natasha. I got up and interrupted him, "Would you mind exchanging seats with me? There's some issue with the compensation details in the agreement."

Charles dropped his hands away from Natasha and looked disappointed as he stood up to go away.

"Thank you," said Natasha as I sat down next to her.

"Why did you agree to sit with him in the first place?" I asked with a scowl. "If he holds your hand like that, can't you just slap him right away?"

"I would have, but he is your photographer. What if he refuses to work with you and you face a loss because of me?" she mumbled, looking away.

"Sometimes, I wonder, what do I do about you?" I shook my head in disbelief. "Do you think he is more important than you? Or for that matter, is anything in the goddamn world more important than you?! When will you grow up and think about yourself?"

She stared at me for a minute, then added, "I know how important this project is for you. All the fights you had with your father were for this one. How could I let someone ruin it for something as small as this?" I looked at her, surprised as she continued, "I know how to take care of myself, but I don't want to spoil things for you."

"Why do you care about me so much?" I asked. I just could not make out what was running in her mind!

She became quiet for a moment, then replied, "I guess it's because I've known you for a while now and have had a relationship with you even though it was fake."

The word fake hit something deep down in my heart, but I couldn't help smiling because of the concern she held for me. Even though she knew our relationship was fake and she was not bound to show any care for me, I meant something to her.

But then, I felt all her efforts were a waste as I was reaching nowhere with this project. "Thank you, but sometimes I think all this wasn't worth it. My dream of making a car company isn't worthy of all these sacrifices."

"Why do you think so?" she questioned, raising her brow as she regarded me.

"I lied to my dad to make him lend me the money. I worked hard, hoping I would succeed, but in the end, I didn't," I sighed. "It failed just like my retail venture in Perth..."

"Everything happens for a reason, and this might have happened for a reason, too. My *Ma* used to say, 'When you do something different, no one stands with you at the beginning. But when you give that work your heart and soul, you will undoubtedly succeed. And after your success, you become a legend!'" she said. "Don't lose hope because your dream needs you more than anyone else. For others, it's just money, but for you, it's your dream, and you need to keep in mind why you started this," she added, placing a hand above mine. Heaving a sigh, she continued, "You did this for your grandfather, so don't let that dream die."

"How did you know?" I asked, quite surprised as I had never told anyone the reason behind my dream.

"I noticed when you explained about your grandfather when we were sitting by the beach at Diveagar. I could see how much those memories mean to you."

In a daze, I watched her for a long minute while she was digging in her bag for something.

I had only shared a glimpse of my past with her. But she had connected the dots and seen it clearly through my soul. Maybeit's the ease with which I talk to her that makes me confess things I haven't done to anyone else.

"By the way, what are we going to do about the divorce?" she asked, turning towards me, breaking my chain of thoughts.

Here she goes again, putting a full stop between us when I'm trying to take our relationship further.

"Didn't get a chance, will do once we return from the shoot," I said and saw her plugging her earphones. Then, I saw her selecting a folder named 'My life' from the corner of my eyes and double-tapping it to play the songs.

She closed her eyes while listening to the music, and I knew she did that to avoid talking to me. It meant she was either hiding something from me or she didn't like talking to me. Why else would she cut me off this quickly, when earlier she used to speak to me for hours together?

I wanted to ask her about her taste in songs and extend our talk, but then I held back. Sometimes, it's best to leave people in their own space lest they feel strangled.

CHAPTER XVI

Natasha

By the time I reached my hotel room, it was six in the evening. Every fibre of my body was screaming for rest, and I was famished. I had not had a proper meal since returning to Mumbai. Without *Ma* around, I had no appetite. And now, having restrained my hunger all this time, it was hitting back with a vengeance. My body ached all over, and I felt dizzy.

I entered the washroom intending to take a warm and relaxing bath, hoping it would wash away the tiredness of waking up early morning to catch the flight till reaching the resort. However, the moment I undressed and stepped into the shower, the doorbell rang.

That was quick, I frowned. I had ordered coffee but expected it to arrive at least fifteen minutes later. Hurriedly, I slid into a dress and opened the door.

"Hey, hi!" There stood Charles, flashing a shameless smile.

"Hi," I uttered warily, feeling uncomfortable in his presence.

His eyes checked me out from top to toe and then lingered over my neckline. He placed a hand on the doorway, leaned a little closer and asked, "Can I come in? I want to watch the football match, but my TV is not working."

"Ah, I have to freshen u-"

Before I could finish, he interrupted, "No worries, I'll just take the couch and watch. You do your thing. I'll not disturb you at all." With pleading eyes, as he added, "It's the last twenty minutes and a significant match, sweetheart!"

I fumbled for a few seconds, looking for a reason to reject, but then, I was way too exhausted to think of anything. "Okay," I mumbled, letting him in. I left the door wide open and switched on the TV before handing him the remote. *This man smelled trouble! Where did Jai find him, anyway?*

"Sweetheart, you can go and change. I don't mind," he said with a faint smile.

I cringed at his blatant effort to flirt and felt like punching his face. But I was in no position to do as I wished. I pulled a chair as far away from him as possible and replied in a stiff smile, "That's all right. I'll wash up after you finish with the match."

"Oh," he raised his brow and added, "It's quite hot in here. Could you close the door?"

"No, it's okay," I protested. "I'm feeling a bit stuffy."

"It's because of the heat! You've got to close the door and let the air-conditioner do its job," he said, standing up to close the door.

My brows knit into deep ravines, and my exhausted mind raced to find an excuse. This was not good. His intentions seemed nothing but evil! I stiffened up, ready to hit him with anything if he tried anything weird.

"Charles? What are you doing here?" asked a familiar voice outside the door.

I breathed a sigh of relief.

"Well, my TV's not working," he replied lazily. "And I've got a football match to finish."

Jai's eyes glanced from me to Charles. "Oh, Italy and Argentina, right?" Jai asked, interest gleaming in his eyes as he entered the room. "Mehta's watching that too, and I was about to join him. Let's watch it together!" Jai gave a friendly pat on Charles's shoulder.

With no excuse to stay back, Charles complied with Jai, disappointment evident in his eyes.

"Mehta, open the door, man!" Jai knocked on Mehta's door, right across the corridor. "Charles and I are here to watch the match with you."

All this time, I was still seated in my chair. Finally, I strolled towards the door and heard Mehta say, "Awesome! I've ordered some wine and snacks!"

I sighed thankfully and was about to lock myself in for the much-awaited relaxing bath when Jai walked back to my room and asked, "Why was he in your room?"

"He kind of barged in to watch the football match here as the TV in his room is not working. At least that's what he said," I replied, feeling exasperated. "I left the door open, but that photographer of yours complained that it's too hot and I should close the door to let the AC do its job!"

"Bastard! Why did you even let him in?" Jai glared at me.

Why was he angry at me? I glowered back at him. "*didn't,* he-"

Not letting me finish, he added while gritting his teeth, "And... you aren't wearing anything inside. Why did you let him in?"

Embarrassed, I crossed my arms over my chest. "Are you my boyfriend or my husband to ask me that in such a direct manner? Why don't you mind your own business?!"

I tried to shut the door on his face, but he stopped me and entered the room. "He must have been ogling at you dressed like that all this time! You didn't mind then, but now when I'm pointing it out to you out of concern, you reprimand me!"

"Look, I told you already. Charles came uninvited, and I didn't know it was him when I opened-" I stopped midway.

"Why the hell should I give you an explanation? You are talking as if I am not wearing anything at all. I'm not revealing anything, and we are not in the eighteenth century!"

"Awesome! Be nice to him!" Jai snapped, utterly riled up. "Hold hands with him and let *him* stare at your peaks! And throw tantrums at *me*!"

I tightened my arms around myself at his mention of my perked-up mounds. But I was furious at him. *Who is he to point it out?* "My wish! I will do whatever I want. Show him or let him touch! You better stay out and go out of my room," I roared. Then, without waiting for a reply, I walked towards him to push him out of my room.

He grabbed me by my arms and threatened, "Don't ever talk to me like that. I may lose my cool."

"If you can talk to me the way you wish, why can't I? You don't own me! I have come for work, but that doesn't mean you can control me!" I vented out my anger, trying to free my arms from his clutches.

His grip was like iron bars, clutching me tightly! I protested and tried to release his grip on my other hand, but he didn't move an inch. He just kept staring at my face as I struggled.

"What has happened to you, Natasha? Why are you behaving with me as if I am a stranger?" he asked a minute later.

"I don't understand what you are talking about!" I exclaimed, trying to squeeze out from his hands.

He pulled me closer into a tight embrace, and I felt like my chest was being crushed into his broad one. His presence affected my mind and his touch, my senses, evoking a myriad of emotions within me. I was brimming with rage because he was making me desire him! I scowled at him and showed him my fury, hoping that he would go away, but he was one hell of a stubborn mule! *Why isn't he going away?* As struggling in his arms was futile, I relaxed and lowered my head. I could never break out of it with my strength.

Jai breathed out a sigh. "You know what I'm talking about?" he asked, lifting my chin up with his other hand.

I clenched my jaws and glared at him. "Jai, I need to rest. I'm here for work. I intend to finish it and go back home."

His pupils darkened for a second, and suddenly he sucked my lips. Releasing my chin, his hand travelled to the nape of my neck while running his thumb over my ears.

I was taken aback by his sudden boldness and pushed him back with my lips tightly closed. But he kept sucking, licking, and biting my lips. When shoving him with both my hands didn't work, I pinched him hard on his arms. Instead of releasing me, he wrapped his other hand around my waist and made it more difficult for me to protest.

Tears of helplessness trickled down my eyes, knowing he might win any second now. I was losing my resolve to fight him, so I closed my eyes and parted my lips, giving into temptation and surrendering myself to him.

His tongue pushed through the gap and swirled, talking in a language of silence, coaxing me with gentleness to relax. His thumb wiped away my tears gently as he stalled the moment with his kiss. Everything around us faded, and I was lost in the cocoon of his arms.

With a swift turn, my back softly hit a wall. Jai's fingers inched his way to my shoulder and slid my sleeves down. Butterflies fluttered inside my stomach as he left my lips and traced the contours of my neck and then shifted onto my collar bone.

Lost in the senses tingling inside me, I let him graze my collar bone and then the slopes of my valleys. My senses were spiralling out of control.

Just then, someone knocked softly on the door. I instantly opened my eyes as if an alarm had been buzzed and woken me up from deep sleep. I pushed him away with all my might. I had to stop him, or undoubtedly, I would repent this later.

He moved away as he was unprepared and tried to catch hold of me again, but I shook my head and jerked off his hand, muttering, "No."

I adjusted my dress to open the door and show him the way out.

He sighed, raking his hair in frustration.

"Ma'am, room service; your coffee," said the server with a smile.

"Can you bring one more and quickly?" ordered Jai, walking to my bed and sitting on it as if he was the rightful owner of it.

"Sure, sir, in five minutes," the boy replied, placing the tray on the table. He was about to pour the contents of the pot into the cup when Jai made him stop. "I will make this for Ma'am. You fetch mine."

Jai was growing more and more audacious! With my hands on my hips, I glared at him. "And why can't you order your coffee in your room?"

He didn't reply but stirred the coffee for several seconds and handed it to me.

I didn't want to take the cup from his hands. I eyed it for a few seconds and took it. "I think you should go. You are a celebrity now after the car incident. Since many people are around here, this may lead to rumours."

"Rumours," he let out a laugh, then added, "That's good! Rumours create publicity, and people will notice our brand."

Is he serious, or is he teasing me? Even though I was hoping that it was just a tease, I felt a little upset. "You did all this for rumours?"

He glanced at me with all seriousness as if he was offended. "I did it because I felt like doing it, not for creating rumours." He walked towards the sliding doors of the balcony and placed his hand on the panes while staring outside. "After staying with me for so long, you shouldn't be saying this."

I sat down to drink my coffee and watched his back flex in anger. His back looked as handsome as ever. My mind started to draw a picture of him standing shirtless. My body temperature was soaring up with the desire, tingling my fingers to touch him bare.

"I think-" he turned around abruptly and smiled, catching me ogling at him. I averted my eyes and focused on my coffee.

He sat down next to me. "I think we should stay together when we go back to Mumbai."

"What?! Why?" I faced him with a frown. "Just because I couldn't fight you and gave up doesn't mean I want to stay with you. We stayed together for the agreement, and we are now done. All that is left is signing the divorce papers."

"Look, Natasha, you can't deny the attraction between us! What's so bad about trying again?" he asked with a shrug. There was a knock on the door, and he said aloud, "Come in."

The waiter placed his coffee on the table and started to pour it for him.

"No need, my wife will do it for me. She knows what I like," Jai said, making me roll my eyes.

"Why are you forcing us together?" I yelled at him the minute the server left.

"Forcing? Weren't you the one who loved to make coffee for me all the time?" he asked.

"It was an agreement that I was bound to," I snapped.

"But the agreement isn't yet nullified, so rightfully you are still my wife," he said, then poured the coffee in his cup and added, "I am not sure what's running in that head of yours, but I have seen you the way you stare at me."

"What rubbish! Mr J, you are just assuming!" I stood up and lashed out at him.

Jai's lips curled up, and that's when I realised I had addressed him as 'J', the way I used to in Perth. I bit my tongue in frustration.

"Finally, you called me 'J'. Slowly, everything will fall in place, and you will confess that you want me as I want you," he teased while sipping his coffee.

"In your dreams! All this feeling of yours is just because I came into your life again, by coincidence. Else you would have forgotten me long back. And these are not called feelings. These are your so-called bodily desires that will go away when you find someone else," I charged at him, banging my empty cup on the table.

I saw him stare at me as if he was going to eat me raw, but I didn't care. Instead, I took out my clothes from my bag and walked towards the washroom, saying, "Please leave once you are done with coffee. I need to rest."

"And what if I tell you all these are not just desires? Open your eyes and take it from me, this is our attraction for each other. Mark my words, six months from today, you will tell the world you are my wife and-"

"Six months from now, I will be seeing someone else and making plans to marry him," I challenged him, walking into the washroom and locking the door behind.

"Fine, we will see! By the way, I hope you have a concealer to hide that mark on your collar bone," I heard him say. I stared at my reflection in the mirror. There was a pink patch near my collar bone. I rubbed it hard, but I knew it was of no use; the damage had been done.

"It won't go, even if you rub it a million times." His faint voice reached my ears from outside as if he was watching me rub it off.

I stamped my feet hard and entered the shower. Switching on the tap, I checked the water before taking off my dress. The very next second, my eyes blurred, and my head whirled. Before I could understand what was wrong, everything blacked out.

CHAPTER XVII

Jai

I was about to leave her room when I heard a thud sound. "Natasha, is everything okay?" I asked, walking towards the bathroom door.

She didn't answer, but I could hear the shower running. Was she ignoring me, or was something wrong? I waited for a minute before trying to get a response from her by teasing her. "Natasha, don't force the mark too much. It won't go! I can do the honours on your other shoulder to make it look even!"

When I still didn't get a reply, my heart started to race. *Something was wrong!* I pushed the door hard, but it didn't budge. I rushed towards the intercom and dialled the reception desk to send someone with a key to open bathroom doors as it was an emergency.

Meanwhile, I kept banging at her door. It was very unlike her to not reply even if things weren't okay. Within minutes, a housekeeping staff arrived with a box. The moment he unlocked the door with a key, I peeked in. Natasha was lying on the floor unconscious while the shower's warm water was trickling down in a small stream near her legs.

"Call an ambulance!" Before entering, I instructed the housekeeping staff and grabbed a towel to wrap it around her.

I picked her up in my arms and placed her on the bed. I changed her into a loose fit, slip-on dress and covered her with a blanket. The housekeeping staff returned a few minutes later and mumbled behind me, "I've called the reception. They are sending the in-house physician for a check-up. He will be here in ten minutes."

"Uh-huh…" I replied, feeling anxious with every passing minute.

"I'll wait outside," he added and walked out. Kneeling on the bedside, I gently patted her face, trying to wake her up. "Natie, get up."

After continuously patting her cheeks and rubbing her palms, she blinked her eyes open.

"Are you fine now?" I asked as she came to her senses. I caressed her forehead and hair to make her comfortable. I sighed in relief when she blinked in reply after a while.

Just then, there was a knock on the door. "The doctor is here." It was the housekeeping staff's voice.

"How did you faint?" asked the doctor, checking the pulse.

"I was about to take a bath, then I…" Natasha faltered as she looked at me, possibly realising that she was wearing a dress now. "I blacked out."

"I heard a thud and thought something must be wrong. I called her, but when she didn't reply, I asked the hotel staff to get the keys." I filled in.

"Oh, good that you were there. By the way, has it happened to you before?" the doctor asked her.

"Once in Perth," I replied.

"Hey, what happened to Natasha? Are you okay now?" asked Mehta, coming inside her room.

"Better now," I replied.

"How did it happen in Perth?" asked the doctor.

I quickly replied, "Lack of proper sleep and fatigue, the doctor had told last time."

"You are her…?" asked the doctor, looking at me.

"A friend," she replied before I could say anything.

"Oh, okay. I thought it was something else," said the doctor with a laugh. Even Mehta was smiling, looking at me.

When I turned towards Natasha, I found her glaring at me. *Why is she seething with fury now?*

"Doctor, how many days of rest would you advise for her? We are here for a photo shoot and wanted to resume soon," asked Mehta.

The doctor checked her eyes and replied, "A day or two should be fine, but ensure she takes proper food and rest. She looks a little pale. I suggest you take her for a blood test. Meanwhile, you can start with these multivitamins," he added, scribbling a prescription on his letterhead.

As I was about to follow the doctor out, Mehta stopped me. "You stay. I'll see him out." He shut the door as they left the room.

"I don't understand, Jai. What are you trying to imply? Who told you to answer all the doctor's questions?" Natasha fired at me as soon as we were alone.

I was not happy with how she spoke to me, but I kept my cool and answered with a straight face, "I was trying to help since you are not keeping well."

"Oh yes and you were indirectly implying to them that something is there between us!" She uttered in annoyance and looked away.

"And why the hell did you keep on removing my clothes? Who gave you such rights?" she asked, holding the hem of her dress in her fist.

Is she crazy? I stared at her with disbelief in her eyes. *Who thinks of that when it is a matter of someone's life?* "Nice, I do fancy doing that, but not in times when you are not in your senses! The day you almost drowned in the sea or now when you fainted, I changed your dress just to make sure you don't catch a cold."

"Next time, even if I die, please don't remove my clothes, and for that matter, I don't want you to even touch me!" Finally, after hissing such hateful words, she averted her eyes.

I wanted to make her look at me right away and put some sense into her! But since she wasn't keeping well, I held myself back and left the room, closing the door shut on the way out.

When I was kissing her an hour ago, wasn't she completely lost in my arms? I might have taken her right there if not for the untimely knock! And now, she doesn't want me to touch her even if she is about to die!

I was raging with fury and wanted to destroy everything in my room. But that wouldn't solve the problem, so I took a shower to cool myself down. After a good long relaxing bath, my anger had washed away, but the sadness remained. I stepped out of the hotel to get Natasha the medicines prescribed by the doctor. Upon my return, I handed it to Mehta and asked him to pass it to Natasha.

A few minutes later, he came to my room. "I gave it to her," he said and eyed me with his brows raised. "You're drinking alone! That's not right, dude!"

While he was away, I had ordered a bottle of Old Monk Rum and roasted nuts to drink away my sorrow.

Dropping all propriety, Mehta slumped on the sofa, filled himself a glass and rested his feet on the coffee table. "Argentina lost! It was such a lame match!" He grumbled on and on and then suddenly changed the topic, "So, you knew her from before."

When I didn't answer, he continued, "I felt that vibe between you two. But I assumed you were enemies, not lovers. What happened?"

"It's complicated…" I uttered, taking a sip. What went wrong? A lot of things… Aloud I said, "All I can say is that she's pushing me away every time I try to get close." Our kiss was still fresh in my mind. "She's driving me mad…"

"So, you love her, don't you?" he asked with his lips curled up.

"I want her anyhow," I stated.

Mehta narrowed his eyes and asked, "To sleep with her and then done? In that way?"

I was silent for some time, wondering what my want was. *Did I really just want to sleep with her, and that's it, nothing else?*

"She creates a fire in me every time I touch her, but I am unable to understand why I want her so much. When she was with me in Perth, it was casual, and she was even ready to give in, but now she's throwing tantrums. It's like she doesn't want me anymore." The more I thought of her, the more frustrated I became. "I don't know what to do about her… I feel like destroying everything that's keeping her away from me."

"Have you ever felt jealous?" he asked.

"Not really, but I don't like that guy buzzing around her… What's his name… Yes, Akash! He is nice to Natasha, and she's unexpectedly very friendly towards him." I filled in my glass and noticed that the bottle was now empty. "Order another one," I said to Mehta, with a wave of the bottle as he was closer to the intercom. "This one's over."

After more drinks and snacks were ordered, I continued, "She's very good to him. He even has a cute little daughter to entice her!"

A couple of minutes later, the server arrived with our orders. "Sir, is ma'am fine now?"

"Yes, I think. The doctor has advised her to rest." He was about to leave when I stopped him and handed him some cash. "Please check on her from time to time and keep me updated. Make sure she eats on time and gets plenty of rest."

"Sure, sir," he said with a smile.

"And one more thing, please book her for a full-body spa and massage. If she refuses, just tell her it's complimentary from the hotel. Bill the charges to this room, and make sure the session is the best one!"

"I will do it, sir," replied the server with a smile and left the room.

"If it was lust, I wouldn't have gone to so much trouble for a woman!" Mehta commented when I returned to my seat.

"She needs to rest and relax. The sooner she revives, the sooner we will be able to shoot the ad." Though I said this to him, I couldn't help contemplating his words.

Mehta chuckled at my reply. "Is that so? But weren't you protecting her before the media the other day? And your face had turned really ugly when the reporters suggested Natasha drive with you!"

I was sure he was enjoying pulling my legs just as much as he was enjoying his drink.

"Rubbish, I would have protected any woman in the same way," I said, taking a gulp of my drink.

"I am sure you would, but take my suggestion; you want more from her than just her body. I suppose you are somewhere in the middle of liking and loving her!" I glared at him while he laughed heartily. "I am definitely going to enjoy this."

.I'm in love with her? What kind of nonsense was that! "One more utter rubbish from your mouth, and I would break your bones into pieces!"

He just laughed it off, and sometime later, he called it a day. He returned to his room while I dozed off. I didn't bother Natasha the next day, but the housekeeping staff informed me of her health. Mehta, Charles, and the creative director joined me in my room to discuss the plans of the ad shoot. The day ended in a flash with only work and no play.

At night, I decided to take a dip inside the pool. The water was warm, and the swim, very relaxing, but I still wasn't sleepy. Every moment I was idle, my mind was occupied with thoughts of Natasha, and unknowingly I was drowning in melancholy. I didn't want to take the help of drinks to sleep tonight, so to tire myself out, I decided to take a stroll at the beach.

I wandered on the sandy coast with headphones plugged into my ears. Sometime later, when I almost reached exhaustion, I decided to return to the hotel. In the silence between the change of music on the way back, I heard someone calling my name. I stopped the music and looked around.

In the darkness, a woman approached me with two men following behind her. The woman's silhouette gradually morphed into a familiar figure, and my eyes widened.

"Jai, wait up!" By the time Natasha reached me, she was panting heavily.

All the anger and frustration I'd felt two days back returned at her sight. My forehead creased, wondering what she was up to.

She caught her breath and turned to the two men behind her. They were police constables, patrolling the beach. "I'm here with him!"

The men eyed me from top to bottom and asked, "Sir, what relationship do you have with her?" asked the police.

For a second, I stared from her to the police, trying to figure out why she was in trouble. Did they think she was a hooker looking for a client because it was so late in the night?

I couldn't help but smirk at her state. She had put me through a lot of heartaches recently; it was time for revenge! My eyes gleamed for a fraction of a second, but I masked it and replied with a shrug, "I don't know who she is."

She gaped at me in disbelief and caught my arm. "What are you doing? They will lock me up in jail!" She pleaded to me, squeezing my arm with all her might and her voice laced with panic.

"Miss, why are you pulling my arm?" I replied, trying to free myself from her grip. Then, turning to the two men, I said, "Sir, I was just taking a stroll. I don't know her."

"Jai, please don't do this to me now. I will be in deep trouble," she mumbled. Then turning to the police, she added, "Sir, he is the company owner with whom I have come here, and we are shooting for his brand launch. Last night, we had a fight, so that's why he is pretending that he doesn't know me."

She looked desperate and clueless as to what to do next. I knew I shouldn't play this dirty joke with her, but I was not done with the frustration she had caused me since the fight.

I blinked my eyes in assurance at the police constable and took out a few notes from my pocket. "Sir, she is lying. I don't know her. These kinds of ladies who roam on such secluded beaches often grab innocent men like us and charge us of rape to make money," I said, moving away from her and standing next to the constable. I passed him the money behind my back without her knowledge. "Put her in jail and teach her a lesson!"

Natasha glared at me. "Jai, what nonsense are you talking about? Sir, please listen. He is angry; that's why he is talking like this. I was just taking a stroll and had no bad intentions. I have come here for work. You can ask the hotel where I am staying."

"Madam, come here quick," said one of the police constables over the phone. He shared the location and added, "We have caught a lady and have to take her to jail."

"Mehta," she mumbled, thinking of something and then pleaded to them, "Sir, let me call someone from the hotel I am staying at."

"Okay, call," one of the constables nodded.

She quickly pulled out her phone from the purse and dialled, but unfortunately couldn't connect, "Sir, there's no network here."

The other constable shook his head with a sombre look, "All women put up similar drama when they are caught this late at night!"

"Sir, I'm telling the truth." Then, pleadingly, she joined her hands. "I did come out for a stroll. I can lead you to my hotel."

"Which hotel is it?" the constable asked.

"Hotel Mayfair Lagoon," she replied instantly.

I finally had pity on her and pitched in before things went out of control. "Sir, I'm put up at the same place. I'll take her responsibility and will drop her at the hotel. You can have my card."

"Okay then, ma'am, we are letting you off because of him. Next time, if we see you strolling all alone this late at night, we will put you in jail for sure!" With these words, the men turned around to leave.

"Thank you, sir," I called out aloud behind them. They glanced back, smirked and waved at us before walking off. "Come," I offered her my hand and added, "Let's return before someone else gets hold of you."

She suddenly faced me and hit me on the chest with all her strength. "Ouch!"

"How could you joke around like that?"

"What joke? I told the truth!" I moved away, rubbing the place she hit. "Didn't you tell me there is nothing between us, and I should not touch you even if you are dying?"

"True, I don't need to touch. I just have to scratch you!" She glowered at me while her fingers tried to claw my face.

"Sir, take this lady. She is trying to touch and harm me." I laughed, trying to protect my face from her. Then, as I moved away from her, I shouted aloud. "Sir, she is trying to rape me, actually!"

The police constables were not that far away. They turned around and gave a hearty laugh.

"You scoundrel, I am not gonna leave you today," she said, running towards me in anger.

Instead of running, I stood upright, and she collided with me, hitting her nose on my chin.

"Ahh!!!" She shrieked in pain, and I caught hold of her chin, making her look upwards.

"Is it hurting?" I asked softly, pinching the bridge of her nose. "I hope it's not broken, although I hope it breaks as your anger always rests here."

She spanked on my hand and then on my chest, "Why are you always troubling me?"

"Sorry, won't do anymore." I wrapped my arms around her and pulled her closer.

She rested her head on my chest and sighed. "I can't walk anymore. Feeling very tired."

Caressing her head, I placed the stray hair strands behind her ears. "Why did you come so far?"

"I couldn't sleep, so I came out for a walk," she said in a shallow breath.

I lifted her chin up and asked, "Should I carry you?"

"It's too far for you to pick me up and walk..." She rubbed her temples, exhaustion evident on her face.

I turned around and kneeled. "Hop on."

"Will you be able to carry me?" she asked, placing her chin on my shoulder and wrapping her arms around my neck as she climbed on my back.

"Yep."

After some time, I heard her giggle. "I feel like a monkey hanging on its mother for support."

"Yes. You are a monkey!" She unclasped her hand around my neck and tried to hit me.

"Be careful, or you'll fall!" I tightened my grip on her and reprimanded.

She leaned on my back as if out of energy and rested quietly.

"Did you have your meals on time today?"

"Hmm..."

"Did you finish everything or peck on your food like a hen?"

"I finished everything," she mumbled and added, "Thanks for the spa."

"I hope that they didn't send a man," I teased, lifting her a bit as she was sliding down.

"Yes, and a handsome one at that," she purred like a cat. "He massaged really well with his strong arms."

"Thanks! How come you didn't realise it was me and let me touch you everywhere?"

"Huh! Very funny!" she retorted and then laughed.

She was about to slip again, so I bent forward and heaved her up. "Are you taking your medicines on time?"

"Hmm…"

"Good. I'll take you for a blood test tomorrow."

"I'm sleepy…"

"I suppose I should carry you then," I said and stopped.

"I haven't slept for the past few days. I am too tired," she mumbled and slid down my back. Then, as she staggered, I caught her and carried her in my arms. "Wrap your arms around my neck, close your eyes. I'll wake you up when we reach."

Ten minutes later, when we almost reached, I asked her, "Where are your room keys?"

"Inside my purse," she said, with her eyes still closed.

I found a housekeeping staff nearby and asked her to open the door with the spare keys while Natasha nestled peacefully in my arms.

I placed her on the bed, tucked her in and was about to leave when she held my hand and murmured, "Please stay with me. I can't sleep."

I wanted to object because, honestly, it was a bad idea! But her dazed eyes and tired look made me acquiesce. I lay down next to her, resting my back on the bed backrest.

She looked tired, but more than that, she looked lonely. I wanted to wrap her in my arms and let her know I was right there, but afraid that she might misunderstand and wake up from her much-needed sleep, I gently combed her hair with my hands and let her rest.

I remained awake for quite some time. I was fighting against the temptation to hold her and make love to her.

Then, somewhere in the middle of the night, I felt her snuggle to me. Her hands wrapped around my waist, and her warm breath ran a tingling sensation all over my body. I tried to move away, but she held me tight and wrapped her legs on mine.

"Oh God, what's this torture!" I murmured, staying put in my position, but slowly, the desire to make love to her was replaced with something beautifully serene. I kept watching her while she slept like a little girl, having a peaceful dream.

Early in the morning, I felt my eyes turn heavy. Just then, I felt her stir beside me. I tried to remove my hand and walk away, but she got up all of a sudden.

"What are you doing here?" she demanded, sitting upright at once.

"Stop..." I said, sitting upright and placing my hands on her bed headrest. "...before you accuse me of anything. You were too sleepy last night and held my hand the whole night asking me to stay with you as you didn't sleep for the past few days."

She stared at me with a frown creasing her forehead.

I continued after a sigh, "So, I was here, unable to let go of your hand and disturb you from your sleep."

"But-" she started to ask.

"For your kind information, I didn't do anything while you were not in your senses, apart from ruffling your hair and kissing your forehead good night. And now that you are finally awake, I am going to my room to take rest. I haven't slept the whole night, thinking I might lose my control," I clarified, walking away from her. "By the way, relax today. We are not shooting and don't go out on the beach alone at night. I'll take you for a blood test later, and don't forget to have your medicine on time." As I walked with my eyes half-closed, I hit my head hard with the wall.

"Shit!" I cursed, clasping my head.

She came to me in a flash and checked on my bruise.

"Couldn't you see and walk? Come, let me put some ice." Natasha pulled me over to the bed and instructed me to sit down.

As she put the ice on my swollen wound, I felt my eyes closing, and I asked her gently, "Can I sleep, please? I didn't catch a wink the whole night."

She didn't respond but lifted my leg up and put a pillow under my head.

I remember mumbling a 'thank you' before drifting off to sleep.

CHAPTER XVIII

Natasha

I didn't know I could torture someone so much, but the way he pleaded with me to allow him to sleep, I knew I had to just let him be.

I wanted to order a coffee but decided otherwise, afraid it might disturb him and managed with the instant coffee sachet from the complimentary refreshments provided. When I returned to the room after a good shower, the rhythmic sound of Jai's snores filled the room.

A chuckle escaped my lips, and I shook my head. He must have been fatigued. I plugged in my earphones to listen to music and sip my coffee. My eyes landed on the man sleeping on my bed. It wasn't the first time that I had seen him sleeping. Observing him sleeping so peacefully always made my fingers tingle to trace his features and pull his cheeks.

As I watched him, last night's events came to my mind. I had gone out for a walk when the police constables caught hold of me. I felt so relieved and thankful to God when I noticed Jai casually strolling not far away. I was sure he would clear the misunderstanding with the police, but then, he refused to even acknowledge me! I was sure he was trying to take revenge for having pushed him away the previous night! I couldn't connect to Mehta's number. My mind had blanked out. More than angry, I was scared that I'd have to spend the night in jail!

However, he offered to drop me at the hotel, and the police let me go. *Now that I think about it, he was smiling at the police.* I pondered with a solemn look. *Did he trick me into this?* Maybe or maybe not... He seemed to be on his way back, unlike me. I guess the timing was just right. I really was lucky to have found him! And he really did carry me back to the hotel!

He was sprawled over my bed, and his head had slipped off the pillow. I clicked a few pictures of him sleeping and then tried to fix the pillow underneath his head. I couldn't help but smile and was tempted to leave a small kiss on his forehead for last night's hard work.

Just then, he opened his eyes. "What are you doing?" he asked, sounding extremely hoarse.

I was only inches away from his face. "I was adjusting your pillow."

His lips curled into a soft smile. "Oh, I see. I thought you were about to kiss me. I don't mind, though." He closed his eyes as if that was the cue for me to go ahead.

"Why should I kiss you? Have I lost it or what?" I retorted and started to move away from him.

Just then, he held my hand and asked, "Can I get a cup of coffee, please?"

I was worried that he would ask something preposterous, but he asked for coffee. It was, of course, within my limits. "Sure. I'll order it right away."

He sat upright a second later and added, "Have it sent to my room. I'll freshen up meanwhile." He got up to walk out of my room.

His honesty sometimes made me blush, and sometimes angry, but whatever it was, I couldn't tell him the truth inside my heart. *I am bound to stay away from him... he is no longer mine.*

***

I stayed in my room the whole day except for a short trip to get a blood test with Jai and another even shorter trip to the hotel's restaurant for dinner. As I waited for the food to be served, I decided to have a video call with Akash and Soha.

After the initial greeting, Akash rambled on about his plan, "We'll be back in India in a month. By then, Soha will be fit enough to travel. All the projects that have been put on hold will have to be taken up on priority."

"You'll be taking me to work with you!" Soha added with conviction.

Akash shook his head while giving a helpless look to his daughter. "You can't, my dear. You need two months of rest before you can start skipping about."

"But I've already been here for a month!" Soha complained with a cute pout.

"Yes, my princess, and you have to rest for another month."

"But I'm bored without you!"

"Then I'll work smart and be with you early every day!"

Unable to convince her father, she made a face. "You'll be with Tanisha Aunty all the time..."

On this side, I kept listening to their squabble with a look of amusement.

"Soha, she is my assistant. I need her to be there," he explained, but Soha was clearly not happy with the explanation. She began to throw more tantrums, and Akash had to eventually disconnect to calm her down.

As I ate my dinner, I chuckled with every bite, recalling Soha's cute little face and her pout.

"Seems like someone is in a very nice mood today," said a familiar voice behind me.

I turned around to find Jai walking over.

"I just had a call with Akash. His daughter, Soha, is absolutely adorable, especially when she creates a fuss and puts her father in a fix!" I remarked with a dreamy sigh.

Jai smirked and came close to my ears. "We can also try. It's not too late."

I glared at him, "We? What do you mean by that? We have absolutely-"

"I get it, ma'am; just teasing! You've already applied for divorce. Although it's not approved yet, it doesn't mean you will stay with me," he said in one breath before I could interrupt him. Then, changing the topic, he added, "By the way, I hope your reports are normal because we plan to start the shoot from tomorrow." He paused and continued, "Be ready by six. We can shoot only till ten as it will become too sunny to shoot after that. Oh, and Tanisha will be coming down tonight with the rest of the team."

"Tanisha is coming!" I was happy that she would be here to support me if I needed anything.

The ringing of his phone diverted his attention. He turned to me before answering, "You carry on, I have a meeting to attend."

"Sure, good night," I said, then occupied myself with the food, but my mind traversed back to the kiss I almost stole in the morning. Though I wanted to deny it, I genuinely longed to be with him. A moment later, I smiled, thinking of the previous night when he carried me on his back. If he continued to act this way, I would be in trouble to control myself.

My mind was in a deep mess and to overcome his thoughts, I called up Tanisha. She readily answered the call and informed me of her room number. She had already arrived! Excitedly, I rushed towards her room.

She opened the door after one knock. However, she looked pale and without any energy. "Hey, what happened to you?"

"I have airsickness," she mumbled with a small smile. "Don't worry, come in."

She looked terrible. My first thought was that if she's airsick, why did Akash make her take a flight? I was instantly annoyed at his thoughtlessness. "Does Akash know about it?"

"Don't curse him. He doesn't know. I came because I'm needed here. With Akash unavailable, things have been hectic, but nothing can be done about that. I'll be fine tomorrow, anyway," she added, shrugging her shoulders.

I could see a reflection of my past self in her, and my heart instantly went out to her. "You take a good rest for now. I'll manage things on my end. Moreover, the team's also here." Before she could protest, I called up room service and ordered soup and a sandwich for her. We then settled on the couch while I expressed my concern. The waiter came with the dinner, put the serving tray on the table and left.

"No, I am okay. I don't want you to be stressed about me," Tanisha said, sipping the soup.

"I will handle on your behalf tomorrow and also explain to others about your condition. Then, it won't be a problem, right?" I said with a warm smile.

Nodding, she uttered, "Can I ask you something?"

"You can ask whatever you have in your mind," I said, reaching out to hold her shoulders.

"Akash and you seem to be more than casual friends. Are you both childhood friends?" she asked, her eyes downcast yet expectant.

"Not childhood friends, but college friends," I replied, thinking of our old times together. "We had many things in common, and gradually our friendship developed into a strong bond. He was always there for me."

For some reason, the smile on her face faltered, and she nodded, "Oh, that's nice!"

"How long have you been working with him?"

"For around three years," she answered and sighed. "But there hasn't been a single day when I've been appreciated for my work..."

She sounded exhausted, not only with the journey but with her work as well. I couldn't help asking, "Then why didn't you quit?"

She flashed a small smile. "Akash is not a bad employer; he does care for his staff. Just that he has never appreciated my efforts."

I could feel a lot of complex emotions fluttering inside her. To lift her mood, I patted her shoulder and consoled, "I am sure he recognises your importance; otherwise, he would have not asked you to fill-in in his absence over here."

"I think you are just saying it to make me feel good," she mumbled, keeping her spoon down. "Besides, he is more concerned about you..."

"Me, yes, he is one of his kind. Always ready to jump in when I need something. You will get very few people in your life who are ready to stand by you, and for me, I think he is that kind of a friend." Though I explained, I wondered where it was all going.

"You love him too?" she asked in a small voice.

My mind snapped hearing those words. *I can never love Akash romantically!* Those were my thoughts, and I said aloud, "I can't love anyone in this life; I don't have the guts to do that. Besides, Akash is my good friend. I don't feel anything else for him."

A smile cropped up her sad lips as her fingers played with the spoon. I opened my mouth to ask her the same question when a message flashed on my phone:

Get some sleep and be ready for tomorrow.

-Jai

"Who is it?" she asked.

"Jai," I said, looking up at her.

"He was very concerned when I dropped by his office to tell him about your absence, as if he would go hell and heaven to find you," she mentioned with a bright smile.

I gave her a small smile, recalling how he had arrived at my village and then saved me from drowning. "He did come to my village to meet me."

"He knew you before you picked up this project?" she asked, and I nodded.

"A good friend, I believe," she tried to probe, but I smiled, not knowing what to say.

"Some people are always complicated to know what they truly mean to you," I said, thinking of our past and present interactions. "I find my relationship with him quite..."

"Complicated?" she asked.

I shook my head with a chuckle and added, "Dangerous."

"What?!" She burst into peals of laughter along with me.

I sighed. "Jai is quite dangerous. I wish to stay away from him at all times."

"I see," she uttered as if she knew how I felt.

"Anyway, rest well, don't worry about tomorrow. I'll manage," I said, taking a leave from her room.

The following morning at five, Jai woke me up by knocking on my door. I sleepily opened the door and asked, "What?"

I'm not sure why, but he stared at me with a dazed look. I waved my hands in front of his face. "Jai! Earth to you?"

He snapped back. "Nothing. I mean, why aren't you ready?"

"Ten minutes!" I remarked, slamming the door on his face and hurrying into the washroom.

An hour later, I was ready with my make up and dress while we waited for the photographer.

Luckily Jai didn't complain when I said Tanisha wasn't keeping well and could not accompany us. However, I was sure her presence would have been better for me. I was nervous and tried to sit quietly in one corner.

"Sorry for the delay!" The photographer barged in and apologised aloud. Then, he asked me to take my position, as he had explained to me on the flight.

Ninja Super Avenue was parked facing the beach. In the background, the pale blue skyline was in contrast to the pearl black coloured car. The waves were crashing gently onto the sandy beach at a distance behind the vehicle.

I was asked to lean on the car bonnet and pose. I moved closer to the car, a little sceptical of myself, placed a hand on the bonnet, and leaned on it, turning on my side and looking towards the sky.

"No, not working!" Charles snapped with a dissatisfied look. "Is there another dress?" he asked, facing the team responsible for the costume. "Red, satin, tube dress and shorter, please! We're doing a luxury car ad and not regular material!"

The designer hurried towards him with a catalogue of dresses. After some deliberation, Charles approved a dress, but its sight made me squirm when it was passed over to me. It was too short for my taste. With the dress in my hand, I slowly walked towards the dressing van, my every step as heavy as lead.

I locked the doors and eyed the dress with reluctance. Then, with a big sigh, I decided to get it over with as soon as possible.

I unzipped the dress I was wearing and was about to let it drop when the door to the washroom opened, and Jai walked out. I clutched the dress close to my chest and screamed, "What the hell are you doing here?"

Jai smirked. "I didn't know you had plans to come here and seduce me. I wasn't ready either!"

"Get out!" With a sullen look, I pointed at the exit.

As Jai passed by me, he glanced at the dress I was supposed to change into. His brows raised in disapproval. "Isn't that dress a bit too short?"

When I eyed him fiercely, he shrugged while walking away. "Not my problem! As long as you are cool."

"Thank you!" I shut the door on his face and turned to the dress with a troubled look.

***

"Lean on the bonnet," Charles ordered. "Rest your head on your hand. Chest out. Show your cleavage."

With his every instruction, my body stiffened, and my mood soured.

"CUT!" Jai's sharp voice stiffened everyone. "This is not an A-rated movie. It's an ad shoot for a car!"

"Yeah, so?" Charles challenged with a quizzical look. "A sexy model for a luxury car will attract a wider audience. It's catchy and makes people stop to view the ad. A little show of cleavage is normal."

The way he put his ideas into words disgusted me.

"No, we will not do this. Try something else," Jai clenched his jaws and stood aside.

Charles rolled his eyes but changed his instructions. This time he lay down on the sand with the camera in hand to take shots from below. Somehow, I felt this was weirder than the previous pose.

"Tsk, tsk," Jai clicked his tongue and shook his head. His face had turned a shade darker. Then, in a stern voice, he added, "I don't think you are focusing on the car. The entire attention is on her legs."

Despite wearing skimpy clothes, I was enveloped in warmth. I had never expected Jai to stand up for me and even object to the world-famous photographer.

After some deliberation, Charles came up with another set of instructions. "Sit up on the bonnet, cross your legs and look at the sun."

I stared at the bonnet. Sitting up on the bonnet did not look feasible in this body-hugging tube dress.

Without warning, Charles placed his hands on my waist. "Let me help!"

I backed off to get away from him. "That's all right. I can do it." I tried to lift my leg up when I heard the sound of something snap.

I froze up in a panic, not daring to move even an inch. Something surely had torn on the backside. My heart raced as my eyes darted around in search of Jai. Where is he? I couldn't find him anywhere, and the helplessness made my eyes well up.

I was in deep trouble now and looked around, but I couldn't find Jai anywhere.

"Move up!" Charles gestured, raising his chin. He appeared impatient, but I was in no position to follow. I tried to blink away the tears and bit my lip, feeling desperate.

"Is everything all right, Natasha?" Jai suddenly arrived from behind the car, holding a water bottle in his hand.

Charles harrumphed. "I don't know what's wrong with her!" He shrugged in frustration. "Crying like a village dump! Can't even give a proper shot! She's not professional! I can't work with her. Get me another model! She can't even sit on the bonnet!"

As Charles continued complaining about my shortcomings, tears trickled down my eyes, and I hung my head in shame. I failed Jai! I didn't live up to his expectations...

"Hold on a minute!" Jai furiously raised a hand at Charles to stop.

"Natasha," Jai turned to me. His eyes seemed to ask, "What's wrong?"

Hesitantly I mumbled, "Jai, I tore my dress."

"Oh, wait for a second," he nodded in understanding and immediately went running to find the designer.

"How could you tear your dress? Are you really a model? It's just a waste of time with you!" Charles flanked both his arms as he continued his hollering.

Jai came running with a skirt and handed it to me.

"What?! She'll wear a skirt this long! You must be out of your mind! This has never happened in my career!" Charles grumbled. "Mr Jai, I suggest we change her if you want your car launch to be successful."

"Mehta," Jai called out aloud while I slipped the skirt above my head.

"Pay him and show him the way out," said Jai to Mehta, ushering me from there.

"What?" the photographer screamed.

"Shooting is cancelled for today," said Jai, calling out to his team.

"Natasha, are you all right?" I heard Tanisha as I returned to the hotel. But I was in no mood to answer her either. I ran as fast as I could to my room and shut the door. Sprawling on the bed, I cried my heart out. I had never faced such humiliation before.

"Natasha, open the door, please," called out Jai from outside. "Listen to me, please. Open the door."

"Natasha, please open the door. Please don't feel embarrassed. It's not your fault," I heard Tanisha say.

"Look, he's been fired, so don't worry," said Jai.

"Natasha..." Tanisha began to say but stopped midway as she started coughing.

"Tanisha, don't worry about her," I heard Jai say. "You take some rest. I'll keep you informed and call for you if the need arises."

Tanisha's voice answered, "Thank you and please keep me posted." Her footsteps died after a while as she walked away.

"Natasha, please open," urged Jai, knocking softly on the door. "I'll just sit here and not ask you anything."

I slightly opened the door and went back to my bed, hiding my face under the pillow.

"Have some water and cool down first," he said, sitting next to me on the bed.

"I don't want anything," I mumbled, sobbing.

"Why are you crying, Nats? He was a stupid creepy man! No one can do anything to you as long as I'm here!" He ruffled my hair softly.

"But you suffered a huge loss because of me, and the photoshoot will also be stalled until you find someone," I said between my sobs.

"Nats, are you crying for such a lame reason? Just because the photoshoot didn't finish? I already had a word with Akash and asked him to get a photographer. This bloody man was a psycho!"

I looked up at him with tearful eyes, "So was it because of that, Akash was saying he is coming to Goa?"

"Yes, I spoke to him a few days back as I had my doubts about this guy. Akash must have arranged for someone, and they will be coming soon." Jai pushed my hair away from my face and wiped my tears.

"But what do we do till then?" I was worried that the entire team would have to wait because of me.

"We'll return to Mumbai for now and come back when Akash is here in India. So that's not a problem," he said with a smile.

"Come on, now get up, don't cry because of that moron!" He lifted me to make me sit up.

Though I was upright, I couldn't lift my head up. Charles's disgraceful comments made me cringe and withdraw into my cocoon.

"Is there anything bothering you now?" Jai glanced at me, his eyes full of concern over my well being.

"How can he say such things to a woman?" I said, looking at the floor. "Big cleavage, men ogle all that. Do men just want one thing in their life? Love, marriage, and commitment don't make sense to them?" I asked, looking up at him. "Why is it that women need to tell men what love and care is? Is it wrong to ask for commitment when you give your everything to that person? Is it not a man's responsibility to treat his women with respect?" Looking away, I mumbled in frustration, "Only sex matters! A woman is just wanted for sex, and when it is done, man's desires are gone!" I paused for a second and added, "And why the hell am I telling you all this? Aren't you the same? Running after women for..." I made eye contact with him, and my words faltered.

"So just because an ill-mannered man behaved this way, all men became the same," he snapped. "Tell me when I was with you, in Perth or here in India, how many times did you find me ogling at someone or say I had sex with anyone?"

I shrugged my shoulders, "How do I know?"

"No one. If you don't know, how can you assume things? If I wanted sex from you, I would have taken you any minute! I know you very well and how to make you succumb!" The compassion he felt minutes ago was gone, and it was masked with glowering rage. "Even if you deny, there is nothing between us, I know what's there in your heart, but I don't know why you are hiding it!"

Goosebumps erupted all over my body at his accusation.

"I don't know about love and commitment because I don't believe in those fairy tales, but I do know how to respect a woman, and I think that's enough!" Though he was scolding me, he appeared more disappointed than angry. "If I had not respected you, I would have taken advantage of you many times by now."

"What nonsense are you spouting!" I remarked, feeling offended. "Are you saying I'm easy? That you'll come on to me, and I'll let you have me! Or do you mean you'll force yourself on me? If you respect me, how can you even think that you can take me any minute? Am I a commodity? Everything doesn't work as you wish. I am not like any other girl you would have met," I stormed at him, standing up. "You don't know about yourself. What would you know about me?"

"What do you mean, I don't know about myself?" he challenged, standing up facing me.

"First, you snore while you sleep! Second, you don't believe in fairy tales because you are afraid of commitments, afraid that you'll be dumped or that your feelings won't be requited!" With an angry frown, I spat out my innermost thoughts about him.

"And what about you?" Jai asked with a questioning gaze. "Do *you* know yourself? You help everyone by going out of your way, and when things go wrong, instead of comforting them, you walk away quietly so that no one knows what runs inside you." He caught hold of my hand in a tight grip. "Am I right?"

I turned away from him, in anger and in pain. His truth was eating me from inside now.

"You always pretend to be happy with Akash so that you can make me jealous, isn't it true? But, you can't deny that you were about to kiss me yesterday while I was sleeping!" He pulled my hand and made me face him.

"What rubbish!" I exclaimed, putting on a brave front. Even though he was right, I would never accept it on his face. "I told you already I was trying to adjust the pillow under your head."

He made me look at him and drilled me like a schoolgirl being reprimanded by the teacher. "And also that day when we were at the village, you were dreaming of us making love, weren't you?"

"All these are assumptions, and even if you kiss me, I don't feel anything because my relationship with you is past repair," I ranted and tried to free my hand from his grip.

"I've had enough of you!" Jai vented aloud and sealed my lips with his. Then, he grabbed my waist and lifted me up. Afraid that I'd fall, I reflexively clung onto him, my arms tightly wrapped around his neck as we went past the bed. Bewildered, I wondered, *Where is he taking me?*

Five seconds later, we were in the bathroom. Releasing one hand from my waist, Jai let me down and put the shower on. Water trickled down on us while he kept sucking my lips. His hand caressed my neck and then tucked at my sleeves, pulling it lower.

My senses hit another level as he mauled my chest with his hand.

"Stop," I rasped, aware that I wouldn't be able to fight with him anymore. But instead of releasing me, he took advantage of my open mouth and plunged his tongue. My breath heaved due to the emotions flowing through me. But his incessant kisses warmed my heart while cooling off the anger which was bursting forth some time ago.

I felt my skirt come off a minute later and slid into a pool near my ankles, followed by other clothing that protected my nudity. The words of protest were dying in my throat with every passing minute.

His touch and kisses clouded my mind. I closed my eyes as the need for him rose in my body. I tightened my arms around his neck. He sucked out the breath from my lungs as he kissed my mounds. He lifted my leg and placed it around his waist to support me from falling.

My hands started to trace above his chest, and I tried to take the T-shirt off his torso. Then, as if he knew what I wanted, he took off his wet clothes and stared at me.

His eyes held a need for me very much like mine. He watched me as if he was seeking my approval and I just didn't know what to reply.

The next instant, he scooped me into his arms. "It won't be wrong if I said, my body wants you as much as you want mine. Since the past six months, no woman has ever occupied my mind as you have."

I looked at him in wonder as he said, "Maybe what I did to you was wrong, thinking you will move on, but the fact is, I needed you more than what I thought was natural." He left a fleeting kiss on my lips and added, "Standing close to you without touching you is torture for me, and every time you challenge me, that there is nothing between you and me, I am shattered. Because I know no one else can take your place in my life."

My body was pressed to him, feeling sensations I had never felt before. But the words he spoke made my heart flutter. All I could think at that moment was the way my heart was beating aloud and making my chest hum with it.

I was lost in his revelations because I saw him so desperate and desirous for me for the first time.

Tears of joy danced through my eyes as I wrapped my arms around his neck and placed my head on his shoulders.

Moving my head away from him, he kissed my forehead with a smile, and then my cheeks one by one.

I laughed as I held his palms on my face. "Where did you learn this trick?"

"I didn't learn. It just popped up. If I had kissed you without the shower running over us, you would have pinched me like last time! So I thought of giving it a try," he added with a mischievous smile. "I guess it worked well!"

I hugged him again and placed my head on his chest, feeling really pleased inside. He stopped the shower and wrapped a towel around me and another around him. We then stepped into the room.

Thinking of the intimate moments a few seconds back, I blushed and wanted to hide away from him. Instead, I pretended to search for something in the mini-fridge and took out the ice cream tub.

"Feeling hungry... you want some," I asked, taking out a scoop.

"You have it." He took a seat on the sofa and sprawled his legs on the bed.

"Hmm, yummy!" I said, putting a spoonful in my mouth and pretending to moan in pleasure. Aware that he was watching me, all my hair on my neck stood up erect. In a flash, he stood behind me and took away my ice cream tub.

"You don't need to fake a moan when I am there," he teased, putting the ice cream tub back into the fridge.

"Hey, I am hungry!" I tried to take it back, but he pushed me on the bed. "I am hungry too." His tongue-in-cheek comment left me in a lot of nervous anticipation. I blushed, trying to crawl backwards while he pulled me holding my legs, and I was right under him.

Our eyes met, and I found my breath becoming shallow. A thousand questions were running in my mind, but as soon as Jai kissed my lips, it went numb.

The warmth that spread across my limbs and body made every inch become alive. He undid the knot of the towel with the flick of his finger. I could feel small jolts as he traced his mouth on my curves and then sucked my skin at places that made me feel relished as a woman.

I remember the times we had made out. He was quite rushed, unlike this time, where he was gentle and exploring me as if I was an artwork he had to mould and get it perfected.

I was moaning, humming, rasping, talking nonsense each time he applied a different method to stroke his fingers over my body.

Then just as the first rain quenches the thirst of dry soil, he entered into my core with slow strokes filling me with pleasant sensations all over my body.

He pecked my forehead, laced his hands with mine and then placed his head on my chest.

As he dug deeper into my core, I could feel my veins overflowing with warmth and sending jolts of ecstasy I had never felt before. I closed my eyes as we unleashed the moment of togetherness, and I drifted off to numbness spreading through my body.

Teardrops spilled down my eyes as the pain of not having him so close all these days was finally replaced with blissfulness.

He looked up at once and shifted to my side, "Are you fine, Nats? Are you hurt?"

"No, I am just..." I smiled as I choked up. "Happy!"

"I thought you were in pain like the first time we made love," he said with concern in his eyes.

"You knew I was vi-"

He kissed my cheeks, then mentioned, "I was angry at myself when I realised that you were a virgin. I thought you were joking about fairy tales and stuff."

"Then?"

"You gave your first time to me. I was pleased but also felt guilty because I had taken advantage of you. I felt maybe you should have waited for your perfect one, rather than having it with me," Jai said, brushing my cheeks with his thumb.

"I got carried away and-" I said and paused. I was a little reluctant to reveal the feelings concealed deep within my heart.

He questioned with his silent stare.

"Well..." I summoned all my courage and uttered, "I... I felt that you were the one for me, and so in my stupidity, I thought that if I could give you whatever I had, you might-"

"Change," Jai completed my words. "But nothing of that sort happened, right?"

"Yeah, I never thought fairy tales don't come true. I believed in them with all my heart, maybe it was childish, but these beliefs were real to me. When I was a kid, even though I didn't have enough money, I always thought I was the luckiest to have Mom, Dad and a caring brother, but they left." My breathing hitched as I shared my deepest feelings. "So, expecting you to reciprocate was much akin to expecting a miracle. I had to get a hold of myself and face reality, so I cut off all connections... Hoping that if you are out of sight and you'll be out of my mind..."

Having bared out my heart and my vulnerability exposed, I was expecting some reaction from Jai, but he was quiet and appeared to have phased out.

A second later, he flashed his sweetest smile. "I like your second version of love rather than the fairy tale one, where you expect someone to stand beside you at all times and care for you always," he said, scooping me in his arms. "Though this is also not too easy."

A thought occurred to me. *He was probably with me because he thought we shared fantastic chemistry. Or maybe he doesn't love me and is here because of guilt, or perhaps he is just infatuated with me...* My head reeled under the innumerable possibilities, and my face instantly fell.

"What happened?" he asked, and I shook my head.

"I think you should return and meet with the crew. They might be looking for you," I said, placing a hand on Jai's cheek.

"I don't think I can go now," he complained, snuggling to me.

"Why?"

With a small laugh, he kissed my lips tenderly. "I am too tired and lazy to leave you and go."

Although he was not in love with me, I pretended that he was and smiled at him in reply. Then, I placed my head on his chest, trying to feel bliss in his arms.

CHAPTER XIX

Jai

While snuggling closer to Natasha, I drifted off to sleep. *I don't know what happens to me when I'm with her. I relax and get sleepy.* I fell asleep in her room yesterday morning and rested like a log until I felt her presence near me. In my dreams, she kissed me gently, waking me up while she was standing close in real life. Dream mingled with reality, and I reached out to her. When I noticed her frown, I realised that I was awake and Natasha was right before me!

I woke up somewhere late in the afternoon, feeling hungry and saw her sleeping next to me. She was covered in a blanket up to her shoulders, looking like a temptress. I couldn't stop myself from kissing her shoulder blades.

She purred and brought her knees closer to her chest. I held her chin and gently turned her face towards me. Her eyes opened slowly, trying to push off the dreams that blushed her face.

"I guess you were dreaming of something beautiful," I commented, taking a feather-light kiss from her soft lips.

She nodded her head, combing my hair with her hands.

"Should be about me then," I teased.

"Not really. I dreamed of *Maa* and Soha. I am excited about meeting Soha," she said with her eyes sparkling with excitement.

"Hmm, Akash will be here in a month," I said, curling her tresses with my fingers. They were soft to touch, and her eyes danced animatedly.

"So what time is the flight tomorrow?" she asked with a frown.

"I have asked my secretary to book one as soon as possible. I will finish the pending works by the time Akash makes it to India," I explained, scooping her into my arms and looking at her face as she blushed for the millionth time.

"I need to go to the washroom." She wriggled free from me and walked away. I wished to remain in bed and wait for her, but a call on my phone made me get up and attend it., "Hello, Dad."

"They are with the lawyer, Dad," I answered. "Why should I lie? It's signed and submitted to him." And then, I suddenly realised that the lawyer must have told my father about the divorce papers being destroyed in the fire. "Oh yes, I forgot about th-"

Furiously Dad cut in. He wasn't ready to listen to a thing. All he wanted was to get my divorce settled at the earliest.

"But what is the rush, Dad?" I asked, finally unable to bear his need for urgency.

"Once you get divorced from this fake marriage of yours, I have set up a marriage alliance for you. She's the most eligible girl in Perth," he said, sounding as confident as ever and then added, "You will be floating in money with this marriage, and we will become number one in this business!"

I felt like someone just punched me in my gut. My father just saw me as a money-making machine. "Okay, Dad, will do as you say. I'll call you later. I'm in the middle of something important."

I disconnected the call and took a deep breath, processing all the negativity that my father had passed onto me through this call.

A second later, I felt my blood drain, thinking Natasha was there with me in this room and she must have heard everything I said. I turned around quickly to explain, but thankfully, she was still in the washroom.

I heard the sound of water and sighed. I knocked on the bathroom door, and when she stopped the shower, I said aloud, "Natasha, I'm heading out to speak with Mehta. We need to make some changes in the plan."

"Sure, go ahead," I heard her reply.

As I went out to the restaurant section, I found Mehta sitting there alone and talking to someone on the phone.

"Hi," I greeted and sat down next to him.

"Will call back, honey," he said and disconnected the call.

"Wife?" I asked with a smile.

"Of course, who else will I call honey?" he smirked, taking a bite of his food.

Amused at his reply, I replied, "Girlfriends. You can call them honey, can't you?"

"This lifetime, no! I am content with my wife and my family." A notification beeped on his phone, and he swiped it with a smile, then texted his reply.

I chuckled. "You're acting like a college boy, Mehta."

"You know when you have someone to take care of you, ask how you are doing and be genuinely concerned for you, half of your stress and worries go away," he smiled, looking at me.

I stared at him for a second. His words sounded ridiculous to me. "What do you mean by 'they will take away your worries'?"

"What I mean is, the presence of your loved one calms your mind. You might have thousands of troubles but knowing that someone is with you no matter what, you will not be concerned with those worries so much," Mehta answered.

I looked away, finding no sense in his talks.

"That day when our Ninja Super Avenue was in trouble, if Natasha wouldn't have shown courage and accompanied you, the reputation of the car and of our brand would have been at a huge risk even if you would have driven it alone," he explained, watching me intently. "Take my word, not many partners stick together when it comes to risking their lives. But Natasha has my respect for standing up for a man who was so mean to her!"

I looked away, knowing that he was correct.

"So, what have you decided?" asked Mehta, sipping his coffee.

"We will have Akash come in-"

"I'm not talking about the launch. About Natasha, have you figured out whether you love her or is it just an infatuation?"

"It's complicated," I replied and averted my gaze. "When I'm with her, I forget the world, but my reality keeps reminding me that she does not belong to my family. My father has found me a bride," I said with a wry smile. Somewhere deep inside, it hurt terribly that I didn't speak my mind before my father.

"Can't come clean before your father, I suppose," he said, reading my mind.

"Not when all my dreams are backed up by him," I answered.

He got up to answer a call but stopped and gave me a piece of his mind. "Remember this, no matter who it is in front of you if it's important for you, I bet you will speak up, else it will be just a casual affair like everything else."

A notification on the phone diverted my attention. My secretary had emailed me the flight details for our return journey.

I sighed, thinking about my Dad's words and Mehta's. *It's true. We speak up when something is important to us. But Ninja Super Avenue is just as important to me, and if I go against dad, he won't let me have a single penny. If he comes to know that I have no plans to submit the divorce papers to the lawyer, another hell will break loose!*

I don't know what to do with Natasha. I always fight with her, asking why she needs a divorce. I tell her to reconsider, but I am unsure at the back of my mind. I'm afraid of how I'll spend the rest of my life with her. She is pretty dreamy, and I might not live up to her expectations or say my family will not let me live up to her expectations.

Sitting alone in the restaurant, eating my food, I stared at the people coming and going. Not finding it amusing, I started to sketch a car. Pleased with the design, I returned to my room to draw a better version in my sketchbook.

It took me an hour to sketch and colour the car design. I glanced at it with satisfaction when it was done, but I still wanted to take other people's opinions. So, I posted it on my social media sites. A feel-good sensation radiated from within me, but at the same time, I wondered how many people must be having a hidden talent that they never get to show to the world!

Then all of a sudden, it hit me, how about opening a bespoke boutique in my retail store in Perth? We could offer customers a choice to hire our in-house designers or design their own dresses. Then, the store would stitch it up for them. We could also offer to provide a custom label for clothes designed by the customers. It would be like setting up their own brand. *This might make the shop popular, right?*

I rushed out of my room to look for Natasha. I wanted to discuss the plan with her, but she wasn't in her room. Overwhelmed with the idea for the retail store, I went out for a walk at the beach.

I called up Chad to get his views on the plan. He pointed out all the cons of the idea. "You would have to recruit quality designers and people to sew the clothes. This would add to your expenditure. In addition, whether or not there you have orders, these employees would have to be compensated. Moreover, the designs given by the customers might not even be feasible."

His concerns were valid. "First of all, we could pay the employees based on commission per order. This way, they will also be enthusiastic about bringing in clients. Secondly, the customers designing their own clothes would have to submit their designs with the materials. Next, our designers would have to attest to the feasibility and draw it out for them. Then, once confirmed, we would proceed to have it stitched," I suggested. "The idea is to give the customers the satisfaction of wearing something of their own imagination and have it labelled with their name."

"Won't it cost it too much to label each one with the customer's name?" asked Chad.

"Not really. These days, the logo can be easily designed digitally and printed on clothes as if printing them on paper. So, of course, it won't be as cheap as buying the ready-made stuff. But, since it bears their signature and their style, they will be willing to pay more," I explained.

"That's true," Chad replied after some thought. "Something unique as this should make them shell more money and help you earn your profits." Chad sounded convinced of my plans. "I think there is no harm in trying for a few days," he added.

Happy to get his assent, I said, "I will ask my team to work on it right away. If possible, could you look into it while I'm away?"

"That's not a problem. I will look into its implementation!" Chad offered enthusiastically.

I sighed, feeling relieved and satisfied. Then, with a smile, I strolled energetically. *This idea would work!*

A few minutes later, I received a call from one of my business rivals. He asked me if he could buy the car design from me. At first, I thought he was joking, but when he offered me ten lakhs as payment, I paused in my tracks. He wanted me to design the details and share them with him. He was even ready to sign an agreement and disburse the money.

A minute later, I called up Mehta and one of my friends to get their opinion. "Give me a minute. I'll get back," said Mehta. He called me back a few minutes later, "I don't think he is gonna use it to make a car."

"So, he was playing a prank?" I asked, feeling angry at that man for wasting my time.

"Every year, an automobile magazine company launches a competition, where the best automobile design is showcased on their front cover, and the winner is given a prize of-" he said and paused.

"How much, man?" I asked, irked at his tricks to piss me off.

"Two million dollars," he said in a whisper.

My lips curled up into a huge smile as I sat down on the sand, heaving a deep sigh. This amount could cover many of my expenses, and then I wouldn't have to ask for money from my Dad!

A ray of hope emerged within me; to be independent and make my own decision. I wanted to share both the news with Natasha, so I called her number, but she didn't answer.

Unable to keep this to myself, I returned to my room and drew more sketches. However, it wasn't until late evening that I felt hungry and called the restaurant for dinner. I called Natasha to check if she had her dinner or could join me, but she didn't pick it up. Checking the time, I thought she must have slept and decided against disturbing her.

CHAPTER XX

Natasha

I was about to enter the washroom, but I stopped to pick up a dress from my bag. Behind me, I heard Jai answer a call. He put the phone on speaker, as a matter of habit. His father's voice loomed from the other end. Quietly, I entered the washroom and closed the door, my ears unwittingly eavesdropping on the conversation.

Silent tears poured down my eyes when I heard their plans. But then, I wasn't as devastated as the last time. Instead, I thanked God for saving me from falling into his trap.

A thought occurred to me, *If only I had someone of my own, I might not long for Jai anymore.* So, I spent the next few hours in my room researching adoption policies in India. Gaining knowledge distracts you from your emotional stress and puts you in an enlightened zone. I was surprised to know there are only a handful of organisations taking care of the female child population. It's considered riskier, and many Indians do not wish to adopt a girl child.

What's more, to adopt a child, one should have a solid financial progress card and a good family. Not fulfilling either criterion, I looked for other ways to help the orphan children and keep myself busy.

The more I read, the stifling in my chest caused by Jai and his father felt like soap bubbles in the air. Compared to the problems of these children who were abandoned to face society because they were deemed unworthy, my problems seemed nothing.

In a split second, as if I had found my calling, I decided to take up this job of looking after such children as my responsibility. An email from Jai distracted my attention. He had sent me the return tickets.

I wish I didn't have to return to Mumbai. I sighed, feeling restless. I couldn't wait to finish Jai's campaign and do what my heart desired me to do.

It was challenging to avoid Jai if I stayed in my hotel room, so I hired a cab, left the phone at the hotel, and went out to travel around the city.

The combination of the water, sky and greenery all around calmed my mind and relaxed my tormented soul. There were times I wished I had company to click pictures, smile, laugh and share jokes, but sometimes, you need to travel solo to figure out yourself. And I am glad I did just that! I roamed around the entire day and returned only when I was dead tired.

There were multiple missed calls from Jai, and I purposely ignored them, sending out a message. Had gone around the city and left the phone at hotel. Tired. Will call you tomorrow.

The next morning, I went for a walk by the beach and then left for the airport on my own, informing Tanisha of my plans.

When I reached the airport, I received a call from Jai, "Where are you?"

"At the airport, getting my security check done," I told him and disconnected the call as I stepped into the aircraft. I was about to take my seat on the flight when I noticed the man next to me. He was none other than Jai.

"We will come back again. I guess you know that. You didn't have to check out everything in the city in a single day! We could have gone out together," he reprimanded gently, getting up from his seat and giving me space to move inside.

"I know, but I wanted to." I pressed the 'call' button on the overhead panel and took a seat. When the air stewardess arrived, I asked, "Please could you get me a glass of water and also a sleeping mask?"

"Sure, I'll be right back." She hurried away and returned within minutes with whatever I'd asked.

"You are going to sleep now?" Jai asked, looking at me with a frown as I pulled the mask over my eyes.

"Power nap," I said with a smile and closed my eyes. I didn't want to have a conversation with him, for I was sure he would make out I wasn't interested in talking with him.

"Ma'am, you need to straighten your seat until the flight takes off," said the air hostess, and I obliged, pretending to be sleep deprived.

"So, where did you run off to yesterday?" Jai asked as the captain made the take-off announcement.

I shifted in my seat, then with my mask on, I said, "I visited North Goa. Returned late."

"I hope everything is fine with you," he asked, putting his hand on mine and tracing the veins in my palm.

"Yes, everything is fine. I am just too tired," I said, removing my eye mask and giving him a plastered smile.

"Good, I thought it's one of those moments where you want to keep hiding under some random excuse," I heard him say.

Such a two-faced guy he is! I fumed inwardly, and then ignored Jai as if I didn't hear anything.

I was a little self-conscious as I could feel his gaze on me, but soon, I dozed off. My wish to open an orphanage for girls manifested in my dream, and I found myself having a good time building it up. Before I knew it, the flight landed in Mumbai. I opened my eyes with a smile and glanced at the person next to me. Jai was reading an automobile magazine, a radiant smile adorning his cheeks.

"I am trying to get here," he said when he noticed that I was awake.

I raised a brow and asked, "As in? You want your car to be showcased here?"

"No. I'm hoping my sketches will be showcased here," Jai answered, his fingers roving over the car on the front cover of the magazine.

He was talented in designing cars. I'd seen his sketches before and felt they were really appealing to the eyes. "You have an amazing talent in designing cars. I'm sure you'll make it here!"

In an instant, he turned towards me and stared at me for a moment before saying, "You don't know how much your words mean to me!"

My heart skipped a beat hearing him, and all my resolve went for a toss. Did I hear something wrong yesterday? We stepped out of the aircraft, and I didn't get to talk to him anymore. He was occupied with his team, and I felt it was for the better. My mind was a confused mess and made me have second thoughts on my decision to stay away from him.

However, I couldn't resist turning one last time to look at him before taking a seat in my cab. And then I found his eyes hooked on mine.

I knew I had made a mistake staring at him like that, but it was too late to pretend otherwise. He dismissed his team and walked straight towards me.

"Mind if I come with you?" he asked.

I frowned, unable to comprehend his intention.

But even before I could reply, he said, "Thanks," and slid into the cab, gently pulling me inside.

Goosebumps made me aware of how much his presence impacted me. I was almost sticking to the door, feeling suffocated and restrained.

"Nats, can we stay together for a few days?" he asked a second later.

My senses snapped back to reality, and I turned to look at him as he fidgeted with his phone. "I feel there is some pull between us... and the separation we went through... somehow has magnetised our desire for each other." His eyes were glued to my face, expecting a favourable answer.

"No, we can't," I said abruptly, making him look at me baffled. I had never said 'no' to him on his face before. "It will be a mistake on my end to agree to this. Moreover, I wanted to add that whatever happened between us in Goa was my foolishness. I want to move on with my life and do something I always wanted to do."

"Mistake?" he hissed at once.

"Yes, I got carried away, which I shouldn't have. But now, I want to focus on my dream. So, once this project is finished, I will work on that." I told this to him with conviction.

His forehead creased, and he raised a brow. "You got carried away multiple times, is that so?" It was as if he didn't listen to anything else I said.

"Yes, it was a mistake, and yes, I got carried away multiple times. You know how it happens when you don't do it for many days." I shrugged my shoulders. "Then suddenly, when you come across someone your body is familiar with, you get carried away. I think it can happen to anyone or with anyone. Maybe if I had gotten close to some other man, I would have felt the same."

He let out a dry laugh, the one which made my skin crawl with fear and sadness. I had hurt him badly.

"That's ironic!" he remarked with a scowl and glared at me with those eyes which had turned a shade of grief. "You are correct. It can happen to anyone and with anyone!"

I felt my throat choke as I gulped my fear in. Probably this would be the last time I was sitting so close to Jai.

"So, then I should make a move," he shrugged his shoulders and patted on the driver's shoulders. "Stop the car for a second."

Things were going too fast for me to mellow it down, to make sure he wasn't as hurt as he looked.

"All right. See you then, Natasha, when-" he said and then paused before his eyes turned icy, "probably when you would have moved on with your life."

I wanted to ask, 'Are you okay?' But instead blurted out, "Yeah, bye, take care!"

His eyebrows shot up, giving me an angry stare as he opened the car door. I turned away to avoid his eyes.

"Natasha?" I heard him call my name.

"Yes-" I hadn't even said the word when he surprised me with a kiss on my lips. My eyes were wide open while his were closed.

But to my surprise, it wasn't like any of the kisses I had shared with him earlier. He was sucking my lips hard, and it was hurting me.

I tried to push him away, but instead, he bit my bottom lip once more.

He moved away the next second, walked out, and instructed the driver, "Drop her safely."

CHAPTER XXI

Natasha

Dreaming is easy but working to turn it into reality is altogether another thing. Nevertheless, I wanted to start working for the orphaned children immediately, so right after leaving my suitcase in my room, I took a deep breath, ready to start.

I knew Mumbai was a city where I could find thousands of orphans who needed help. The faces of children who beg around traffic signals came to my mind, and I made my way towards the nearest traffic signal where I could find them.

I spotted a boy selling flowers and decided to approach him. "Hey, what do you do?"

The boy turned towards me and smiled hopefully, expecting me to be a potential buyer. "I sell flowers, Ma'am. Do you want to buy them?"

"Yes," I nodded. "But tell me, do you have parents?" The words choked my throat as if thinking it was enough to make me feel alone and unworthy of anything in the world.

"Yes, Ma'am," he replied indifferently but picked out the best flower in his hand and offered it to me. "I'll give you a discount, as you seem to be a good lady. Only ten rupees for this red rose."

"Thank you," I chuckled at the boy's attempt to sell his goods. But I had to push on and ask more. "Do you know someone who needs support and doesn't have a family?" He looked here and there, speechless at my question. He seemed a little impatient as if I was stopping him from doing business by asking unnecessary questions. "Ma'am, I need to work. If I don't sell these roses, my family will not be able to eat."

"I understand, but I need your help to help other children," I said, gently placing a hand on his shoulders.

"There could be many who need help, but right now I must go," he said, looking a little desperate towards something behind my back.

I turned to look at what he was staring at but couldn't figure out what it was.

"Ma'am, do you want to buy a flower?" he asked impatiently, and I handed him a hundred rupees note.

His face gleamed with a broad smile as he handed me all the flowers in his hand.

"Now, are you happy?" I remarked, realising that I had finally struck a nail. "Can you tell me if someone needs help?"

"Thank you, Ma'am," he said, walking away with a contented smile. He stopped a short distance away and added, "You can find many who beg and live on the streets. Bye, Ma'am."

Saying that, he ran away with a smile.

I was surprised at the unthankful behaviour he displayed. At least he could have pointed me to someone who needed help. *What work could he have apart from selling flowers?*

I let my disappointment in him not let me down and looked for more children, but every time I was driven away as soon as their intention was fulfilled. Finally, I couldn't hold my frustration anymore and grabbed a kid by the arm. "If you'll answer my questions, I'll give you money."

The girl child paled as if something painful had stung and paralysed her.

"Hello, Ma'am." A voice behind me made me turn. A moderately dressed man gestured at the girl to get going.

She instantly pulled her hand away from me and scampered away.

"Yes?"

He crossed his arms over his chest and had a menacing look on his face. "Ma'am, I have been watching you for quite some time. Why are you troubling the children?"

"Troubling?" I gave a dry laugh. "I wasn't troubling them. I'm here to help them."

"Ma'am, I'm not sure how you want to help, but they are working here to feed themselves. If you bother them like this, they will not have earned enough to eat."

I was perplexed at the man's accusation. "What do you mean? I've only been here for thirty minutes!"

"It's just thirty minutes for you, but it is a matter of food for them," he said with a meaningful gaze.

Before he could continue, another man looking older than the first one joined us. He was dressed in a t-shirt and shorts, but unlike the younger man, the quality of his clothes seemed better. "What happened? Why are you not working?"

"*Bhai*, I was just explaining to her not to waste the time of the kids," the younger man answered.

The older man turned to me. "Ma'am, what work do you have with the kids?"

"I was asking the kids if they know anyone who needs help... like children who are orphans, who don't have parents-"

"Here, everyone has parents, and they send them here to work," he said with a dismissive tone and turned to walk away.

"Work, you mean begging?" I was surprised.

"Yes," answered the man, turning back. "How else will they survive?" He took a step closer and eyed me with a stern look. "I suggest you stop digging your nose into their business. It'll be better!"

I was speechless at his rudeness. Is he making them beg? Somehow, he seemed to be the handler, forcing the children to do his bidding. Finally, I picked up my courage and faced him head-on. "Excuse me? I want to meet their parents, else I will go to the police and tell them that you are making the kids work illegally!"

He scowled and then stepped closer, just inches away from my face. "How many will you meet? They are all the same. They don't have time for such small issues. Every day, a new person comes and tells them they will help, and then after spending two or three days, they walk away, turning a blind eye," he added.

"I'll still meet them!" I remarked in a challenging voice.

He looked at me for a second, then something caught my arms and off went my purse, "Hey!" I shrieked, feeling utterly lost. "Catch him! That's my purse!"

A boy ran away with my purse at lightning speed. I turned to the two men. "Please get my purs-"

I stopped midway, noticing their big smile, "What the hell!!" I retorted in frustration and went running after the boy.

I chased the little boy from the main street to the narrow zig-zag lanes until he suddenly stopped. We stared at each other, heavily panting.

He took out a note from my purse, then walked closer. I was on the verge of catching hold of him and reprimanding him when he handed me the bag. "*Didi*, you shouldn't come here again. These aren't good people. I snatched your purse to drive you away from them. You should leave right away, or you might land up in trouble. But..." he hesitated for a second and added, "I have to take some money back so that they don't suspect me of helping you."

I was suddenly at a loss. The child seemed very young, maybe seven or eight, but he had quite an insight on the situation here. "Can't you go to the police?"

"What can you do when your own parents send you here to earn money?" he muttered, holding his chin down. "It isn't easy surviving without money. My mother works in the construction of buildings, but doesn't have work on many days. There is no shortage of such labourers here, but there is a shortage of work. The days when my mother doesn't get work, I earn and feed my family."

"Do you mean they give you money in return for selling those items on the street?" I asked, taking my purse from his hand.

He nodded silently. "I must return to work, but please don't come back here."

"But I wanted to help and support you all..." I mumbled, my mind racing fast to come up with a solution.

He looked at me with grief-stricken eyes. "By the time you can reach the needy ones and help them, you would have landed in a lot of trouble. These men, the handlers, don't want to lose us."

He walked away without looking back. I sat down by the pavement, lost in the confusion created in my mind. *What can I do? Where can I go to help them? And where should I start?*

All I wanted to do was help someone and feel good, but this wasn't as easy as it seemed. However, I didn't give up and decided to seek help from NGOs. After a lot of research, I visited a few of them. Most of the people working there were volunteers. They primarily worked in various other organisations, and on the weekends, they contributed to the poor with food and clothes.

I participated in such activities for a couple of weekends. Still, I realised there was a big gap between the people who volunteered in NGOs and the children who actually needed help. We delivered food and clothes only to a handful, and that too only to the children who came in our contact and were not in the wrong hands.

My mind was in a mess thinking of all this, and a month passed away just like that. I wanted to do something, but the money I had with me was neither enough to help the children in a big way nor did I know of anyone who would support me to help the children.

I tried all my means and settled to use the internet to my advantage. I opened a social media page and a website to generate supporters, but unfortunately, there was no footfall on the links.

Finally, I decided to do what I could do best: cook at an orphanage for the children without any fees. I guess this is what I needed, for I felt lighter in my heart as if I'd done something meaningful.

A few days later, I received a phone call from Akash, informing me that he was back in town with Soha and insisted on meeting me. I promised to visit her that very evening.

I felt overwhelmed with happiness from the minute she spoke to me. I was eager to meet her just as she was to meet me.

The feeling of someone liking you makes you high, and I was feeling the same. I didn't have any relationship with Soha; however, the bonding with her was precious to me beyond words.

The moment I arrived, little Soha was all smiles and jumped to hug me. It was a delight to hold her in my arms and squeeze her little body into mine.

"I like Natasha aunty, not Tanisha aunty!" she immediately chirped.

"Soha, you shouldn't talk like that," said Akash. "Say sorry to Tanisha Aunty."

Tanisha, who seemed immersed in her files, stiffened at Soha's words. She gave me a small smile, ignoring the little girl and her rude comment.

"Sorry," said Soha unapologetically and zoomed towards her room. Akash eyed her and followed behind, his expression ready to scold her.

"I'm sorry, don't take her words to heart," I said, walking over to Tanisha.

Tanisha shook her head and gave a dry smile. "That's fine. She didn't say anything rude. She just expressed herself. Anyway, where were you all these days?"

"I've taken up a job as a cook at an orphanage near my place," I said, feeling proud.

"Wow! That sounds nice!" Tanisha remarked, her eyes glowing with respect.

Right then, Akash walked in. "Part-time modelling and part-time charity work, you have a big heart, my friend! You are the best!"

"Well..." I took a breath and continued with a bright smile, "No modelling after this. I enjoy working at the orphanage and want to keep that as my priority. As for filling my stomach, I think, 'll just take up a simple and easy job."

"Are you sure about this?" asked Akash, raising a brow.

I nodded. "This will give me peace and also enable me to repay my mom."

Tanisha's phone began to ring before Akash could ask me more. She answered and hurriedly stood up. "Akash, I need to go, something urgent has come up," she said with a flustered expression as she arranged the files she was working on.

"Is everything all right?" Akash inquired with a frown.

"My... my fa- a relative of mine is admitted in hospital," Tanisha replied as she hurriedly organised the files and rushed towards the door.

"Oh! Then you better hurry up!" Akash nodded. "And call me once you reach the hospital. If there is anything I can do, let me know."

Tanisha stopped before stepping out and nodded her head in acknowledgement.

"She's sweet!" I remarked about Tanisha once she leaves.

"Yes, she's good, and I'm happy with her work," Akash answered, returning to the sofa. Finally, he let out another sigh and faced me. I could make out that he wanted to say something important, and I was sure it wasn't about Tanisha. "Natasha, I need a favour..."

"Yes, tell me." I raised my brows, wondering what kind of favour he wanted.

Akash weaved his hands through his hair, contemplating whether to speak up or not. "I'm not sure how to put it..."

"Just tell me, Akash. We've been friends for quite a long time. So you don't need to hesitate like this."

He took a deep breath before he began. "Soha seems to have become very attached to you. Since our return, she's been asking for you non-stop. I've tried to explain to her that you can't always be with us as you have your own life, but she's acting spoiled, and I don't know what to do." His eyes almost turned helpless when he added nervously, "Could you move in with us to help Soha recover? She nee-"

"Okay," I cut in, nodding my head.

"What?" His brows arched up with a blank look as if he didn't understand what I said.

I smiled at his reaction. *I guess he didn't expect me to accept his invitation right away!* "I said, I'm okay to accompany Soha," I said, stretching my arms as I settled on the sofa. "I was planning to move somewhere anyway. Living in that big house without *Ma* is very depressing. You could sublet a room to me, and I could be with Soha as long as you want me to be!"

I expected Akash to rejoice, but he still seemed nervous and out of sorts for some reason. "What's wrong? You don't want me to come?"

"She needs a mother," Akash replied, locking eyes with me. "I want you to be her mother."

Everything froze as I stared at him and he at me. My mind was blank while Akash's eyes were expectant. Soha suddenly appeared, jumped on the sofa and wrapped her arms around my neck. "Yes! I want you to be my mother. Natasha, Aunty, please!"

I had always wanted a daughter like Soha. What could be better than having Soha as my daughter than someone else like her? But agreeing to become her mother meant more than just being a mother figure... right? I had second thoughts and wanted to ask Akash about it, but Soha's pleading gaze and sweet face made me give up my apprehensions. "I will, happily," I smiled, hugging her back.

She tightened her delicate arms around me and poured small kisses on my face.

Akash just watched us, his eyes welling up with happy tears. "Thank you, Natasha!" His voice was choked as the anxiety was released. "Thank you... You don't know how happy I am!"

Soha skipped out of my arms and into Akash's. "You got what you wanted!" he remarked, pulling her cheek.

"Yes!" Soha screamed joyfully.

Akash glanced at me and added, "After we are done with the campaign, let's have a small ceremony and announce our wedding."

I felt my breathing hitch at the word 'wedding'. The word held a deeper meaning in my life. I was getting cold feet, but... I glanced at the father-daughter duo. They looked ecstatic. *I love Soha and Akash is a very precious friend. I guess it is all right to agree... after I let him know my not-so appealing secret.*

"There's something I need to tell you," I said with a sombre look, walking towards them and added, "...before we make the wedding announcements."

"What is it?" he asked, his smile washing away at my expression.

He placed Soha on the ground, and she announced in a happy mood, "Okay, Auntyand Dad, you talk. I'll go to my room and sleep happily!"

Once we took a seat, I told Akash about my contract marriage in Perth, carefully keeping Jai's name out of it. "After I returned to India, the lawyer's office caught fire, and the papers were destroyed. So, we need to once again file for divorce, and until then, I'm still legally married."

Akash listened intently. A myriad of emotions flashed across his face as I relayed to him the events of my life. In the end, he pondered for a while before asking, "Are you sure the papers were really destroyed? What if it was all a pretence to stop you from leaving?"

"Nah, it's not like that." I shook my head, and a wry smile came to my lips, thinking of Jai's conversation with his father on the phone. "From the beginning, it was a contract between us for our mutual benefit. We both got what we wanted from the agreement. The divorce would have happened had it not been for the fire. Moreover, he will be getting married soon. His father has found him a bride. The only thing is that I'll have to visit Perth to file the divorce papers once again."

"Why can't you sign the papers and courier it?" he asked.

"He said physical presence is required in the court," I explained.

"What? I don't think so. It is accepted everywhere..." Akash replied with a thoughtful look. "However, yeah... the court may request your presence when they receive the papers and want to know your final decision."

I was puzzled because it was the same thing I had thought when Jai had asked me we had to go to Perth to settle this.

"Who is this guy, anyway? Give me his number. I will talk to him," Akash said, breaking my chain of thoughts.

"No, don't worry. I will speak to him," I said instantly. I didn't want him to know that the man was Jai. "I just wanted you to know before we went ahead with this wedding."

"Even if you wouldn't have told me, I trust you," he said, placing his hand on my knees.

"Thanks," I uttered, feeling both happy and sad.

"By the way, we'll be flying to Goa next month for the photo shoot." He smiled at me, tucking the stray strands of hair behind my ears, and he added, "I hope your divorce is finalised soon."

I smiled, even though hearing about the photoshoot for Ninja Super Avenue brought about a nervous chill to my body.

CHAPTER XXII

Jai

On the Day of the Photoshoot, Goa

She had said, we don't have anything between us, but every time I was alone, I kept thinking about her. I wanted to give her some time, so I didn't chase her. But, I was looking forward to the shoot. I was informed that Natasha would arrive with Akash and his team a day before us to get the arrangements done.

I felt as if it was deliberately done by her. Furious was a short word to address my anger, but then Mehta told me that Akash's daughter was also accompanying, and that's why they had arrived earlier. *I understand the girl has undergone the operation recently, so precautions are necessary, but still, Natasha could have informed me about this directly... right?*

When I arrived at the hotel, I was impatient to meet her, so I immediately enquired at the resort's reception. However, I was told Natasha Meher had booked a room but was yet to check-in. With no other choice left, I called Akash, but he disconnected the call right after informing me that he was away on a trip with his family and I should contact his secretary, Tanisha, for updates.

I called Tanisha and met her in the lounge over a cup of coffee. Since I was meeting her, I thought I might as well discuss the revised schedule. The previous photoshoot was cancelled, Akash had found another photographer, and it was to be done with the video shoot. The ad was supposed to be *au naturale* with the beach in the background giving it the effect of 'simple yet elegant'. After we went over the plans, I asked, "By the way, where's Natasha? I wanted to have a chat with her about the ad."

Tanisha slightly stiffened at my query. She plastered a business-like smile and answered, "She's away with Akash, his mom and his daughter. They are celebrating Soha's birthday."

"Oh, I scc," I answered with a nod in a casual tone. "Are they returning today?" Though I pretended to be cool, I was far from feeling it!

"Yes, they'll reach tonight since the shoot starts tomorrow."

I stood up to leave. "Thanks for the update, Tanisha. I suppose I'll meet her once she is back."

"Hmm," Tanisha nodded and added, "Well, I'm not sure whether it'll be a good idea to disturb them that late at night." When I frowned, she added, "Akash and Natasha are to marry soon. I thought I should tell you since you seem to be concerned about Natasha so much."

"What?!" My facade cracked, and I squinted my eyes at her. "When did this happen?" My surprise knew no end! I felt stifled in my chest and also betrayed... Why didn't Natasha tell me about this?

"Akash proposed to her, and she agreed. That's all I know," she looked away, a hint of pain on her otherwise expressionless face. "Well, see you tomorrow," she gave me a small smile and walked away. I kept staring at her back, getting smaller and smaller until she vanished after turning a corner, but nothing registered in my head. I stood frozen stiff, my mind blank.

The waiter's voice broke my trance. The piece of news didn't go well with me, and I marched off to the beach to take a stroll accompanied by emptiness. I had left her alone to gather herself, and I could persuade her again, but it was now evident she didn't want to stay with me. *She was definitely attracted to me! We had such good chemistry! Then how could she do this? Did she honestly think of our time as a 'mistake'?*

I know I shouldn't stop her from deciding her future, but it hurts like hell! I have to ask her what's on her mind! Damn it! She's still my wife! I dropped on the sand, the pain in my chest making it difficult for me to breathe. I spent a long time there on the beach, breathing heavily until I finally calmed down. After all, what she wanted to do with her life was her wish. She had already told me to my face that she wanted to move on.

I returned to the resort, feeling lifeless. For a long time, I held myself, cooped up in my room, but as the night started to unwrap, I couldn't control it anymore. Before I knew it, I was standing in front of her door. But my hands were not moving up to ring the bell. Something between us had changed when I came to know she was about to marry Akash.

Finally, I found the courage to ring her bell, having the urge to know everything from her mouth.

I could hear the TV's sound, but why wasn't she answering the door? I waited for ten minutes, assuming that she might be in the washroom and rang the bell for the second time. When she still didn't open it, I said aloud, "Natasha, open the door, please." Afraid that she might have collapsed again, I contacted housekeeping and explained to them the situation. Within minutes, they obliged, and I rushed in. I found her sitting on the balcony, holding her face to her knees. Relief coursed through me, and I thanked the housekeeping for their help before turning back to Natasha.

"Natasha," I called her softly while walking over to her.

"Go away!" she turned to me and screamed. "Leave me alone!"

What happened? Why was she crying? Did he do something inappropriate with her? That bastard!

I asked her gently, "Natasha, can you tell me what happened?" I tried to inch my way towards her. She looked distraught, as if something inside her had broken. I wanted to hold her and give her my support. "What is it, Natasha? Please tell me. Your silence is killing me!" I was next to her now. I lightly patted her back and caressed her to help her calm down.

"I can't, I simply can't," she said through her tears. "Please leave me alone. I will be fine."

I was annoyed at the way she was pushing me away. The sound from the TV was adding to my irritation. I walked off to find the remote and switch the damn thing off when a familiar face on the TV screen caught my attention. It was Atul. I felt my heart tug in pain.

"A man found dead in gang wars in Mumbai," said the news reporter and went on describing the situation. The reporter continued with his opinion of how families are stranded by the death of their kin and added, "The gang members do not care about their deeds and involve themselves in gang wars."

I slumped on the chair, feeling numb. *What could I do or say now?*

"They are my parents," Natasha's feeble voice reached my ears. "All this time, I thought they were dead!"

My own voice felt choked, unable to think of what I needed to say.

"All these years, I was crying over their sudden death. I was praying for them to be blessed, wherever they were. Today, I finally came to know that they are alive! They didn't ever come back to check on me!" With her hand clasped over her face, she cried fitfully. "I don't know what to say. I feel like the most unfortunate person on Earth! God, I don't know what wrong I did to deserve all this!!!" she wailed out in grief.

I pulled her in my arms and let her cry on my shoulders. "Natasha, calm down. You couldn't have done anything in this situation."

"I don't know whether I should feel happy to know that they are alive or feel sad and cry for my brother's loss. I feel like a fool, unable to sort out myself," she said in between her sobs.

She wiped away her tears. Then, looking at me, she said, "But for once, I want to know why didn't they ever come back to check on me. What was my fault for which they left me alone to suffer?"

Her cries made me panic. She might do something to herself if she is left alone. I let her cry as I sat down next to her on the floor and ordered food for her.

She insisted on not eating, but after forcing her to take a bite or two, I stayed put and made sure she rested well. However, she pushed me away and asked me to leave. I was reluctant, as I knew she was suffering. Finally, after ensuring that she had calmed down, I left her room. She promised to rest but wouldn't let me stay.

With a heavy heart, I moved out from there. I tried to sleep, but thoughts of Natasha and her pain kept me awake. I couldn't rest even for a minute. I don't know why, but I felt terribly bad for her.

CHAPTER XXIII

Natasha

I knew I wasn't amongst the privileged class, but I was happy with my family. But then, they suddenly went on a trip, leaving me behind with the relatives and never returned. Though I was told about the accident, the realisation didn't sink in as I was just a child.

At first, I didn't understand why my loving relatives suddenly stopped me from going to school and made me work at home. Then, their pampering changed to scolding and bullying for mistakes I didn't even commit. Finally, the scolding changed to beatings, and my confused, immature mind could not fathom the reason behind it. Then, someone told me that I was an orphan, and that's how orphans are treated. I was supposed to bear it all like a mum slave, but I could not stop my tears. Dreams turned into nightmares, and I often woke up crying for my mother. I chanted every God's name that I knew of, but no one came to my rescue.

I fell ill, severely ill. The torture, the helplessness and the fear were too much for me to take, and I started suffering from seizures. Finally, after the second time I collapsed, I heard my Aunt say to my Uncle, "She's sick and of no use to us anymore. All she does is cry all day. We should get rid of her. I don't want to feed her when she can't even work now!"

I knew they were speaking about me. Again, I felt broken and betrayed and the tears streamed down my eyes. I didn't know what I could do. The following day, they left me at the home of Uncle's friend, with promises to pick me up the next day. I held onto my aunt and cried, begging her not to leave me behind, but she made a sweet face and said in an equally lovely voice and coaxed me to stay put, promising that she would return soon.

One night became many, but they didn't come back.

By God's grace, I found Miss Karuna Meher, a generous young lady in that house. She took me into her fold, and I started calling her *Ma* earnestly. Then there was no looking back. She was all I needed. My prayers were answered by God when I met her.

But now, after so many years, when I saw my parents on TV and realised that they were still very much alive, I felt betrayed. They didn't seem to be having memory loss, so the only possible reason why they left me meant I was a burden to them.

As a daughter, it was impossible for me to accept that they left me just like that to suffer in the world on my own.

Even if I tried to console myself, saying their betrayal led me to *Ma*, an angel on Earth, I couldn't toss away the thought that they made me live like an orphan. And now, with *Ma* gone, I once again felt like an orphan.

One miserable thought attracts another; with Jai's arrival in my room, all my depression burst forth. He had been exceedingly sweet in Diveagar. Even during my last time in Goa, he had been more caring and understanding than he had ever been during our so-called marriage. It was evident that he had a soft corner for me. A tiny hope sprouted that maybe we could get back together.

But then I heard him speak to his father. He was about to marry someone else. Whether he was being forced or it was his choice, I don't know. All I know is that he said he was working on the divorce.

Though he had not spoken much about the divorce, hearing him talk to his father about it pricked my heart. Why did he make love to me when he still wanted to separate? Was he trying to use me?

I was already reeling due to the heartache Jai had caused. So the betrayal of my parents was like a final nail in the coffin. His visit to my room added to my pain. His concern for my well being seemed like a farce! *Why was he doing it? Couldn't he understand that I didn't want him in my life again?*

But despite all this, in his arms, I felt as if someone had put balm on my sore soul. I badly needed someone to hold me then, but I knew that expecting truth and honesty from him was no good, so I drifted away. I had to stand up on my own without his support. I guess love isn't for everyone, so probably marrying Akash would be best. At least, he was a good friend who always stood by me, not to mention his daughter who was an adorable darling who truly loved me.

I didn't know when I drifted off to sleep in the morning after crying endlessly all night. Those tears represented my misfortune and my unrequited love for Jai.

The next morning, I woke up really early, around five in the morning, unable to sleep anymore. While brushing my teeth, I glanced at my reflection in the mirror and saw swollen eyes with dark circles all around staring back at me. My hair was in a bad state, and overall, I looked like a mess!

I chided myself for being so weak and decided to bring about a change!

I ordered a sumptuous breakfast and coffee in my room. I'd had enough of being gloomy; I needed the energy to uplift my mood!

After applying a cold compress to my eyes, I took a long warm bath, hoping that it would wash away all the negativities within me. Then, I took my time to get ready. I stared at myself once again in the mirror when I was done.

Dressed in a white floral sleeveless dress, nude lipstick, a little blush on my cheeks, hair tied in a stylish updo, I looked fresh and confident, ready to take on the world!

Since it was still early and the shooting was scheduled to commence an hour later, I decided to take a stroll along the beach.

"Natasha Aunty!" Soha's chirpy voice sounded behind me.

My lips curled into a smile even before I turned around to face her. She was rushing towards me, her eyes glittering with excitement.

I kneeled down to hold her in my arms.

"How are you, Aunty?" she asked ever so softly in my ears.

"I missed you," I replied, hugging the petite little doll. *Yes! She is all I need and nothing more!*

She pulled away from me and cupped my cheeks. "I missed you too, but a little less since I didn't know you'd miss me so much!" She grinned lovingly, placing her arms over my shoulders.

I pulled her into a bear hug. She wasn't the one who needed warmth; rather, it was me who desperately needed her cheerfulness. Her feelings towards me were genuine, full of innocence, unlike the spiderweb-like lies of the adults.

"Good morning, Natasha," Akash greeted me, and we both turned to face him.

I flashed him a smile. "Morning!"

"Can you look after Soha while I get things ready for the shoot?"

"Sure," I nodded, and Soha and I went ahead with our stroll. We walked for some time, collected the tiny conch shells, and settled on the sand to build castles.

Soha and I were deeply engrossed in building our castle not far from the lashing waves. An hour later, after much hard work, we succeeded in making one. As we stared at it, our eyes gleamed with accomplishment. I felt alive!

A shadow fell on the castle, making us look up with a huge smile. I was expecting it to be Akash, but it turned out to be Jai, and my smile faltered.

"Seems like you girls are having quite a lot of fun," said Jai, sitting down next to Soha on the sand.

"How are you, little angel?" Jai extended his hand towards Soha. "Your dad said you are a true fighter! But, I must say, I don't have the courage and strength like you. I have failed in a million things," he added while shaking her grainy palm.

She giggled and replied in a quirky voice, "That's okay. Everybody can't fight, but you need to be happy with whatever you have!"

"Well said!" Jai nodded with an appreciative look. "Now I know why Aunty is a fan of yours." He winked at her, and she turned to me with a smile.

"Do you want to play with us? But we are building castles as we love fairy tales. If you don't like it, you can make anything else." Soha patted on the castle wall, making it steady.

Jai scratched his chin and surveyed the castle. "I suppose I can build a wall around it so that your kingdom is well protected, my princess," he said and bowed down to her as if greeting royalty.

This earned him another giggle from Soha, and she nodded her head fervently in approval. After that, Soha and

Jai chatted, exchanging ideas on the wall while I continued with what I was doing as if he was invisible. I didn't wish to spoil the peace I felt at the moment.

A few minutes later, I felt a presence around us, and I glanced up to see what was happening. Ninja Super Avenue was silently rolled near us on the sand. The lights and camera were being set up.

My eyes locked on Akash, and I mumbled out, "What's happening?" He, the photographer, and the creative director were all staring at the camera lens, pointed in our direction.

"Seems like he is playing on something…" Jai voiced out, surveying the surroundings.

Akash glanced at us and said aloud, "Continue what you are doing."

I stiffened up and became a little conscious while Jai continued to build the wall around the castle as if he didn't give a damn about what was happening around.

"Nats, what are you doing sitting idle? Make something!" Jai's command brought me back. I smiled, forgetting the set-up around us and decorating the castle using the shells we had collected.

Soha kept us involved, twittering like a bird as she instructed us on her ideas. They chatted and laughed and chuckled and roared as if the world around had turned into a haze. And, I was happy, listening to their banter.

Finally, when the castle wall was done, Akash walked over and announced, "All right, guys! We're done! Let's take a short break." When he noticed my questioning gaze, he smiled, "It was an impromptu decision. The three of you looked just perfect with what we had in mind, so we decided to capture it!"

Unknowingly, I sighed with relief. The shooting was done without much effort! Soha tugged on my dress and extended her arms towards me. "I'm tired!"

As I carried her in my arms, she asked, "Can we have breakfast together?"

Though I was full and wanted to return to my room, I nodded with a smile. A cup of coffee will be good!

A sunshade with tables and chairs was set up not far from where we were, and refreshments with packed boxes were laid out. I took a seat with Soha at a table. While Soha munched on the assortment of dishes in the box, I sipped on the coffee.

Jai, Mehta, Akash, the creative director and photographer, made themselves comfortable on a nearby table, reviewing the stills from the shoot.

"The shots have come out well," stated the creative director. "A little bit of editing, some music and we'll be done."

"That's good," stated Jai.

"Ah..." the photographer pitched in. "We need a few stills of Natasha and you. Let's get them after breakfast."

As I overheard their conversation, I swiftly turned and interrupted, "I can't!" I didn't want to pose with Jai!

Akash glanced at me. His face was expressionless, but his eyes had a perplexed look in them. "Nats..."

That's when I realised my reply had sounded stronger than I intended.

Before Akash could continue, Jai said, "It's all right. We'll do it tomorrow. Is that okay, Natasha?"

I didn't answer but returned my attention to my table with a frown. Today or tomorrow. I'm not okay about it at all!

The meeting was dispersed a few minutes later. Jai and the rest walked away. Akash came to our table and asked me, "What's wrong?"

"Nothing!" I snapped at him. "I'm just fed up with his antics and don't want to be with him. Instead, I want to spend time with Soha and if you have a problem with that, let me know." With this, I returned to my coffee while Soha eyed Akash and me but did not utter a word.

"Natasha, look-"

"I told you already," I stood up angrily. "I'm doing this for you; this one photoshoot, and I'm done. I want to go back where I belong. I can't live in this false world and lie even if it's for the camera!" I knew I was taking my frustration out on the wrong person, but somehow, I just couldn't hold things inside me anymore.

"Uncle, your handkerchief has fallen down," said Soha aloud, making me aware of the third person in the room.

"Thank you, Soha," I heard Jai say in a sad tone and making me aware he heard what I told Akash.

I closed my eyes, repenting what I'd said but then sighed. At least, I'm not putting up an act like Jai!

"Akash, can I have a word with you?" I heard Jai ask. With a nod, Akash walked away with him.

CHAPTER XXIV

Jai

I don't know what's happening. *Why exactly is Natasha angry? All I know is that she cannot stand me! She probably hates me... Shit man! Where did I go wrong???*

As Akash and I walked out of the sunshade, I felt like a thousand needles pricked my heart. But I didn't know what I could do to not be hurt. I didn't want to trouble her anymore. Since she didn't want to see me, it was best to let her be. So aloud, I said to Akash, "I guess she's tired. Let her rest well today, and we'll finish the stills tomorrow. Just keep it simple so that it doesn't stress her out."

Akash seemed to be deep in thought all the time. I found him glancing at Natasha and then at me. "I think she is troubled about something. She was okay while shooting, and suddenly she became upset. I've never seen her this angry before."

"She's going through a lot..." I thought of how I found her last night. Anyone facing the situation would crumble from inside. The fact that she was still here today and working was commendable!

"Yes, her *Ma* was everything for her," Akash replied with an understanding nod.

I heaved a heavy sigh. "Yes, but what happened last night was far more shocking for her."

"Huh?" Akash faced me, his brows raised up. "What happened last night?"

Didn't she tell him? That was my first thought. But then, maybe I would have done the same in her shoes. I hesitated for a second, whether to tell him or not, because it was her personal matter. I glanced towards her seat, but she was nowhere around. I guess she had left with Soha. After a second thought, I told Akash everything I knew. He was her college friend, and they seemed pretty close.

"I never knew that she lost her parents in an accident," Akash replied with an astonished look. "Moreover, I would have never guessed that her *Ma* was not her biological mother!" Then he frowned and added, "But having said that, I didn't understand why she was taking out her anger on you. Though she was okay during the shooting, I think her mood snapped when I spoke about the cou-"

"Mind if we drop in between the discussion Jai," I heard a familiar voice and turned around to find Samira and Chad standing behind us.

"Big bro!" I smiled and hugged Chad, feeling relieved seeing them. *Relieved? Yes!* Because I thought now that Samira was here, Natasha might open up and be at peace.

"Hey, Jai!" Samira greeted with a sunny smile, her hand hooked around Chad's elbow. "Where's Natasha?" she asked, her eyes dancing in eagerness to meet her best buddy.

"Well, she's playing with Akash's daughter," I said and introduced Akash to them.

"So, you're her friend from Perth!" Akash gave a genuine smile while shaking Chad and Samira's hands.

"Yeah, we are just friends, but Jai here is much more than that!" Chad gave a friendly pat to my shoulders.

"Was," Jai gave a self-deprecating smile. "Not anymore. She's pushing me away, is all I can say now..."

Akash seemed to sense that something was amiss, frowned. "I'm sorry, I'm not able to follow. Is there something I'm missing here?" He looked at our faces and added, "And do you know who her ex-husband is? The one who is not willing to divorce her?"

Chad and Samira gazed wide-eyed at Akash and me.

Before I could think of what to say, Samira replied, "I think Jai is the best person to tell you that. Now, can someone tell us where we can find her?"

"I think she returned to the hotel," I replied to Samira and gave her Natasha's room number.

"Are you her ex-husband?" asked Akash right away the moment Samira and Chad left to find Natasha.

I turned to face him. I knew this was my only chance to reveal everything to him and leave what happens next to destiny. It was as if my life depended on his judgement now.

"Yes, I am still her rightful husband," I corrected him.

"Do you still love her?" Akash asked with a serious look. His eyes were scrutinising me as if trying to figure out my honesty.

"Honestly speaking, I don't know what love is," I said, facing the sea and pushing my hands in my pocket. "I think about Natasha all the time. I want to protect her, stand by her, and make her happy. My family is quite prejudiced, and she lost her job because of that. I don't want her to suffer because of me." I paused for a while and added, "To be frank, when I see her with you, I feel she is at ease. She is thrilled whenever she is around Soha." I felt my throat constrict as I spoke. I confessed my worst fears to the man who could be said to be my competition, but for some reason, I felt better. I wonder why...

Akash was also facing the sea, but still, I could feel his gaze on me. "Tanisha told me that you had visited her village after her *Ma* passed away."

When I nodded, Akash asked, "And also that you had pushed her to accept the campaign, or my company would have to pay two crores for breaking the contract. Is that correct?"

"I needed a reason to keep seeing her," I confessed.

Akash was very quiet for a while, as if contemplating over something. His thoughts were masked behind his expressionless demeanour, but I didn't feel any kind of animosity coming from him. After a while, he just sighed and suggested, "Just get your act together. You should figure out what you are looking for before it is too late." He paused, and we both faced each other. Our eyes met, and he added, "Because as far I can see, she loves you."

I was genuinely surprised at his words. I knew Natasha felt something for me, but lately, it seemed more like hatred than love. I don't know how, but I had a feeling that I had let her down. "What makes you think so?"

"First of all, her eyes are always following you. And when you look her away, she purposely avoids your eyes," explained Akash. "The day we met at your office, you were rude to her. Which was kind of strange, but what was stranger was her reaction. She was pissed off as if her fuse had blown. Though she denied it, I knew right away that she knew you from before and was reluctant to acknowledge it."

When I didn't reply, Akash added, "Her hatred towards you explains how much she loves you, and such extreme hatred arises from extreme love. It's a natural response to protect ourselves when we fear being taken for granted and also when we don't want to get carried away by our feelings."

His explanations made complete sense.

After a short pause, Akash added, "By the way, she agreed to marry me."

"I understand," I huffed out, feeling like a moron. *Why did I open up to him? Did I think he would back off if he thought I was her husband and loved her still?*

"From what I know of her, it is very easy to make her happy. She just wants honesty, and I guess you couldn't give her that. She believes in fairy tales, and all she desires is to be loved back as wholeheartedly as she loves. So maybe you couldn't earn her trust, and that is why she is pushing you away." His words were like daggers piercing my chest. Akash took a breath and continued with his assault, "I think you should get the divorce finalised and let her move on."

The helplessness led to anger, and I felt something crawl on my skin. I was angry at no one but myself. Who else could I blame for this?

"I'll go and check my daughter. Take care and think about it," Akash turned around to leave.

He had walked back a couple of steps when I called him out and said, "Send me the ideas for tomorrow's photoshoot."

Turning around, he gave me a nod and left.

***

An hour later, Chad joined me in my room. "So, tell me, what's going on." He had left Samira to spend some time alone with Natasha. They had met after nearly seven months and had a lot of things to catch up on.

Even though it was still morning, I ordered some drinks and snacks to give us company.

"Same old things," I replied with a shrug. "Dad's like always, butting his nose into my business and making things complicated. Everything between us is like a transaction of the barter system; do this, and you'll get this! I'm fed up listening to all this! But you know what's worse? I'm unable to stand up for myself!" I gnashed my teeth and gulped the drink in one shot.

"Calm down, bro. You need to stand strong for yourself! And by the way, your retail business is doing good after implementing your creative studio corner plan."

"Still!" I chided.

Chad consoled, "Jai, remember, the moment you stand up for what you really want, things will start falling in line!" He looked at me over the rim of his glass. "The question is, what is it you really want to stand up for?"

"For Natasha," I uttered immediately. "I don't want to divorce her... I want to be with her."

"Hmm, I see," Chad nodded in understanding. "So, have you told this to her?"

"I don't think I have the courage to do so," I confessed. "And now Natasha has agreed to marry Akash."

"Oh, I see," Chad nodded again and took a sip of his drink. "But are you sure she is happy about marrying him? I was with her this past hour, and I don't think she looked happy about it. On the contrary, she looked quite stressed."

I blinked and stared intently at Chad.

"Jai, confessing is never easy. There is always the fear of being rejected." He leaned forward and looked me in the eye. "Even I wasn't able to confess my love to Samira until she said she was going to leave Perth and stay in India forever with her parents. At that moment, everything blurred out, and I felt that if I didn't hold on to her and tie her to me, I would miss her terribly!"

"Then did you confess to her, right away?" I asked with a chuckle.

"Nope, I just confessed that I was the man from the pub she had met several years ago who had advised her to move on," Chad replied with a smile lingering on his face.

"Then?"

"Then what? That confession was not enough," Chad said, walking towards the window. "I had to gain her trust. I promised her that I would always be there for her and stand by her no matter what! You know, when someone's first relationship ends on a bad note, they go through a lot of pain. So, moving on for them is quite difficult. They don't trust anyone easily, even if you mean the world to them. They prefer to hide in a shell and ignore your love until they are made to confess."

"So did Samira confess her love to you?" I asked, walking over to him by the window-side.

"She did when Natasha told her, 'You are worse than Pallavi!'" Chad laughed.

"Natasha made Samira confess!" I exclaimed, quite surprised at the revelation.

He nodded. "Overcome with jealousy, Samira confessed right away that she loved me right from the start. She had recognised me long back that I was the same guy from the pub."

"So, before you came to know that she was the same girl, Samira had already figured out that it was you! But why didn't she tell that to you?" I asked, surprised that women could hide their thoughts so plainly under their sleeves!

"Her marriage with Arjun had failed miserably, and she was afraid that she would make the wrong choice and fall again," explained Chad.

My thoughts drifted towards Natasha. She never confessed about her having a boyfriend. Moreover, she was a virgin. Any guy could have fallen for her. She could have used me for good as her husband if she would have wanted.

"Jai, what happened?" asked Chad, wrapping his hand around my shoulder.

"I think I'm the only one who has made her suffer. I don't understand how to make up for my mistake," I asked. Then, taking a sip from my drink, I added, "The evening I carried her on my back, I felt that I could do this for life and would not get bored or ever repent."

"If you seriously feel for her, you will find a way," Chad said with a smile.

I wanted to meet her right then and was just about to excuse myself and run to her when I received a call from Akash.

"Natasha wants to complete the photoshoot today. After that, she wants to return to Mumbai by the first flight tomorrow," said Akash as soon as I picked up.

"Okay, where do you suggest we meet?" I asked.

"Meet us in an hour at the beach," he said, disconnecting the call.

"What happened?" asked Chad as I slumped down on the couch.

"Natasha wants to finish the shoot today so that she can fly to Mumbai tomorrow morning," I said, wondering what urgent work she had.

"Calm down, give her some time," Chad suggested and pulled me up.

"I guess I don't have that," I gave him a wry smile as we stepped out of the room. "She and Akash intend to marry as soon as I divorce her," I told Chad about the fire at the lawyer's office and how happy I was when I found the papers were burned.

"Jai, I am sure you love her more than you think you do," Chad gave me a meaningful look. "Your position appears complicated because you aren't aware of your feelings! It is not the importance of the relationship that keeps us together, but the force that pulls us towards each other that makes us stay in a relationship. If it was just an infatuation, you would have divorced her and moved on. But you don't want to move on. In fact, you are jealous of her getting married. This all means only one thing-" Chad paused as if teasing me to figure out the answer on my own.

"What?" I asked, impatient to know what he had to say. Sometimes, it is more difficult to ascertain your own feelings than others!

"You love her!" Chad relayed his conclusion. "I think you should confess to her before it is too late."

"Sorry for eavesdropping, but I have something to say." Akash's voice made us turn. He was just a couple of steps behind us. "I know how she stood up for you after the incident at Malshej Ghat. I've seen the videos. And I also sat with the creative director while he shot the ad today. I could see the longingness in her eyes," said Akash. "It's like she knows you are her world, and yet she denies it for some reason."

"She refuses it because she doesn't trust me anymore. I have broken her heart once and hence is reluctant," I said with a small smile. My eyes started to glisten, realising how I lost her because of my own foolishness.

"That doesn't stop her from longing for you," he said, passing his phone towards me. "Have a look."

My heart skipped a beat as I looked at the short video. Natasha's eyes followed my actions, and her face radiated a small smile each time I laughed talking to Soha. Even though she denied having feelings for me, her face depicted how much of an impact I had on her. Throughout, her eyes were observing me intently, talking about the expressions of her heart.

"Jai, you would make an awesome father," added Chad, looking at the video.

"Yeah, that too," Akash chuckled, and he eyed me with a frown. "You've cast magic on my daughter! She rarely speaks to strangers, but she seems to have fallen in love with you!"

I smiled inwardly at their compliments. I never imagined myself having a family. *However, when I think about being a father in future, I just know I want Natasha to be my partner and the mother to my children!*

I thought of holding my daughter in my arms with Natasha on the other side. The feeling was overwhelming, and I felt a tug in my heart.

"Jai?" I heard Chad call out, and I came out of my daydreams.

"I was just happy looking at..." I fumbled for the right words but couldn't figure out what to say. I felt a strong urge to rush over to Natasha and bare my heart to her. I just had to confess to her now! It was now or never! "I was just happy looking at her happiness while playing with Soha. I realised all Natasha ever wanted was someone that she could be happy with."

I smiled as I swiped through the photos and uttered, "I need her more than anything else in this world. Nothing makes sense without her. All this company, family, and everything else that I am trying to achieve are meaningless in front of her."

"Hmm, I see," Akash sighed. I saw him in deep thoughts, making some hard decisions. "Jai, I'll give you a week to confess to her. See what she decides. If she agrees, no worries, but if not, you will give her a divorce and let her decide her future."

Even though he sounded like we were trading her, I had no option. I had to get her anyhow!

"Thank you!" I said, giving him a hug.

Akash said in a grave voice, "I know how it feels when you lose someone you love. And I don't want her to lose her heart for the sake of mine."

"Right," said Chad, keeping a hand on Akash's shoulder.

"She's agreed to marry me to avoid you and move on, but I am sure she will regret the decision in her heart all her life," said Akash.

His honesty tugged at my heart. He was a really good friend of hers and was doing everything for her happiness; otherwise, I didn't deserve the chance.

"Thank you, my friend," I said again and hurried away to look for Natasha. Unfortunately, I was short on time, and she was avoiding me like the plague. I didn't know where to start as each step felt like I was walking on broken pieces of glass.

CHAPTER XXV

Playing with Soha had calmed me down, but I was overcome with guilt for having screamed at Akash. He was nowhere at fault. Everything was because of Jai! Ever since we met again, all he wanted was to get close to me, get touchy-feely with me! And I'm sure his act of concern was just so that he could have sex with me!

The thought of the word sex brought forth the memories of our encounter in the shower. I blinked away the tears, cursed myself for skipping a beat at every drop of a hat and closed my eyes shut.

But no matter how much effort I put into strengthening myself, I cry... I become soft and silly.

As Soha was tired, I left her with her grandmother in their room and returned to mine. Blurry eyed, I tried to insert the key in the keyhole, but for some reason, it was showing me an attitude much like Jai! Everything wrong in my life was his fault! So, while cursing him under my breath, I tried to insert the key again.

An unexpected touch on my shoulder made me jump and whirl.

"Hey, sweetie!" Samira greeted with a big and warm smile.

Wide-eyed and in a daze, I stared at her for a few seconds. "Samira!" I cried out happily and engulfed her in my arms.

She rocked me back and forth, like old times, smiling ear to ear.

"Hi, Natasha!" Chad, a few steps behind, let me know of his presence.

"Hi, Chad," I replied, wiping away my tears. I opened the door to my room and let the two in. "Would you guys like some coffee?" I asked.

"I'd love to," replied Samira, slumping down on the couch. "This one's been a rushed journey!"

"Ah!" interrupted Chad. "Why don't you girls catch up while I look for Jai?"

"Sure!" Samira nodded, waving him away.

When the door closed after Chad, I slumped down beside Samira. "I'm sorry, Sam-" I started to say, but she placed a palm over my mouth.

"At first, I was angry at you for skipping my wedding, but then I realised I would have done the same," she consoled me.

Tears glistened in my eyes as I hugged her and cried my heart out. "Sam, things have In so bad the last few months...hic... I don't know where to begin...hic..."

She knew about the fake marriage and *Ma*, but I still wanted to tell her on my own. I tried to speak between tears, but the incoherent voice sounded gibberish, and I cried even harder.

"Shu..." Samira tried to calm me down while patting my back. "I know it all. Jai told us everything."

I sobbed and sobbed as my body quivered in her embrace. She gently caressed my back as if lulling a child.

When I had calmed down enough to continue, I whispered between my gasps, "My real parents are alive."

"Really?" Samira leaned back to look at me with surprise in her voice. "That's great news!"

Was it really great news? I hung my head down, thinking about my childhood.

When I didn't reply, Samira continued her queries, "How did you come to know? Do they know about you?"

I shook my head and told her about my childhood.

"I don't get it," Samira uttered with a frown. "They knew where you were. So why did they never return to take you?"

I shrugged my shoulders, "Maybe, I was a burden to them."

"You know," Samira lifted my chin and looked me in the eye. "It's all right to assume at times, but at other times, to get your peace of mind, you should find out the truth. I think you should visit them and talk directly."

"Yeah... I guess," I sighed. But before that, I would have to wrap up the photoshoot, and my mind was reluctant to face Jai!

"By the way, what's up with Jai and you?" Samira held my hand and tucked my hair behind my ears. "How come you two are working together?"

"One thing led to the other..." I said, thinking of how things transpired, completely out of my control. "I needed money to take care of *Ma*, and nothing was working out. So I decided to try out modelling and incidentally my college friend, Akash, was the Advertising Director. His company had just signed an agreement with Jai's for their rebranding campaign, and that's how I landed here." I paused for a while and added, "If I had known Jai was the owner, I would never have come here."

Samira wrapped her arms around my shoulders, making me rest my head on her chest. She gently fingered my hair as if pampering a child. "He screwed up big time. But you know, he's not that much of an asshole. At least that's what I feel... He is genuinely concerned about you. He didn't need to rush to your side when he heard of your *Ma*'s news. But he did, didn't he?"

"I thought so too!" I remarked, my chest hurting at his mention. "But all he wants is my body. He is just infatuated with me. He doesn't really love me. His father has arranged his marriage with some rich girl, and he agreed."

"Oh!" Samira was taken aback. "I thought he was in love with you... maybe not..."

"Akash asked me to marry him, and I agreed," I added while Samira was deep in thought.

"Huh?" She blinked at me, her eyes questioning my sudden decision.

"I need to move on..."

She sighed, understanding how I felt and kissed my forehead. "Of course, my darling. It's for the best!"

After a while, I sat up straight. I felt much better after letting it all out. It was time to face my fear! I washed my face and ordered some coffee. "I should wrap up the photoshoot and return to Mumbai. High time I met my real parents."

Samira smiled. "Of course!"

After finishing my coffee, I called Akash and told him about my decision. "Sure. The weather seems good. I'll get things ready in an hour and give you a call."

After I disconnected the call, I had an idea and turned to Samira. "Do you want to meet Soha? She's Akash's daughter, an angel!" My eyes glittered in enthusiasm at her thought as I pulled Samira even before she agreed to meet Soha.

***

Soha was playing with Barbie's Cinderella set when her grandma let us into the room.

"Aunty!" she jumped up at our sight. I hugged and introduced Samira to her. I played with her for a while, and Samira chatted with her grandma.

When I joined them, Samira said to me, "You seem to like her too much! Your eyes turn affectionate, and it is evident how much you dote on her!"

I glanced at Samira and beamed, "When I'm with her, I'm just happy! Besides, she reminds me of the mini-me. Like me, she doesn't have a mother, so I think I associate well with her thoughts. I guess that's why I like her so much."

"Hmm," Samira nodded, her eyes on Soha. "Growing up without a mother is quite difficult... and you should be forever grateful for having found someone like *Ma*, who took care of you so selflessly."

After a call from Akash, we said goodbye to Soha. While Samira went to find Chad, I hurried towards the photoshoot. The stylist ushered me into a van when I arrived at the location. I was dressed in a lacy floral dress with red flowers. My hair was tied in french braids, and my eyes were accentuated by subtle eyelashes and mascara.

The moment I stepped out of the van, someone whistled.

My first thought was, it's Jai, and my legs froze. But when I faced the direction and found it was Akash, I silently let out a sigh of relief.

"You look lovely!" he said, walking over to me. "Come, let's get going. Everything's ready."

"Thank you," I replied, following behind him. But for some reason, the nape of my neck felt itchy. By the time I reached the car parked in the sand, I realised the hook of the dress on the back had come undone, and a few strands of my hair were stuck to it.

I called for the stylist, and she made me sit in the car with my back to her to fix the problem. After properly hooking the dress, she had to redo the latter half of my braid.

"Akash, where is Natasha? When are we starting the shoot?" Jai's voice made me stiffen up.

"Yeah, looks like she is missing," said Akash with a chuckle.

I jumped out of the car to make my presence known and remarked with a straight face, "Can we do the shoot fast? I am tired!"

Jai let out a laugh. "Your tantrums are no less than that of a supermodel's!" Then, before I could retort, he turned to Akash and asked, "What's the sequence?"

As if that was the cue, the photographer appeared and explained it to us. "All right! You are to stand beside the car. Jai, you have to hold her waist, pull her close and lean down on her. Natasha, you'll have to bend your knees and lean back. Look into each other's eyes as if the whole world has blurred out. Understood?"

When we nodded, Jai turned to me and asked, "May I?" He held out his hand to mine.

The moment I slid my hands into his, he moved forward, held my waist with the other hand and pulled me closer. My heart started to sink when I leaned back.

"Jai's perfect, now look into his eyes, Natasha," the photographer's voice sounded from a distance.

"You'll not find anyone else who looks at you this way in the whole world," Jai said, his eyes gazing intently into mine.

I frowned and stared back at him. *What is he up to now? Why can't he just keep quiet?* "This is not a video shoot. But, please, can you not say anything?" I said to him with a straight face.

"This is a video shoot, honey! Make up some lovey-dovey lines," he smirked at my flustered expression.

"What?" I straightened up and stared from Jai to Akash.

"Oh yes, I forgot," Akash said apologetically. "Natasha, please act along. Say something nice, whatever you feel in your heart!"

What the hell! I felt like stomping my foot and walking away.

"Okay, let's start again," said Akash.

Jai pulled me closer in a flash, and I gasped for air in his arms as he bent me down and looked intently, "I didn't know I loved you until now. From this day onwards to the last day of my life, I will be forever yours."

I blinked, looking lost in his eyes as he said those words with conviction.

"I don't know what to say," I started to stammer, unable to think of anything.

"Close your eyes," he said, placing his hand over them, "and just feel us... Think of how you felt about me in Perth and say something."

His soft voice was like magic, and I was transported to the moment we spent on the cruise ship. "I don't know whether I should trust you or not, but my heart beats every time I see you..." I heard myself murmur.

"Natasha, I'm a fool for letting you go just like that. I want us to be together again, feel the lows and highs of life together..." Jai's voice was mixed with love and longing.

I opened my eyes in disbelief. He sounded way too real.

"Change the position," said Akash's voice boomed from the loudspeaker.

Jai lifted me up and placed his arms on my back. He looked me in the eye, "You and I are made for each other, Natasha. Let's give ourselves another chance."

I wanted to refute and say so many things, but I smiled, and no words came out of my mouth. We were doing a shoot and were surrounded by a crowd.

"Mama!" called out a little voice, and I turned around.

Soha came running towards us.

Before I could predict what was going on, Jai lifted her up in his arms. He swayed her in the air and wrapped her closer in an embrace.

"Here you go, Natasha. Your fairy tale is complete," he said, kissing my forehead.

Claps roared as he said that, and Soha slipped down from his arms.

"How did I do, Dad?" Soha skipped towards and asked Akash.

He gave her a thumbs up. "You did fantastic, my little angel!"

I stood rooted to the spot with a bewildered look on my face. What just happened? One moment we were doing a photoshoot, the next moment a video while recollecting our times in Perth. And just when I uttered my deepest desire, Soha entered the scene, and it was all over!

I could not clearly define how exactly I felt right then. I was perplexed, no doubt, but also relieved. The feelings of love that I was unable to confess otherwise, I told him now. Yet, I was also sad because being loved back was a futile dream.

"Shall we go, Natasha?" asked Jai, reaching out for my hand.

I nodded, breaking out of my chain of thoughts.

Mehta came forward clapping, "Akash, I must say what a wonderful capture. 'A complete family ride, for that special fairy tale experience'. What a caption, my friend!"

"Oh, the last part of adding my daughter to the scene and 'fairy tale experience' in the caption is from him," Akash said, pointing at Jai.

I looked at Jai as he held my hand. I was baffled, thinking why would he suggest something he doesn't believe in!

"This calls for a party," said Mehta, shaking hands with Jai and Akash. "Let's meet up in the hotel lounge at six!"

"Absolutely!" agreed Akash and turned to me, "Nats, please join us."

"Sure." I nodded and excused myself to change out of the clothes. As I changed in the van, through the tinted glasses, I saw Samira and Chad strolling hand in hand in the sand. My lips curled into a soft smile; they looked good together, and I was truly happy for them.

***

When I arrived at the lounge at six in the evening, the party had already started. People were huddled in groups, some chatting, some drinking, and some dancing to the songs being played by the DJ.

I spotted Akash and made my way towards him. Before I could catch up with him, he picked up two drinks from the bar counter and walked away. I was almost at his heels and was just about to call out to him when he handed one glass to Jai, and they clinked their drinks. "You are awesome!" I heard Akash appreciate Jai. "How did you come up with that fairy tale idea?"

My hand that was raised to reach out to Akash faltered. I took a step back, but my ears strained to hear Jai's reply.

"It's all because of Natasha. She's crazy about fairy tales!" Jai chuckled, sipping his drink. "After losing her, I realised, a woman needs to be cherished. What could be a better example than a fairy tale experience with their dream man?" He raised his glass and added, "And thanks to you, I got the opportunity to confess my feelings to her. It's so hard to open up!"

"That's fine. I gave you a fair chance to do your bit," Akash replied. "But it was you with the dialogues."

"I just thought it would fit in well with the theme," Jai said, looking ahead. "Moreover, it was simple, and I was sure Natasha would pose well without feeling awkward; else, she would fret, making it all appear on her face!"

Akash nodded. "Right! She is a bit sensitive that way..."

"I know, that makes everything all the more scary! I don't know how she'll react when she comes to know the truth about her family." I heard Jai sigh.

Akash glanced at Jai and asked, "You mean, her real family?"

When Jai nodded, Akash asked, "How did you know them, anyway?"

I glanced at the back of Jai and Akash with a frown on my face. Why were they talking about my biological family?

"I grew up with his brother. We were childhood friends. I don't know how he ended up being a gangster," Jai replied.

I froze at his statement. Then, clenching my jaws, I stepped between the men. "Is the fun around here over that you are digging on my other personal issues?!"

Jai and Akash both jolted as they glanced at me. Jai started to clarify, "Natasha, we weren't talking bad about you. We-"

"Thankfully, I heard what all I should. Thanks to you both, I know where I stand, and also, thanks for letting me know you knew my brother. I hope the surprises you have up your sleeves end here because now, I am fed up," I yelled and then turned to leave.

"Natasha, I didn't know he was your brother then," he stated.

"You didn't know he was my brother, but when I told you my story, you realised the truth but stayed mum. You took advantage, knowing I was lonely!" I vented on his face and then turned away towards the door. "It is not your mistake. I trusted you to be at least a good friend, but you couldn't even keep that relationship!"

"Natasha, you are wrong!" Jai rushed after me. "I very well know how to keep my friendship. I agree I have made mistakes, but I have stood by you always!"

His words made me stop and turn around. "Stood by me as in being faithful and loyal like a dog? Isn't that what you said on the cruise... only dogs can be so faithful!"

Jai clenched his jaws and said, "I remember saying that. But didn't you say love meant caring for a person, missing that special someone in your life? Sharing all your life with that person and that one kiss from them is all you need to survive!"

"Ah, great, so you used all that to gain my trust. Thank you, and also thanks for using me!"

"Natasha!!" he called aloud, but I banged the door and came back to my room and locked it.

Packing my bags, I called for a cab; however, I found Samira standing there when I opened the door.

"Natasha, what's wrong? Jai said-" she started to say.

"Do whatever you want but don't take his name before me. And please don't stop me as well. I'm going to Mumbai," I said, giving her a hug. "I must go now."

She nodded her head, giving me a peck on my cheek, "Take care and call me once you reach."

As I turned to leave, I saw Jai standing there. Ignoring him, I walked towards the exit, but he came near my cab, "Natasha, it's not good to leave in a hurry. At least listen to what I have to say!"

"I don't want to listen!" I screamed at him. "Because all you do is lie! I can't trust you anymore!" I opened the door of the cab to step inside.

He said behind me, "Let me come with you, please."

"Jai, I want some peace now. Leave me alone! And email me the papers."

"Wait!" Jai held my hand, stopping me from moving inside. My heart raced, thinking he was about to kiss me like last time.

"Jai, I don't want any more dram-" I said and inched behind to be away from him.

He pulled me tight in his grip and hugged me. "Natasha, I have broken your heart before, but believe me, all I want in my life is you! I have been running around the world to set up my business and whatnot, but the thing that really calms my mind is *you*."

My feet wobbled hearing his straightforward words. I could see he was straining himself to speak up. I felt like I should give him a chance, but acknowledging the pain he had given me recently, I chose to ignore him. "I'm not the same Natasha anymore. So let me go. I need to figure out many things," I said, pushing him away.

"Natasha, you are correct in your thinking, but please give me a chance," he demanded.

I stared at him, my brows furrowed. I had to end this stalemate or else he wouldn't let me go. I sighed and uttered, "Give me some time to think."

His hold on my arm loosened, and I slouched on my seat. He stood there tugging his hands inside his pocket while I wiped the wetness dropping off my cheeks. "Let's go," I muttered to the cab driver.

Memories and mistakes flooded my mind while tears dropped from my eyes. During the entire journey in the outstation taxi from Goa to Mumbai, I kept my eyes open, but his thoughts made me feel guilty about my decisions. It was late in the morning when I reached Mumbai. As soon as I entered home, I lay down on my bed and slept like a log due to mental and physical exhaustion.

***

The next morning after I got up, I searched the internet about my brother's death. I wanted to get the contact information of my parents. After hundreds of calls to various news channels, I finally got the address. But when I got there, no one answered the door. My incessant knocking alerted one of the neighbours. When I told her that I was a relative, she immediately gave me directions to a hospital.

I reached the hospital and enquired about them. I was nervous, and my heart started to weaken with each step I took.

"Yes, who are you looking for?" asked the lady wearing a pale yellow sari, with its borders crumpled. She was feeding something to a man lying on the bed. She looked familiar. The only things I noticed were the dark circles around her eyes and wrinkled face. The man on the bed looked familiar too, but his bones looked more prominent than his skin. I felt my throat choke up in pain as I associated the word 'parents' with them. They were my parents, but I didn't have the courage to confess it to them.

I looked around the hospital ward, where my father was lying. It was very peculiar and smelly. Unable to bear the sight of them suffering so much, I enquired about them with the nurse.

"He has appendicitis. He needs surgery, but they don't have money, so we are waiting for funds. We have asked them to go to the government hospital, but they aren't willing to leave," said the nurse.

I wanted to argue with the nurse. If this was the condition of a private hospital, what would be the position of a government hospital? But I knew it was better not to waste any time. "Okay, please arrange for his operation. I will pay the bills right away." I felt at ease when the nurse carried out the formalities, and the operation theatre was arranged for him.

Sometime later, as the hospital staff took him to the operation theatre, the nurse explained to the lady, "It will be a minor operation, and he can be discharged in a day or two."

"Thank you so much for all this help," said the lady to the nurse.

"Not us. She paid the bills," said the nurse pointing towards me.

The lady came to me with her hands joined, thanking me for the favour. I felt like holding her hands and telling her that it was unnecessary, but I couldn't. I just gave a small smile and nodded. No emotion was coming through me. I observed them but didn't feel like I belonged with them. Maybe it was because they had left me to struggle when I needed them.

When you don't connect emotionally in a relationship, you don't feel anything for the person. I felt the need to help them because of humanity, but otherwise, I did not feel anything even though I met them after so many years.

I went to get medicines mentioned by the doctor. When I returned, I saw the lady hugging someone while he was holding the hands of the man lying on the bed.

Maybe some well-wisher, I thought and went inside. However, to my surprise, the lady saw me, hurried over to my side and hugged me at once while crying. "My Lali! My daughter! I missed you all these days."

"No, I am not your daughter." I panicked and tried to move away, but I couldn't move an inch. I looked up for help, and to my utter surprise, I saw Jai standing there holding the man, who was my so-called father.

My eyes burned with fury as I stared at Jai. *This is not done at all!* I said to myself and forcefully removed her hands from me.

"No, I am not your daughter, Lali. I am Natasha Meher, Miss Karuna Meher's daughter," I said with chagrin and moved away.

"I'm sorry, my child. I understand what you must have gone through, but there wasn't a day I didn't cry for you. My girl, we were helpless. We didn't have enough money to support your upbringing," the lady tried to hug me.

"No! You don't understand what I went through," I shrieked even though I was aware of my surroundings. But, I didn't give a damn! Because only me and my *Maknew* what I had gone through! "You shouldn't be called a mother, nor you a father," I uttered, my voice full of spite. "I did what I thought I should do to pay back for what you did for me when I was a child, and now I don't need to be with you, just like how you left me."

I turned around and walked out of the ward, dismissing the calls of the lady echoing in the background, asking for forgiveness. All this would have never happened if Jai hadn't interfered. I wish I could just take him out of my system once and for all. *Yes, I had gone to ask my parents why they left me, but seeing them, I didn't feel anything. So, I thought I would just help them and walk away. After all, why should I give them a chance to know that I am alive and doing good in my life even without them?!*

But whatever thoughts I had, Jai had to intervene, foil my plans and drive me crazy!

As I rushed out, I recalled how he had held the lady. That was enough for me to feel betrayed by him again.

I wanted to coil into my cocoon, and go back to the warm love of my *Ma*. So I left for my village, booking a cab right away. Now, my reason for coming to Mumbai was anyway done!

CHAPTER XXVI

Jai

Whosoever said, 'Once you are in love, everything will fall in place', hadn't met reality. I wonder why your heart acts like a crazy machine when it starts loving someone.

I rushed out of the hospital, consoling her parents that I would bring her back, but before I could catch up with her, she boarded a cab.

I don't know why this girl had a habit of running away when it came to facing things. I followed her cab but lost her in the heavy traffic. However, I could guess where she was headed as the route led to Diveagar, her village. The sky had turned orange, and sundown was not far, but the village was still an hour's drive. I had driven down from Goa last night, rested for just a couple of hours before starting off again running after Natasha. The exhaustion was slowly starting to take over my senses, but I could not stop to rest. I had to speak to her!

My eyes felt heavy suddenly, and I lost my grip on the steering wheel. Sometime later, someone opened the door and patted my cheeks, asking me my name and address.

I felt lifeless as I fell down from my seat into the man's arms out of the window.

"Phone, Natasha, my wife," I said faintly, then blinked my eyes, drifting into a slumber before Natasha's smiley face flashed for a second.

I smiled as I murmured, "I love you."
***

I woke up with a giddy feeling. My eyes at first couldn't adjust to the bright lights of the room, but then eventually,

I could see the pastel blue walls.

"Nurse, call the doctor! He is awake!" said someone urgently, and I turned my head in the direction. It was my bro, Chad.

He caught my gaze and came to my side. "How are you feeling now?"

I nodded and noticed the IV drip connected to the back of my palm. The voices of my mother and father reached my ears, and I tried to widen my eyes. Mom and Dad were hovering over one behind the other, with an anxious look, asking innumerable questions. Behind them stood Samira, her face just as worried as the rest.

The face I was looking for was not there. I closed my eyes but opened them again a few minutes later when the doctor arrived. He sent everyone out and took his time to examine me. He asked me a couple of questions, and when I answered them to his satisfaction, though in a croaking voice, he smiled at me and said, "You met with a road accident. Thanks to modern technology and airbags, even though your car overturned, you just have two fractured ribs, a concussion, and some internal bleeding in your spleen." He then flashed a playful smile and added, "In case you are wondering, how long you've been knocked out, you've not slept for long, only for seventy-two hours!"

Taken aback, I stared at him wide-eyed before giving him a faint yet grateful smile. The moment he pulled back the curtains around my bed, mom and dad rushed in through the door.

"How's he doing?" Dad was the first to ask.

"I'm all right," I answered.

The doctor nodded, agreeing with me and added, "He is doing quite well for the accident he had, but we'll keep him under observation for two the next two days."

Mom and Dad sighed in relief, and the creases on their forehead flattened. The doctor gave a few instructions, to which my parents nodded obediently.

"Where's Natasha?" I asked the moment he left.

"Why would she be here?" Dad questioned back, raising a brow.

Before blacking out, I clearly remember asking someone to call her from my phone. Did she really not come? I felt disappointed but asked, "Does she know I met with an accident?"

"She knows," said Dad avoiding my eyes and added, "It's best you forget about her and move on with your life."

Chad and Samira had entered the room some time ago while the doctor laid out his commands. I glanced at them for an affirmation. Instead, Samira avoided my gaze while Chad said aloud, "I'll let everyone know you are awake." Then, without a second look, he and Samira walked out.

My mind numbed out. The entire day passed by. Many people visited; doctors, family, friends, relatives, associates, but the one my heart was desperately waiting for, did not arrive. How could she not come and visit me? She was ready to sit next to me and risk her life while I drove to Malshej Ghat, then how could she not come now when I had such a major accident?? I was sure if she knew about my accident, she would travel from heaven to hell to see me. And here it had been three days, but she had not visited! It was hard to believe.

Something's wrong! Something is dreadfully wrong! My heart refused to trust my father's words. There had to be something I was missing!

I thought of speaking to Chad, but he didn't drop in after the morning visit. As the day came to an end, the dissatisfaction from her absence started to get on my nerves. Is she so angry that she doesn't want to see me, even though I'm in this state?

I was losing my mind over it, and then my father appeared before me, holding a brown envelope. He took out the papers from within and placed them on the bed-side table. "Here, sign these."

The moment I glanced at the bold header on the front page, I knew what it was, and my jaws clenched. They were divorce papers.

My father passed me a pen and added, "She signed the papers and handed them to Chad."

I threw the papers away. "I don't believe it. Must be one of your tricks."

"My tricks?" My father gaped at me, his eyes narrowing with every passing second. "What will I get by tricking you? You can check the signature and verify whether it's hers or not." He picked up the papers from the floor and placed them back on the table.

"Your wish, but don't delay it. We'll sort this out before returning to Perth. I can't let you stay here alone and work on that lethargic car of yours which always puts you in trouble," he said, taking a seat on the attendant's bed.

I looked away from him, and he continued, "First that girl, then this car company, it has ruined your life. I think it's better you start a car company or whatever damn thing you want in Perth, where the resources are good, and people are worth it."

His words made my blood boil. If this is what he thought of me, it was high time for me to clarify that I was free to do whatever I wanted in my life!

"Jai," said Chad, entering the room. It looked like he wanted to say something, but reading the tension between my father and me, he quietly walked in and pulled a chair.

"Dad, you never understood what I wanted in life." I let out a wry laugh." All you've ever done is try to influence my wishes and desires with money."

"What are you saying?" he blurted out, turning towards me in disbelief.

"I think if not for your terms and conditions, I never would have played around with Natasha's feelings! I would have taken her seriously in my life. You influenced me to believe that there would be many girls like Natasha who could be bought with money," I uttered, feeling a dull pain in my heart.

"You'll find plenty of girls much better than Natasha for sure-" he started to say.

"Yes," I interrupted him. "You can find girls much better than Natasha with money like you said, but there is only one Natasha whom I love more than anyone else."

"You have gone mad after your accident!" he snapped.

"It was Natasha who believed and trusted me with my dreams. She stood by me even though she knew the car might be a huge risk for her life," I defended my love.

"Then why the hell did she not come?" he demanded, standing up.

I made eye contact with him and asked, "If she didn't come, then how the hell did you come to know about my accident?"

Dad flinched and became quiet. But the next second, he recollected himself and replied, "Chad informed us."

I turned to him and asked, "Chad, how did you come to know?"

Dad turned towards Chad. Though his back was facing me, I could see that he was gesturing something.

"Chad, how did you come to know about my accident?" I asked again, hoping he wouldn't lie to me.

"Natasha called me up after she had reached the hospital where you were admitted," Chad replied, looking at me while ignoring Dad's stares.

I felt my heart skip a beat. A smile erupted on my lips. I just knew Natasha would have come!

"Then?" I asked Chad.

"I called up uncle, and he-" Chad started to say.

"Listen, whatever it is, I can't bear the sight of her!" Dad butt-in. "I had told her to forget about you in Perth, but she found a way to reach you here again. I should have paid her to keep her away! Girls like her will do anything for money!"

What did he say to Natasha in Perth? My ears perked up, and I felt like my veins would burst anytime with anger, but I kept my mouth shut. It seemed like he had said something incorrigible to her. Come what may, I shall get him to confess.

He took a breath and continued, "As she has already signed the papers, it means she doesn't want to stay with you. So then why are you creating a fuss and refusing to sign the papers?"

"How did you get these papers?" I asked. My brows creased as I corrected myself, "How did *she* get these papers? I never gave them to her."

"She asked me to give them to her," Dad said without blinking a lie.

"Is it?" I challenged him, raising a brow. I knew my dad very well. He indeed would have stated some terms and conditions that compelled her to sign. Otherwise, there was no way things would have happened so quickly while I was asleep!

"Jai, I don't want you to think so much about this girl. Get well soon, and we will go away from this messy place," he said, throwing tantrums like a wealthy businessman caught up in a small town cow shed.

"I am not going anywhere from India, and I'm also not leaving her," I affirmed, watching him intently.

"Oh, God! Why have you become so foolish?" Dad looked frustrated, as if I was a complete failure despite all his troubles to groom me. "How many times I have told you, think rationally! You must always weigh your pros and cons, act like a businessman. Learn something from Chad," he added, pointing at Chad.

I let out a small laugh.

"What is so funny?" he asked.

"I always envied Chad because each time you told me to follow him, I felt inferior. I felt so wrong in my own eyes. Like I didn't deserve anything, I was just worthless. Since I always compared myself to him, I felt utterly helpless." I paused and glanced at Chad with a wholehearted appreciation for him. "Then later, I noticed, even Chad made mistakes, but he learnt from them. Moreover, he stood by his independence!" His grandma was totally against his marriage with Samira, but he stood his ground and refused to bow down to pressure.

Chad smiled back at me and nodded.

"He followed his decision and stood by Samira when she needed it. He also brought the father and daughter together, even though he didn't need to." Chad's smile grew with every word I spoke about him.

"I always envied him but never saw how much he sacrificed for everything he achieved in his life," I paused, taking a sigh. "But now I don't envy him anymore. Instead, I look up to him, not as my competitor, but as an elder brother whom I will always look up to because whatever he has achieved on his own, I have to still do that, and I know

I can do it," I said with conviction.

"Jai, without my money, you can't do anything, and this car business will be a flop just like your retail business!" Dad chided.

"Uncle," Chad joined the conversation. "Jai's retail business has made half a million profit last month. He brought in some changes which the customers are responding to very well. Even though he was here focusing on his car company, he managed his retail business as well," he pointed out objectively.

"Dad, my car company is doing good. When our company's reputation was targeted, and the reporters were flocking, challenging the safety of Ninja Super Avenue, Natasha stood by me, took the ride with me, to prove that it was safe to ride," I said. I then added, "In fact, it added as a viral boost to the sales."

Dad calmed down for a second, unable to say anything.

"Oh! By the way, Dad," I looked up at my father with confidence. "I have signed a deal with Asia's biggest automobile magazine, where I have to provide a new car design every six months, and they would pay a million dollars for each design."

While Dad stood bewildered, unable to comprehend what I just said, Chad let out an enthusiastic cry. "Oh my God! That's just awesome news! Congratulations, bro!" Chad walked over to me and patted my shoulder.

"Dad, trust me, I can take care of my car as well as the retail business, but none of this will make any sense to me if Natasha is not by my side." He fiddled with his pen as I said.

"After years, I figured out what I want in life, just because of Natasha. I believe *love* teaches you to reach out to new levels, especially when you want to protect and care for the ones you love," I said, a smile stretching my lips.

I never believed I would say these things to Dad, but right now, I was overflowing with emotions for Natasha, which made it easy for me to fight with the world.

"Dad?" I called out to him, hoping to hear what was running in his mind.

Just then, the door opened, and mom walked in. She looked at me, then over to Dad and said, "I was standing outside listening to your conversation."

"How can you even think of all this, when he was fighting for his life?"

Taking a deep breath, she continued, "I can't ever forgive you for that and I have never suggested you anything because I believed and trusted that you will do good for Jai, but-"

Dad looked at her, puzzled. She sighed then walked next to him, "We have only one son, and he is sure of what he wants. This time, let's not give him any terms and conditions. I think he will do well on his own."

Mom held Dad's palms in assurance while exchanging glances with him. "Years ago, I trusted you with my love, and today as well, I trust you with the same love. I have always kept quiet and accepted your decisions out of this love for you." She took his hands in hers and then continued, "But please listen to his heart as well. Everything can't be weighed with money. We should let him do what he wants."

"But what about us, our dream to settle down while he takes care of everything in Perth?" Dad asked. "Who will look after my company?"

"I am sure he will do something about that as well, and times are changing. He can take charge of the company from any place in the world," she reasoned. "But right now, if he doesn't get what he needs, we may not be able to call ourselves his parents."

"You don't understand. Natasha is not up to our standards. What will we say to our friends and family?" Dad argued.

I was about to say something when Mom showed me her palm to stop. "Just because our status has changed over the last two decades, did you forget that we also come from the middle class?"

"Ours was a different case. We didn't have to answer anyone, but now people will question us! Remember how they questioned her when she was with us and told, good, that she was gone. She doesn't fit in with us." Dad objected with a sullen look.

I felt like laughing at Dad's thoughts. I wished to put some sense into him but kept silent. Luckily, Mom was talking on my behalf for the first time.

"You know I never listened to Jai because I knew that as a father, you would do good for him, but I never knew that for you, society came first, not Jai!" She sounded extremely disappointed. "If Jai likes her, it's all we should ever need, not her status, not any society."

As she stopped talking, Dad fell quiet. He looked troubled as if he was being force-fed a bitter medicine. After what seemed like a very long time, Dad breathed out a dejected sigh. He patted her hands softly and nodded assuringly. Finally, he glanced at me and said, "Well then, if you know what you need and have decided to stand by it, I won't become a hurdle in your path." He stood up and patted my back. "Wish you all the best, my son! Every father desires that their son lives up to be independent and grow to become a mature man. I suppose, today, you. have become one, and I am happy for that." He glanced at the divorce papers and let out another sigh as if thinking of something. Everyone's eyes were on him.

"I forced her to sign the papers," he mumbled, sounding apologetic. "I told her if she loved you and wanted me to invest in your company, then she should sign the papers and never appear before you."

"How could you!" Mom exclaimed and made him face her.

"Dad, how could you!" I exclaimed at the same time.

He scratched his head and looked away. "All right, all right. I'm sorry! Look, I'm tearing it away. Now I won't come between you!" With that, he took the papers from the bedside table, tore them into pieces and threw them into the dustbin. He then clumped down on the attendant's bed, his face hanging down.

"You can be so mean at times," *Ma* grumbled, making a grumpy face. "I don't know why I fell in love with someone so mean and tricky like you."

I smiled at my mother. I think this was the first time I'd heard her accusing him of anything. He kept his head cast down, listening to her scolding without a single retort.

"You've always behaved like this to get what you want! At first, your target was me, and now it's our son!" she charged him.

"How did he target you, aunty?" Probed Chad with a big smile while holding my other hand in his, enjoying the sweet barter between mom and dad.

"He threatened that he would drink poison if I didn't agree to marry him, and then, later on, I found out it wasn't poison at all. It was some cough syrup!" Mom grunted in anger.

"God, dad! How could you do this?" I joked, but mom seemed to get angrier at my jibe.

"That's not all! He confessed about it one evening when he was completely drunk! By then, you had already come into our lives, and I was in love with this insane character," related mom, sitting down at the foot of my bed.

"Now, what can you do, mom?" I nudged her to make more for such revelations.

"I will divorce him!" she stated bluntly.

Dad jumped upright. "Why divorce after all these years? And I confessed that I made a mistake, so why do you want to separate? Where will I go without you?" His voice quacked in panic.

"Then promise me, you won't play any more of your tricks on our son or me!" She stood up and glared at him fiercely.

Dad walked towards her and held her hands. "I promise! I've already got my lesson, and trust me, I won't do any more of such things ever!"

Puppy eyed, he looked at her and pleaded apologetically a couple of times more. Mom finally agreed and let him hold her in his arms.

"Now, your turn," said Chad, squeezing my hands.

I nodded and asked, "Please get me out of here and also, can you find out where she is?"

"Though you're scheduled to be discharged the day after tomorrow, let me see what I can do. And she's in Diveagar," he said. "Sleep well tonight. I'll drive you there tomorrow."

CHAPTER XXVII

Natasha

Sending out a message to Akash and Tanisha that I was heading to my village and need some alone time, I put my phone on mute. However, thoughts took a toll on my mind and I was exhausted by the time I reached home, but more than that, I wanted to hold onto *Ma's* old clothes and feel her. After your dear ones leave you, their belongings are the only thing left to give you their warmth. I closed my eyes and cried, clutching them in my embrace.

"You are my *Ma*and no one else can take your place!" I consoled myself. My *Ma* did so much more than my actual parents ever did. So, even if they apologised a million times, I couldn't feel anything for the people who left me to face an unknown world at such a tender age.

"Jai, I'll never forgive you," I muttered, the pain he had put me through still fresh in my heart. Every time I have tried to shake him off and take care of my life in my way, he has barged in unannounced and made a mess.

It all began because of my idiotic heart, which skipped whenever Jai came to pick up coffee at The Grind.

I had fallen for his charming looks at first sight! To discourage myself, I refused him entry into the cafe a couple of times, stating that we were closed, but deep down in my heart, I always waited to see him.

When I had to leave The Grind, one of my many regrets was that I would never get to see him again. However, destiny made him my boss at the retail store I applied to work for.

Falling in love with him was easy for a crack nut like me, but even after the day I had decided to move on, destiny brought him right before me again.

Why did it happen this way? I felt frustrated! When we are supposed to move on from things or people, why do we keep thinking of them?

It is all my fault! I need to keep my mind occupied, or I'll keep thinking of him at all times! But my newfound purpose of helping orphan children seemed like a distant dream. Cooking at an orphanage wouldn't help other children who needed support. I had to think of an out of the box solution to this problem. I knew, only then would my heart be at peace.

The incessant ringing of my phone made me come out of my thoughts and I lazily reached out to answer it, without checking the caller ID. "Yes?"

"Your husband has met with an accident. He looks serious. We are taking him to a Gokhale Hospital in Jaigarh," said the man in a panicked voice.

Fearing the worst, I forgot to breathe, my legs gave away, and I landed on my knees.

"Hello?" The man asked, getting no response from me.

In a shaky voice, I answered and took down the details of the hospital. The town was an hour's drive from Diveagar. I grabbed my bag and rushed towards the bus stop to catch one of the frequent buses travelling towards the town.

Just as I settled into the bus, I sat wondering if it was the wrong number. Immediately, I checked the call logs on my phone. The last incoming call was from Jai's number.

My heart started to sink, and I clenched my fist for strength, hoping for him to be safe through my tears.

Why did he follow me? He had met with an accident last time as well when he had come to see me after *Ma*'s death! *Why does he always come after me? Why!*

I sprinted out of the bus and raced towards the hospital. Panting, I reached the reception and enquired about Jai. He was currently in the Emergency Room undergoing treatment for his injuries. I wasn't allowed to enter, so I waited outside, restlessly pacing for any news of him.

The moment a doctor stepped out, I stopped him and asked, "Doctor, Mr Jai Sharma. How's he?"

"And you are?"

"His wife," I immediately replied without a second thought.

He nodded. "Mrs Sharma, your husband has a superficial injury on the head, two broken ribs and internal injury in the spleen. He's lost a lot of blood and needs immediate surgery to stop the bleeding. We need you to fill the forms and sign a no-objection certificate before we proceed."

"Yes," I said faintly.

The nurse handed me a form, "Please sign here and mention the relationship."

My heart was beating loudly, the sound almost audible in my ears as I wrote my name, and then signed.

"Relationship?" pointed out the nurse.

My name was scribbled below his as the caretaker. A strange feeling passed through me as if he *did* belong to me and no one else! In the relationship column, I filled 'WIFE' in bold.

The nurse took the form from my hand, while I wiped the beads of sweat from my forehead. *Fear is so powerful that it can usher forth your deepest desires and strike you straight, making you aware of what you cherish the most.*

My own life was never so important to me, but for him, I would have sacrificed mine without a second thought right then. Tears poured out of my eyes, telling me I loved him more than anything in this world. He was not just someone my body desired. He was connected to my soul.

No matter how much I'm hurt by his actions, I'll still love him till the end of my life.

All I wanted was for him to live a happy life!

I found an idol of God at the hospital lobby and bent down before the Elephant God with all the faith I had ever had in my life. "Please save him. I have no one else apart from him." I begged Him, kneeling down on the floor.

As I looked towards the emergency room, I saw nurses rushing in and out. My heart began to sink, thinking he was in danger, but I didn't leave my faith or move an inch from where I was praying for his life.

The only hope I had was God, and today He must listen! *I have been through many troubles in my life, but if I lose him, I will not be able to live.*

As if talking to God, I promised, "Once he gets well, I will tell him how much I love him. No more fights and no more complaints. Please just save him."

Uttering these words eased the pain in my heart as if a burden had been lifted. While I was pretending to be his wife, I believed in my heart that he was mine but had never said it to him even once.

I had tried several times, but the fear of rejection made me stop every time. Finally, two days back, when he confessed his love to me during the photoshoot, I knew it was the right time to say that I loved him too, but I didn't because I kept judging him.

"Ma'am, your husband's phone." A voice above me made me look upwards. I saw a man holding out a phone towards me. "I'm sorry, I forgot to hand it over before and had gone for an emergency in my family."

"Thank you," I said, then out of curiosity, asked him, "How did you reach me?"

"Before he fainted, he said, 'Call Natasha, my wife.' And I called you from his phone," he said.

More tears rolled down my cheeks. Even when he was in a near-death state, he addressed me as his wife...

"Thank you for bringing him here," I said to the man, wiping my tears.

"Don't worry, he'll be fine. God always protects people who love each other," he said with a smile.

I smiled back, hoping his words were true. *Because for once, I have no fear in saying that he loves me more than I do.*

Time ticked incredibly slowly. After a long time, he was rolled out of the Emergency Room and placed in the ICU.

His doctor found me and smiled. "The operation was successful, but he needs to be under observation. You can meet him when he comes to his senses."

I nodded, sighing with relief. Then I swiped his phone to call Chad. While swiping through his call logs to get Chad's number, I saw my name entered as 'Natasha - wife.' A small smile played on my lips, feeling happy seeing the word 'wife' next to my name.

I called up Chad and informed him about the accident. No sooner had I hung up when the phone buzzed with an incoming call from Jai's father.

"Uncle, this is Natasha. Jai had an accident while coming to my village. He just had a surgery, and the doctor has kept him under observation," I said in a single breath.

"Why the hell are you there with him?" he barked aloud. "Why did you contact him again? I should have known you needed money! Didn't you give your word that you'll never meet him?"

"I didn't meet him deliberately. We met by chan-," I tried to explain, but he didn't let me speak.

"Tell me where he is."

I told him the address slowly while he noted it down.

"Wait, I will call you again on this number," he said, disconnecting the call.

A nurse rushed towards me and said, "The doctor wants to see you."

The doctor explained to me the moment I reached the ICU doors. "Mrs Sharma, your husband is stable for now, but his pulse seems to be erratic. Therefore, we recommend you immediately transfer him to a hospital in Mumbai."

I panicked and called Chad.

Within minutes, he arranged everything and called me back. "You get the papers. I've arranged for an air ambulance which will bring you to Ariel Hills Hospital in Mumbai, along with the doctor."

I was waiting for the chopper Chad had arranged when a man dressed in a formal suit approached me. "Ma'am, Mr Sharma asked me to hand this to you."

I was wondering which 'Mr Sharma' he was talking about when he extended an envelope towards me and added, "Sir would like to have a word with you." He then passed on his mobile.

"Natasha," Jai's father boomed from the other end. Before I could greet him, he started off with what he had to say. "I've sent you the divorce papers. Sign them and hand them over to my associate."

"Wh-what..?"

"If you love Jai and want him to succeed in life, then you'll do as I say and sign the papers. Otherwise, I'll pull out my support from his car company."

I was aghast and tears welled in my eyes. He left me no choice but to concede... He was always this ruthless!

When I mumbled an incoherent 'yes', he added more instructions for me. "Chad will be there in a chopper in the next ten minutes. You can leave now."

"Let me at least accompany him to Mumbai!" I pleaded, feeling helpless.

"With a doctor and Chad there, you are not needed. I don't wish to talk to you regarding this. You've already caused a lot of trouble in his life. I don't want him to suffer anymore!" His father raged on and on as if I was the reason for all the problems between father and son. "You stay away from my son. Jai will be returning to Perth, and he will marry someone who matches our status. Just sign the papers and let him move on with his life, away from the cursed life you have!"

The phone slipped from my hands and crashed to the ground. His harsh words were enough to make my knees go weak, and I staggered, as my hands fumbled for support. The man in the suit held me and led me towards the waiting area in the hospital.

At first, he offered me some water, and when I calmed down, he asked me to sign the divorce papers.

I looked at him, streams of tears flowing down my eyes. *Yes, I am jinxed... why else did my parents leave me at an early age? My Ma passed away suffering from cancer, and twice Jai had an accident because of me.*

I took the pen from the man and signed the papers without any hesitation. A few minutes ago, I had finally accepted that he was my life and had signed the forms as his wife, but now I was signing this paper which would cut off all those ties and remove me from his life.

Chad found me at the waiting area and said, "All set, let's go."

I handed him the divorce papers.

"What's this?" he asked.

"Divorce papers," I said, the pain pinching my heart.

"Divorce? You want to divorce him now, at this time, when he needs you the most?" he asked with a deep frown.

"I have to, for him. I have caused him enough trouble. So now, it's time to step back. Bye, Chad. Leave. He needs to go to the hospital soon," I said, wiping the tears from my eyes.

"Natasha, I don't think you are doing the correct thing! I'm taking him, but I'm telling you, you'll repent later," he said and left in a rush towards the waiting chopper to take him and Jai.

One last look at Jai with all his systems messed up because of the accident and his face clamped to a breathing mask, and I knew I did the right thing. He didn't belong here.

"Natasha, are you sure you won't come?" Chad asked, boarding the chopper, and I nodded my head which was spinning by now because of the pain in my chest.

Unsettled, he looked around to come up with something, anything to make me accompany, but then he glanced at Jai, who was lying on the stretcher with the oxygen mask attached to his nose. His face turned grim as he gave up his attempts to persuade me. Jai needed immediate attention. Everything else could wait.

I saw them fly high up in the sky, and knowing Jai would be safe without me, I left the hospital with a heavy heart.

CHAPTER XXVIII

One day turned into two and then three but at a snail's pace, and finally, I received a message from Chad that Jai had regained consciousness and was doing fine. The anguish and distress I was reeling under over Jai's wellbeing, lessened but the heartache and despair I had been suppressing all this time came back with a vengeance.

I had no complaints or anger towards him. I loved him in the past, I love him in the present and would continue to do so in the future. But he could not be mine, as I was a cursed being. So staying apart was for the best...

I was lonely, still I had to live and survive. I cried for the whole day until there were no more tears to shed. Our times together flashed before my eyes. And then, I felt a strange calm the next day. Whatever I did, I could hear his voice as if he was with me, giving me his piece of mind.

I went for a walk by the beach and returned with a big family pack of ice cream. The quiet of the house, coupled with the loneliness of my heart, was maddening, so I switched on the TV to watch a comedy.

Nothing seemed like fun anymore. I forced myself to eat mouthfuls of ice cream and uplift my mood.

Just then, the sound of the doorbell made me glance at it languidly. I looked at the time. It was almost three in the afternoon, nearly time for the housekeeper to come and do her daily chores. There was nothing much for her to do except clean the house. Sometimes she was early, and sometimes she was late. But it didn't matter to me.

Dragging my feet, I opened the door without glancing at her and returned to my place on the sofa where my ice cream awaited me.

I heard her close the door, but the usual greetings followed by non-stop chatter did not follow. With a chuckle, I settled down. Yesterday's scolding to the maid to keep quiet had worked! But then, she stood by the door instead of going ahead with her work. *What's wrong with her now? Does she not want to work anymore because I scolded her, or does she want a leave?*

"What is it? Please finish the work soon and get going," I said, my eyes fixed on the spoonful of ice cream. I forced another mouthful and frowned. Ice cream is said to boost your mood, but it wasn't helping. Should I try chocolates?

Aware that the housekeeper was still there but silent, I asked, "Do you want to take a leave, or do you want to quit?"

"I know I met with an accident, and you are sad, but ice cream? Serious.ly? Isn't it just too much?" I heard Jai complain.

I slowly looked up in the direction of his voice. This time, it was accompanied by visuals. I knew I was hallucinating, but it was a welcome sight. I smiled and replied, "No, it's not. Everything's over..." My voice faltered, and I frowned again, staring at the ice cream. *This is not working. I should get chocolates!*

"But at least pretend a moan as you did while you had the ice cream, the last time we were together," he said.

"Yeah, right!" I rolled my eyes. Even his hallucination was teasing me, and I instinctively retorted. "Go away! Your mirage is just as bad as you!" But the very next second, I repented my outburst and cast my head down. Then, in a melancholic voice, I said, "No, stay... this is better than having nothing to myself."

"Hmm... that's true," I heard him say. "I feel it will be better to hug you to erase your loneliness."

I didn't say anything as his footsteps approached me. He took the ice cream from my hand, placed it on the coffee table and took a seat next to me on the sofa. Then, he embraced me in his arms.

The warmth around me felt good, and I was lost, dazed at the familiarity for some time. I missed Jai terribly. No matter how much I tried to mask the pain and loneliness, I could just not get over it. I was losing my mind, for sure! It started with his voice. Now my psyche had reached another level to make me hallucinate his vision and his warmth! The pain was simply indescribable. Fresh tears rolled down my eyes, and I sobbed, "Jai... I'm sorry... I miss you... but... but..."

The arms around me tightened. "Shu-shu-shu..." He laid tender kisses on my head as he cocooned me in his embrace. "Nats, calm down, my baby. I'm right here."

I shook my head, refusing to believe. "You're a dream, and you'll go away..."

He caressed my back and held me lovingly. "I'm here with you. I won't go anywhere without you."

"I know you will," I murmured, wrapping my arms around his neck and placing my head on his shoulder.

"I won't. I promise. I'll be with you, forever." The sweetness in his voice sounded strange. He had never said such words before. It was as if the hallucination was muttering my deepest desires. But vaguely, it felt natural, and I lifted my head to glance at his face.

"Jai," I mumbled, blinking my eyes to make the hallucination go away.

But he remained there. With my brows furrowed, I ran my fingers over his face, from his head to his temples, cheeks, his jawline... He stared into my eyes and let me feel him. Then, as my fingers traced his lips, he opened his mouth and gently bit on it. I flinched at the pain, and my eyes widened.

I gaped at him. A jumble of inexplicable feelings made my heart pound hard.

"You're here..." I muttered almost inaudibly.

He nodded, running his palm over my cheek to my hair and pulling me closer.

I resisted, still staring at him without blinking my eyes. That's when I noticed a plaster on his forehead.

"You really are here!"

"Yes, I am, Nats. For real, not your hallucination," he said, leaning over and kissing my cheeks.

Tears started flowing down my cheeks. As he looked at me, I moved my fingers, gently tracing his wound. It seemed he had a few stitches there. Then recalling his father's words, I dropped my hands down.

Standing up from the sofa, I moved away. "Jai, you must go. I don't think we have a future together. I am unlucky. With me, you will only find troubles in your life."

"No matter what happens, I will stand by you and be true to you always." He held my hand and continued, "You don't have to worry about anything that Dad said. Everything has been taken care of."

I shook my head in panic. "It's not just that! I-I... There are so many things! I'm ill-fated, Jai, and being with me will bring you troubles!"

Jai tried to reach out and hold me. "You're nothing of the sort!"

"But I am!" I argued aloud, taking a step back.

"You're not!" Jai remarked louder than me and clenched his jaws. "You are a strong woman, like your *Ma*. You are someone who has always stood by me!" He closed the gap between us and cupped my face, his eyes staring at me tenderly. "And now it's my turn to stand up by you," he said, kissing my forehead ever so softly.

I felt something melt inside me.

He rested his forehead on mine and held my face with both his hands. "I missed you, Nats. I was waiting for you."

More tears trickled down as I closed my eyes. "I was asked not to come to Mumbai with you."

"I know, honey..." He kissed my forehead and once again wrapped me in his arms. I thought of pushing him away because his father's words resounded in my ears like an indelible truth that could not be refuted, but my greed took over my rationality. I wanted to spend some more time in his warmth.

Then, Jai parted and glanced at my face. He pecked my lips and added, "I do wish to make love to you right away, but we have visitors."

"Huh?" I stared at him dumbfounded. His words just didn't register in my head.

He fingered my hair to straighten out the tangles, wiped my tear-stained cheek with tissues and led me towards the door. "Come on, they are waiting."

I was still in a daze as I followed him out, and then my eyes widened at the familiar faces. There were two SUVs parked outside with Samira, Chad, Jai's mother and his father standing there. At the sight of his parents, panic rose within me, and my legs turned to lead. "I-I'm sorry, I didn't know. Sorry to keep you waiting." All my joy withered away, and my voice croaked, "Please come in." I gestured towards the open door with my hands, but my heart felt heavy. I had no desire to face them.

His mother was the first one to take a step towards us. "Natasha, we've come here to apologise." She reached to where I stood and caught my hands. "We've wronged you terribly. Please forgive us."

The unexpected apology put me in a trance. Before I could react in any way, Jai's father reached us and added, "And thank you for saving our son's life." He looked embarrassed as he fumbled for words, "I-I shouldn't have forced you... to sign the divorce papers and leave Jai."

My eyes widened in disbelief. *Am I hearing things?*

"I realise my mistake and want you two to get back together," he added.

Did he mean I could stay by Jai's side? As his wife? Those damn tears threatened to flow out as my breathing became erratic and my body quivered. Jai's mother, who was still holding my hands, squeezed them as if she could understand my state. I didn't know what to say. Everything was just too sudden. Her eyes flickered pleadingly as she said, "Natasha, we want to take you with us to Mumbai."

I was hesitant yet willing. I wanted to say yes but was afraid. Without warning, I was struck out of Jai's life, and without notice, I was being invited again. I looked at Jai; everything was happening too fast...

"Ah..." Jai interrupted my chaotic thoughts. He placed a hand on my shoulder and pulled me to his side. "Actually, give us a couple of days. I want to spend some time with my wife, and then I'll bring her to Mumbai."

His sudden gesture made me red in the ears, and I glanced at him sideways. His eyes were twinkling with delight. Then, embarrassed, I cast my head down.

"This ambience.... We'll not get in Mumbai." Then, he gazed down at me and asked, "If you're okay, can I stay with you for two days before returning to Mumbai?"

No sooner had I nodded when Chad chimed in, "That's a great idea! Uncle, aunty, we should give them some space and return back first. They will come back in a few days anyway," with a smirk, Chad winked at Jai.

"Yes, that's true. Let them stay together for a while. After all, they have been through a lot!" Samira said, climbing the steps to my house. She gave me a warm hug. "Come back soon. We'll be waiting for you."

I nodded with a smile as she kissed my cheeks. "Bye, Nats, take care. I'll wait for you."

I waved at them as they boarded the car and left as suddenly as they had arrived, leaving Jai behind. As I watched the cars drive away, Jai moved closer to my ears and whispered, "I'm waiting inside."

I stood there for some time until their car turned around the corner and vanished out of sight. Then, slowly, I walked back inside, feeling a little awkward to be alone with him. Before he came here, all I wanted was to see him once and hug him, but now, I felt shy to be alone with him.

When I went inside, he was surfing the channels on the TV. "What do you want to see?"

I sat on the single-seater sofa. "Anything you want."

"Is there anything to eat? I'm famished," he said.

"I'll make something," I said, heading towards the kitchen. But when I checked the supplies, there weren't any vegetables except a few potatoes and tomatoes. Thankfully I was not short on the grains! Therefore, I decided to cook *Dal Khichdi* and a tangy tomato curry.

"I didn't know that you can cook," Jai said, entering the kitchen.

I almost jumped at his voice, then replied, "Yes, I do know. I often helped *Maa* in the kitchen. In Perth, Samira and I often tried our hands at new dishes, but I never got a chance to show my expertise at your place."

"Nice, so many things to explore about you," he said, tossing the tomatoes up in the air, then chopping them into fine pieces.

"You know how to cut vegetables?" I glanced at him in awe at his tomato slicing skills. "Who taught you to do that?"

"Your mother," he replied, busy peeling the potatoes and continued, "When she was staying with my grandpa."

After a brief pause, he continued, "My grandpa employed them as helpers after he found they were survivors of a bus accident and didn't have any money to return home."

I stopped chopping and reflected on his words.

Jai diced the potatoes and turned towards me, "When you are poor, you aren't given many choices in life. You need to make harsh decisions. They had to stay alive and look after their son, who was their only child right then."

"What about me then?" I asked, looking at him.

"They assumed you were doing good at their relative's house. After all, those relatives were very nice to you, weren't they? They treated you like their own daughter, gave you sweets, bought you new dresses, but your parents didn't know you'd be wronged once you started living with them."

"How did you know?" I snapped with a bewildered look.

"When I was here the last time, I had immediately recognised your parents, Vimala Aunty and Ashok Uncle. Right then, I didn't find it appropriate to tell you about them because I had to know why they had left you behind. So on my return, I enquired with them about you on a casual note. I had often heard them speak of a daughter, but I had never paid much attention before. I listened to all their stories this time around, but I didn't tell them about you." Jai paused and looked at me. "I wanted to talk to you about it before letting them know, and then Atul's incident happened. Things spiralled out of my control, and you ran away from me before I could tell you the truth."

"Why didn't they come back once they were fine after they got a job at your grandfather's place?" I asked, crossing my hands above my chest.

"They assumed you were doing good and though they worked for my grandpa, they were still in a dire state. Feeding one child was tough, and feeding two would have been tougher. They never once doubted the relatives and their treatment of you."

"But they were my parents. How can they be so cruel?" I asked, not willing to accept the reasoning to leave their child like this.

Jai held my arms and replied, "In a way you can say, it was wishful thinking on their part. I know it is selfish, but when faced with the cruelty of life, one needs to take drastic decisions and make hard choices to survive."

Jai tucked my hair behind my ears and held me close. Suddenly, I was reminded of the children I had met on the streets in Mumbai when I was looking for orphans, whom I could help. Their parents had sent them to beg on the streets for the sake of food. The boy seemed miserable and helpless when he confessed his situation to me.

I dropped my eyes down, deep in thought. I was terribly hurt when I came to know my parents were alive. But, unfortunately, the circumstances made them make such a hard choice and leave me behind. Maybe I can't blame them, but that doesn't lessen the physical and mental abuse I went through.

"Well, they made their choice based on many assumptions. From what you said, I can't really blame them, but I can't reconcile with them either. At least not now..." I said, looking up at Jai.

"I'll not force you to," he answered, hugging me in his arms and added, "We'll meet them only when you are ready."

I nodded, placing my head on his chest.

"Something is burning," he said, twitching his nose.

I looked at the stove to find the curry leaves charred black in the frying pan. In a hurry, I removed it from the fire without using the pincer. "Shucks!" I exclaimed in pain. I'd burnt my fingers.

Jai immediately held my hand and placed it under the open tap. "How can you be so stupid?"

"It's nothing, leave it," I said, trying to pull my hand.

Instead of letting me go, Jai tightened his grip and brought my fingers close to his lips. Is he going to kiss? I almost laughed at his ridiculous action when he started to blow at my fingers. "Is it fine?" he asked while I was eyeing him with a lot of interest, feeling nice about this special treatment.

"Feels awesome. I've never received this kind of special treatment," I replied with a smile.

He pulled me closer to him, and then wrapped his arms around my waist. He kissed my earlobes with his lips, "I think you should put the gas off before the house catches fire."

"I need to cook," I said, almost moaning in his embrace. "My husband is hungry."

"Oh yes, that I am for you right now," he said, kissing the nape of my neck with soft strokes that made me melt from inside.

I felt my breath become fast as he sucked the skin above my collarbone, gently sliding his lips down my sleeves. My hand clasped over his mouth. His eyes that were glazed with desire turned to me questioningly.

"Are you sure you're physically fit to indulge in such activities?" I asked, raising a brow.

He let out a loud laugh and then mumbled, "It's tough to resist you!"

I pursed my lips and pushed him away. "Go away. I have to cook for my husband!"

He let me go but held me from behind and started kissing my nape. "I love you, wifey," he murmured breathlessly.

All my suppressed emotions surfaced at his confession. How much I yearned to hear these words from him! And now that he uttered them, I couldn't hold back myself anymore. Tears welled up, the happy kind, and I turned around, wrapping my arms around his waist. "I love you too, and have done for a long time..."

***

As I cooked, Jai rested in my bedroom. He had been discharged from the hospital, but he still wasn't completely recovered. His confession opened the numerous knots in my heart, not only the ones he made but also those made by others. I felt blessed, as if I could now face the world confidently and even win all battles without hesitation.

It was more than a fairy tale for me, where he was my prince charming beyond my reach. At the end of the struggle that I went through, I finally had him by my side.

The aroma of the *khichdi* made me realise that it had been days since I had eaten properly. *When everything falls in line, your appetite for food also comes back.*

I smiled as I served the food in two plates and turned around to take it to the bedroom when I saw Jai standing at the kitchen door with his hands crossed above his chest.

"It's ready. Let's eat!" I said, gesturing at the plates.

"I am ready too," he said, walking closer and giving me a tight hug, then kissing my lips hungrily.

His hands then crawled inside my t-shirt, and I grunted, "It feels ticklish! Go away, or I'll drop the plates! Let's eat food first," I added almost pleadingly to move away.

"Then?" he asked, pinching my waist.

"Then sleep. You need rest," I said, still trying to move away from Jai.

"All right, as you say, but not before you tell me why you didn't confess earlier that you loved me," he said, taking a plate from my hand.

"I didn't want you to feel pressured or that I was trying to bind you to myself and take advantage of you," I replied, following him.

He asked over his shoulder, "So when did you realise you loved me?"

I stopped and gazed at him. "Are you taking my test?"

"No, just wondering. Wasn't it when I used to visit the cafe?" he asked, raising a brow.

My heart suddenly started to race as if I had been caught in the act of committing a crime. "How did you know?"

"It was evident from your face. Every time you teased me, saying, sorry, we are closed," he said with a smug look, taking a seat on the sofa.

"Smart!" I retorted, not at all happy to know that I was so transparent that he could read me. "But did you know then?"

He shook his head.

"Then when did you come to know?"

He brought a spoonful of *khichdi* near my mouth and divulged, "I felt it many times, like when you explained what love means to you when we were at the yacht. The second time was when we were here the last time. You were moaning my name in your dream, but when I asked, you said it was Akash."

I watched him as he fed me another bite and said, "And many other times, like when I brought you back to the hotel on my back and muttered many things. But that time and all those times, I ignored it, as I felt that I was not the right one for you and may not be able to keep you happy."

"So now?" I asked, this time feeding him from my plate.

"When my accident happened, I thought I was going to die. But then, for a brief moment, I saw your smiling face, and I knew I had to live for us," Jai said, watching me. "Then I realised how much you meant to me!" He took a breath and continued, "Nats, I was just fading away to death, but it was you and your love that I craved so much that I knew I must live to confess and make us get together!"

My lips widened at his confession, and I kissed him on his lips. "You made the best decision! I would have felt dead without you. I tried to move on, but without you, my heart doesn't stay in its place."

I confessed to him how I worked at the orphanage as a cook to look after the children and my interaction with the street children.

"I wished to help them, but it's way beyond my capacity," I said, giving a sigh. "So, I will continue to work as a cook to support the children as much as I can."

"I know you want to do this for your *Ma*," said Jai, kissing my forehead. "I think you should continue working there. You will find peace in that work."

I smiled, nodding profusely when he took me in his arms. Safe and secure was what I felt for the first time after several years, just like when I was a kid with *Ma*.

Epilogue

A year later, Perth

I looked at my reflection, and my pulse raced in panic! I had never imagined things would turn out this way!

"Natie, are you ready?" asked my mother, coming to stand by her side.

"Yes, I am, but I'm a little nervous," I said, holding my mother's hand. She squeezed it tight, just the way I remember she used to when I was a kid. She then said, "This is your day. The family you always wanted!"

"You remember?" I raised my brows in surprise.

She nodded, "How can I forget your face when you said, '*Aji*, when I become big, I want to marry a man who will love me like you do!'"

Mother's face became a little sad, but she dismissed it and added, "Trust my word, Jai would take care of you much better than I ever could."

"Mumma, don't be sad. I realise what you did was your only way to save us, rather than making the entire family starve," I consoled her. Teaching and cooking for the shelter home kids made me realise life is not so easy for people who don't have enough to survive.

I had worked with an NGO for some time and started my own a few weeks back. But working there made me see life differently and understand that we all are born with our fortune. Some have spoons made of gold to feed them, while many have no spoons at all. However, we all must go on and not succumb to life, saying, 'I can't,' because once you give up, everything becomes more burdensome.

How we overcome our struggles positions us as strong or weak.

Two months after my reconciliation with Jai and his family, when I met my own parents, I didn't have any regrets; I had forgiven them.

Jai invited them to stay with us for a while. Then, every evening, after I returned home tired from my long hours at the NGO, we had dinner together. It was delightful to see how well-acquainted Jai was with my parents. My father, who rarely spoke to me when I was a child, often tried conversing with me. One evening, after the meal was over, I heard him asking my mother about my well being. There was awkwardness written all over him.

Then one day, I sat beside him and said, "You can behave normally with me. Let bygones be bygones."

He smiled and unexpectedly hugged me and cried his heart out.

My mother ran her hands over my shoulders, breaking the chain of my thoughts. "You were always my favourite. You were kind, happy, and intelligent, always eager to learn something, but Atul was quite the opposite. Because of his complaining nature, no one liked him," said my mother. She heaved a sigh and continued, "That's why we took this tough decision of letting you go. Moreover, we thought our relatives loved you and would care for you. But when Jai told me how you were thrown out by them and were sheltered by someone else, I realised we had done injustice to you."

Her tears poured out, and I felt terrible for her as a woman. But, after meeting the mothers at the orphanage and children's home and listening to their confession about how life had made them take the most challenging decisions, I was now able to understand each of those women's conditions myself.

"*Aji*, is this what you will do? Cry on my wedding day?" I asked, and she quickly wiped away her tears. "My mistake, let's go, my Lali. Jai and everyone must be waiting for you."

I hugged her, and then, taking a quick look at myself in the mirror, we walked out. Jai's parents had organised a small function, inviting relatives and friends to celebrate our togetherness.

***

A year ago, the commercial for Super Ninja brought more success than anticipated.

Apart from the official advertisement, another set of photographs from the photoshoot became very popular. They were candid shots taken by Tanisha and posted on social media.

Ninja Motors gained a good foothold in the Indian market, generating crores of revenue in the very first year! Jai was now busy coming up with a design for his next car, targeting the small car market.

Slowly and steadily, everything had fallen into place and I was really excited to take the next step towards my happiness.

As I entered the hall, Jai walked towards me and stretched out his hand, "Come on, Nats, I have been waiting for you ages!"

I smiled, placing my hand in his. My father stood at the far end with a broad smile. He looked content now that I was embarking on a new journey of my life. I smiled back at him. He blinked his eyes in reply, blessing me for a happy life from where he stood.

While I walked down further with Jai, I saw Samira and Chad smiling wide. Samira's parents stood to their side, followed by Chad's parents, and then Jai's parents.

Jai's mother walked over and held my hand, "Your mom said you desired a big family when you were a kid. Look, we all are here to welcome you to our family!"

I was moved. I hugged her and muttered, "Thank you!"

"Natasha Aunty, you look wonderful!" exclaimed Soha, walking through the crowd and pulling my arm.

I noticed she had a smile on her face after a long time. The news of me moving in with Jai instead of marrying her father, hadn't gone well with her, and she was silent for a few days. It went on until Tanisha had spoken to her personally and helped to ease the tension. Her smile radiated more as Jai winked at her, standing next to me.

I lifted her up and asked, "Where is your dad?"

I saw Akash walk towards us along with Tanisha.

"Congratulations to both of you," said Akash.

"Couldn't be possible without you," said Jai and hugged him.

"Anything for my best friend. I knew she was marrying for the sake of avoiding something but didn't know it was you until I saw you both at the beach playing with Soha," said Akash.

"You must be kidding! I didn't drool over him then to make you think like this!" I uttered in surprise.

"It was clearly written on your face how much you wanted him," Akash confessed. Then holding Jai's hand, he added, "It was that moment. I knew I had to give Jai a chance so that he could reach out to you and confess his heart."

"I still can't believe you!" I said, shaking my head while Akash and Jai laughed aloud.

Akash said, "Why don't you ask the member of your girl gang then?"

I looked at Tanisha for an answer, and she smiled, saying, "It was inked all over your face that you loved him to the core. We could clearly read that it was only him who could make you the happiest!"

I accepted her words with a smile, then dragged her close to me, "Was it the same way I see on your face for Akash?"

She blushed and moved away, spanking my hand and then adding, "Don't talk nonsense! It's nothing like that."

"We'll see! Samira and I have placed a bet on it already," I whispered again.

"What are you both whispering?" asked Samira, walking towards us.

"Nothing, Nats has gone mad in love with Jai," Tanisha uttered when I chimed in, "and she in love with-"

I clamped my mouth midway as Tanisha pinched my arm.

"Who is Tanisha Aunty in love with?" asked Soha inquisitively, while Akash turned pale.

"With you, my darling," said Tanisha, bending down and hugging Soha lovingly.

"By the way, Tanisha, you just stole the show with the photograph. I can't really thank you enough for that picture you took," smiled Jai.

"Jai, don't exaggerate. It was just a friendly click, I really liked the background and couldn't keep my hands off," she said, smiling widely.

"Still, that photograph of yours broke the records and made Ninja Super Avenue a limelight," I confessed, feeling proud of her.

"But it was Akash who advised us to keep that picture instead of the one clicked by the professional," Jai said.

Akash smiled as he confessed, "I too was surprised at the perfect timing of the photo and didn't know till then that she was such a pro at photography."

"I guess you don't know a lot of things about her," I chipped in, seeing Tanisha's face blush at my words.

"That's true, my mistake. She was right before me and I was searching for a genius photographer all around," Akash shook his head.

"Jai, Natasha, let's cut the cake!" Jai's father said aloud, making everyone walk towards the centre of the hall. It took me some time to forgive Jai's father. After all, he had commented that I was cursed. However, finally both his parents accepted me wholeheartedly.

There was a marked difference in their attitude towards me as compared to before. Their repeated attempts to win my favour at last unwound the knot in my heart, and the barrier that was once there between us, collapsed.

As we made our way towards the cake, Jai mumbled in my ears. "It's not over yet!"

I looked at him suspiciously.

"Just wait." He signalled someone, and a large screen was brought in. He connected his phone with the screen and made a video call.

"Are we ready?" he asked, and everyone nodded a big yes.

"All right then, officer, can you show the surprise to my wife?" he asked, looking at the screen.

A man wearing a white shirt and black pants smiled happily from the screen and nodded, "Of course, it will be my pleasure," and held a baby in his hand. "Mrs Sharma, how is she?"

The man was holding a sleeping baby wrapped in a white cloth. My heart instantly went out to the baby with the cherubic face. Just then, the baby smiled in sleep, making everyone go "Awww!"

I looked at Jai, unable to understand a thing, when the officer clarified, "Ma'am, Mr Jai and his parents came to us five months back and asked if they could adopt a girl. And by God's grace, this girl came to our orphanage just a month back. When Mr Jai visited us, we arranged the papers for you both to adopt her."

I looked in awe at Jai when the officer clarified, "If you'll come to India and sign the papers, we can happily hand her over to you."

I clamped my mouth and rushed to hug Jai. The emotions that I was feeling inside were way beyond my heart could hold on.

"I knew you would love this," he whispered in my ears.

Teary-eyed, I nodded in acceptance. All I ever wanted was someone who loved and understood me. With Jai's sweet gesture, I couldn't help appreciating the fact that I had finally gotten that special love in my life.

And now, adopting this baby girl would make my family complete! It would fulfil my wish of taking care of someone else's child as my own.

"She'll be named, Karuna... after my *Ma*... Is that okay?" I asked aloud. My mother pressed my shoulder and nodded in assurance. "She will always be your guiding light."

My search for *love* was finally complete. I was blessed with an abundance of love and care in the embrace of Jai, his parents, and my little princess.

Keep In Touch

I am so glad you reached this page. I hope you had a great time reading it. Do share your feedback on the story. In any case, I am happy that you picked up this book in the millions you would have come across.

If you wish to connect to a group of positive happy people where we talk about romance and happy life, please join the below link.

HAPPY GO LUCKY GROUP:
https://www.facebook.com/groups/357865542512836

The below link is for abundance generation group. The group goal is to generate more money and remain positive with the law of attraction. I have been a conscious believer of the law of attraction, and as a token of love to the universe, I wish to pass on the techniques of achieving an abundance of money to you. Please join and make a difference in your life.

I desire to attract MORE:
https://www.facebook.com/groups/709402279982029

I am also available on the below social media handles
Facebook: /NVedurla/
Instagram: vedurlanivedita
Twitter: nisha1133
Website vedurlanivedita.com
Email id: nivedita1133@gmail.com
Author profile on Amazon: https://amzn.to/2q3TMlK

About The Author

Nivedita Vedurla started her career as a technical support, moved to software testing and then became a Junior Business Operations Manager at Fabcoders, Goa. She now follows her passion of writing, along with her job as a Software Quality Analyst.

Her first book 'Two Angels' received tremendous love and appreciation from all her readers. Her stories reflect her strong belief in love, faith, and the power of mind. She likes to interact with strangers from all walks of life and gain knowledge about their way of living. This ultimately gives her the wings of imagination to pen down the fantasies which one can relate to.

When she isn't writing, she can be found indulging in reading something or dancing, cooking, or learning something new in her leisure time.

- My fathers Lessons
- The bestsellers wife
- Always with you
- Café House 21
- In Search of You
- All for Love
- The Seeker
- My Difficult Love
- Long lost friend love
- A hiccup in love
- The one I love
- Rhythm in love
- Two angels

Copyright Disclaimer

This is a work of fiction. Names, characters, businesses, places, events and incidents are products of author's imagination. Any resemblances to actual persons, living or dead, or actual events are purely coincidental.

All content posted is original work of the author and no part of the content can be copied, reproduced or posted in parts or whole on any other social media platform, website, publications or published in form of a hard copy without the prior consent of the Author.